Ties to the Hood:
G-Code

Ties to the Hood:
G-Code

Aija Monique

www.urbanbooks.net

Urban Books, LLC
300 Farmingdale Road, NY-Route 109
Farmingdale, NY 11735

Ties to the Hood: G-Code

ISBN 13: 978-1-62286-565-9
ISBN 10: 1-62286-565-0

First Trade Paperback Printing August 2017
Printed in the United States of America

10 9 8 7 6 5 4 3 2 1

Distributed by Kensington Publishing Corp.
Submit orders to:
Customer Service
400 Hahn Road
Westminster, MD 21157-4627
Phone: 1-800-733-3000
Fax: 1-800-659-2436

Ties to the Hood:
G-Code

by

Aija Monique

SHUN

All could be lost in the blink of an eye. Bad decisions, lies, deceit, and betrayal only beget death. After graduating high school, I was determined to get the hell out of the cesspool they called Kern County. There, my future was already set in stone. I was most valuable player of Kern County High School basketball team. Basketball was my ticket out. My life was defined by how many points I could score in a night. I was popular defined by how loud the crowd roared and the shoves and chants of my fellow players.

I often wondered how long that would last if I happened to fall and break my ankle or tear a ligament. I knew one thing: I wasn't going to stand around and wait for that to happen.

My cousin Phil was too hardheaded to listen to a damn thing I had to say. I guess I was the young and naive one. Some of this turned out to be true. I went on to become one of the few and the proud. I was brave enough to address the threats of our lands but naive to the fact that rules and loyalty were fragile when faced with death and confinement.

Leaving the hood in search of a better life wasn't all fun and games. Matter of fact, it was treacherous. They say the good often die young. Well, I did, in the confines of a jail cell, trying to uphold the laws of loyalty and respect. My soul was crushed.

I often looked back to graduation day. My cousin Phil threw me a party. I got drunk as fuck and nearly missed my bus headed to boot camp the following day. I was an official "jarhead," a true marine. I wore that uniform with such pride. I never would've thought I'd be seated on a bus, headed straight to prison.

"Murder?" Taking the fall for my sergeant was the worst mistake ever. Then again, snitching was social suicide, and there was no way my days in the service would last much longer had I stood up for myself. The murder of a gay marine spread through the media like a virus. Protestors from all over were outside the gates of the base and courthouse.

The freedom to fight for your country, gay or straight, was the highlight of the year. I was deemed the bastard who defiled the honor and glory of the armed services across branches. I might as well have stood outside the White House and burned the American flag. I was guilty anyhow. Fernandez wasn't my best friend, but he was a man that stood next to me in our lineup and pulled me over the wall when my leg hit a cramp in the field. He wasn't no fagot, not no outright pink-wearing mutha-fucka. He didn't do much to hide his sexual orientation either. He was the class clown when we got a moment's peace, and a soldier better than many when the time warranted. Still, having respected the man, I didn't take a step out of line as his commanding officer ordered the beating on Fernandez that subsequently caused his death. Back home, Kern County Projects taught you to keep your mouth closed, no snitching allowed. I saw how badly that man was being treated, but it wasn't my business; another rule of the hood I carried with me.

Number one: no snitching. Number two: mind your own damn business. They go hand in hand, really.

Phil was hotter than lava at my leaving the hood. Though he understood my thirst for bigger and brighter things, he felt abandoned. He didn't have anyone else in the hood who was actual blood. His parents were lost to the ways of the world, from drugs to prostitution. To me, the hood equaled death, and that's what most people living throughout the housing complex expected. It was a blessing for a man to reach the age of twenty-one in the hood, and most were highly praised if they reached the age of eighteen.

Graduation was the best day ever. Shit, it was my time to hang loose. I barely made it. But I did, and my next stop would be San Diego Marine Corps Base in California. I wouldn't be too far from Phil. However, two different worlds. My life was looking up. I still looked at a life of staring down the barrel of a gun, but in a world where men were protectors of the people, not one where children are dodging bullets, and young girls are prostituting for a hit.

Graduation was cool until the argument between Phil and me. I didn't mean to hurt him. I actually thought he'd be happy for me. But he felt betrayed. He couldn't stand the fact that I was going to leave him there alone. I can remember some of his rants now.

"You ain't shit without me. I'm a real nigga. You will always need me. Your very life depends on it," Phil said as he pointed his calloused index finger in my face.

That's when all hell broke loose. We actually came to blows. My guts were soft as shit the entire night preparing to leave for San Diego the next morning. I thought I'd never see Phil again, but there he was, waiting to see me off. We were like brothers.

I didn't see too much why Phil was so dramatic about my leaving. He had a sidekick. Cyrus. He was a hothead as well but less groomed in the area of finessing his kills.

He just didn't give a shit unless Phil was talking. Cyrus was there, and he always hung on to Phil's every word, as if he were God or something. Cyrus wanted out too. He was just too much of a follower to express himself.

Funny thing is that Cyrus didn't even live within the gates of the Kern County Projects. The man stayed five blocks over in a quiet neighborhood with his mother. She was a single parent and couldn't afford the luxuries of Nikes and Jordans, but she kept food on the table and a nice roof over his head. Cyrus had options. He could get away with most things, based on the fact that he wasn't labeled as a hood kid.

Even the schools labeled us as underachievers. Kern County Project kids had their own class, as if we weren't good enough to circulate with the general public. Our test scores weren't recorded with standardized testing. We were segregated. I was determined to make a better life for myself. In the end, Phil wanted the same.

Change came due to circumstances that caused both of us to reevaluate our take on life. Friends weren't friends at all. Women were nothing but gold digging tramps, and laws were just made to be broken. Living on the right side of the fence didn't mean law-abiding citizens. It meant clout—who had it versus who had the most.

There I was sitting on a bus going straight into the gates of hell. I had done my time. Still, I get a one-way ticket back to Kern County Projects with my dick in my hands.

Phil

Man, the hood love me. Ain't no point in leavin'. Especially if this is all you know. I have to admit that I was hotter than lava at Shun for leaving. We were a team. My blood. In reality, I know my boy had to leave, but I hated to see him go. He was my motivation to make it in and out of the day because I had someone to care for, watch over, make sure he was straight, you feel me?

Now, I'm here with these half-baked goons that can't trap for shit. Always spendin' before they eat and chasing after pussy. Tainted pussy at that. With no parents and an elderly grandmother who wanted nothing to do with me, I had to make a dolla out of fifteen cents.

I enjoy my life. I come and go as I please, and I am met with respect—or else. My trigger finga is extremely happy, and I take strongly after Beanie Sigel's true statement in State Property, "Get down or lay down." Definite true story for me.

Real shit, with Shun returning home, I couldn't be happier. I was skinnin' and grinnin'. It was a shame he had to do time for some shit he probably had nothing to do with. The entire trial was bullshit. Don't sound like nothing he would put his hands on. The fuckin' media made a mockery of my cutty like he was on the down low. Murdering a gay soldier was almost grounds for public execution, let news at eleven tell it. Shun could give two fucks whether a nigga liked dick. All he ever saw was plan and execution. All I see is the money. For real, for real, if it was a hit. I guarantee it would have been done without a blink of an eye if the money was right.

I put fifteen young men on my squad. I generously gave opportunity for advancement in this business. I only have one rule: respect. With respect, all else follows. With respect comes loyalty, power, and most importantly, affluence. I educate my men on the importance of these things because without it, you can't call yourself a man. The goal of every man should be to answer and to work for no one. However, in order to do that, you must follow protocol. Pay your dues, service your community, and allow for no disrespect.

I admit I'm into making a public display of those who are disloyal. My head is hot. I get excited when I'm presented with the opportunity to prove a point. Shun could never understand that concept. Fear is what makes people move out the way. Shun prized himself in moving in silence, and he discussed discipline heavy while in the service. I can dig it. I even used some of those same phrases when I was training my goons for money and murder. It takes discipline to move this work. I dare a nigga to abuse my work. I don't give a shit if they pay for it. No drug is acceptable except weed.

On to the business of family. It hurts my heart to know that Shun is my only true friend and bloodline. I have children, but my baby momma is dirty as hell and a money-hungry bitch. I take care of mine. I'm just not gonna provide for her selfish needs. I miss my boy, but I am not in a position to have him around. Things get funky real quick out here in these streets, and I'd go crazy if something ever happened to my kids.

I get angry easy and admit that my emotions often override reason. I get like that when I feel as though

I'm being taken advantage of. I don't have parents. My mom was on drugs heavy, and it eventually took her out. The lights went out then. I was nine, and, well, my dad didn't seem to give a shit. He was abusive and a damn pimp himself. He was murdered right on our front porch. Dude came right up behind 'im and rocked his shit. I never respected a man who couldn't stand toe-to-toe with his foe. I made a promise then that I would approach and execute my intentions with no questions. I didn't have time for meaningless arguments. Shun changed me for the best, and, I have to say, so did my son. I focused on the almighty dolla. Without it, I couldn't provide for my son. It was more than my dad ever did for me, so I made right by my seeds. I wanted the best for my children.

Though it seemed I wanted for nothing, that was far from the truth. The street life kept me hungry for more. I became a predator to those who fell victim to my wrath, but in reality, all I truly wanted was love and a shot at a normal life. Sure, my head was filled with anger, but it all stemmed from fear. I couldn't let the streets feel me internally. They would eat me alive. And right now, all I had is my street cred. No matter how bad I wanted to hang all this shit up, I couldn't. Someone would be sure to take me out in a hurry for any show of weakness.

Besides, both Shun and I tried the right way, and it turned around and bit us both in the ass. So for now, it's money and power, and those who get greedy often get eaten by bigger fish, deceived by their own eyes.

PROLOGUE

The Fall

"Aye, but I didn't do it! I didn't do shit, man. Mitch, tell 'em. Sergeant, tell 'em. You know I didn't do it," Shun yelled in a panic as the marshals dragged him out of the barracks in his underwear.

"Come with me, soldier."

Shun caught the eyes of each of his bunk mates' solemn but stern faces as he kicked and pleaded for the same backup he would expect on the battlefield. No one stepped forward. The truth was, over a handful of his colleagues had a hand in harassing Fernandez, mostly lewd comments about him wearing lipstick and soliciting his talent for giving blow jobs. Any one of them could have been a suspect if Shun hadn't witnessed the crime himself.

That was all she wrote. Shun did a nickel in the pen and got out in three years, on account of good behavior. First thing he did was put a call in to his cousin Phil. He wondered what Phil was up to, having heard he was still on that same hype—out there in the hood, drug sales, and petty theft. No telling how many bodies he dumped. All was well. Phil was on cloud nine and excited for Shun to get back home and get this money. Phil failed to talk in code, he was too juiced. Shun, on the other hand, was so afraid of incriminating himself he hurried Phil off the phone. Shun had learned his lesson. Doing good didn't pay off, and, hell, doing bad had the same result, if caught. Do right by the law and end up in the pen, just the same.

He walked out of Wasco County Prison, and the first thing that hit his fresh white tee was a gust of dirt. The soil didn't bother him, though. He welcomed it because there were no gates around it. The guards had the nerve to toss him his Marine Corps uniform from his previous tour as if he were down with the flag. As far as he was concerned, the Iranians could walk right past him, guns blazing. He couldn't guarantee he wouldn't throw on a damn turban and blow some shit up himself. He was done with the "America the Brave" shit. He was ready to tackle a new way of life, civilian life, if his cousin Phil didn't get him into trouble.

He stood outside the gates of Wasco Prison for about fifteen minutes. He was just about to panic until he saw his cutty speeding up in a brand-new, candy-painted, old-school Camaro.

"What's up, ma nigga? They finally let yo' ass out!" Phil said.

"Yeah, man. They let this *innocent man out!*"

"Man, it's good. You out. You served your time. You can tell me. Hell, everybody in prison innocent, right?"

"I'm not jawsin' about this, cutty. I didn't do nothing. His own bunk mates killed him on some ole gay shit. I could care less if that man wanted pussy or penis. Just as long as his gun was locked and loaded when the enemy was lurking, you feel me? It's all good now, though. Granny told me to do right. I listened. Look what it got me. Absolutely nothing. So case closed. You got that work for me I asked for?" Shun asked.

"You know I got it. You know I'm runnin' shit out in the hood now, right? I got these hoes turning triple tricks a night. Got some weed going," Phil answered.

"What about that white girl? You not fucking with that yet? That's where the money at, and clientele? Who you servicing? Them niggas in the hood or you got white bread clients now?"

"What I need from them? I got ma goons, plenty money, and pussy. I'm good. You start fooling around with too many people or adding faulty-ass niggas to yo' crew, and then *wham*—you locked up. Fucking snitches, and them be the men on your team."

"I feel you, bro. I have a plan, though," Phil said with a look of determination on his face. Shun didn't faze much of what Phil said when he had his undivided attention. He was thinking on how he was going to build from his new pals at work. Shun shared no plans with working a 9 to 5, not after Wade approached him at the office.

"Yo, man, know anyone I can score some weed and coke from?" Wade "The Suit" said as he bounced into the men's room. Wade was the rich kid in the office. He always walked around like he had his own theme song playing his head. He bought to please. He only got the job on some hype to prove he didn't need Daddy's money, but his mother was feeding him over five grand a month for supposed groceries and help paying $400 rent for a studio apartment.

Shun finished adjusting his tie in the mirror and turned the water on high velocity. He smirked and wet his dry knuckles rubbing them carefully before looking The Suit in the face. "How much?" Shun replied after seconds of thought that ran in his mind for at least a minute.

"A few pounds of weed and at least a brick of cocaine. Mark made manager for our Los Angeles office, that fuckin' dick! We want to get him fucked up before he leaves."

Shun bellowed in laughter as he usually did at his colleague's less-than-savory humor. The job emulated prison. He was forced to do the tasks assigned to others and wear a uniform suit and tie—orange jumpsuit, same thing. Life was choking the shit out of Shun, and in this very moment, he felt air.

"You got $2,600 layin' around?"

"That and lots more," Wade responded pulling out a huge roll of cash.

"Ma man," Shun said, shaking Wade's hand.

It was on.

Three Months Later . . .

Shun's BMW caught all the ladies' eyes as he rolled into the entrance of Meadow's Lake. He had a drop to make to some rather bigwigs in the upper-class white community of Bakersfield. Phil wasn't at all happy about the choice Shun made to sell cocaine and heroin, but he had to admit he was paid. Soon, Phil asked to join Shun's team.

Money was good in the hood, but it wasn't enough to be rolling around in Bavarian Motor Works, taking cruises and shit the whole nine. Made a nigga really mad. The green-eyed monster had undoubtedly reared its ugly head. Especially since he put Shun on. Here he was, still living in the hood, eating greasy fried chicken, drinking Kool-Aid and Hennessey, while Shun ate from the best five-star restaurants in the country and drank the finest wines.

Phil knew Shun had a few issues about putting him on, but he felt like he could handle his crew. They hadn't proved disloyalty thus far. Phil had to put a few knuckleheads in their place for overstepping boundary drug zones and talking out the side of their necks, but that was about it.

Shun's issue with Phil's organization was quite simple, and he let Phil know about his feelings regarding the whole thing. Basically, Shun felt like Phil wasn't worried about much of anything, like the police and the company he kept. Hell, he didn't know or trust half the cats Phil rolled around. He was fresh out. There was no way he was going to leave his freedom in the hands of the unknown. He did the dirt, Shun was willing to face the consequences, but on his own accord. Phil's folk may appear to be loyal, but that was only because niggas followed his lead. Soon, and this was almost always true, one of his goons was going to do one of two things. Either snitch to take him down, once caught, or plot to kill him. Set him up in order to take his spot. Goons may do the dirty work, but as they work, they learn, and soon, they get old and wise. They want to eat well and sit back too. Order would soon be disrupted if Phil didn't tend to his flock appropriately.

The thing with Shun was that after all he had been through, he didn't follow a soul. He answered to and followed no one. He'd had enough of that in the service and in jail. Shun left the hood, for reasons he thought would prove him to be above the rules of the hood. Only the game don't love you whether you are in or out.

Thinking Back

My grandmother used to say it was not where you lived, it was how you lived. That, and there was no reason for me to accept the idea that because I was from the ghetto I was destined to be a product of it.

So I played basketball while Phil sold weed at the gym's door. I got my grades up while Phil watched my back. Don't get me wrong, I wasn't no pussy. I did my dirt too. Just didn't label myself as no thug, you feel me? I did what was needed to survive.

Phil only protected me because he knew my worth. That's how people are, you know. Yeah, we fam, but his dad was a crackhead, and his mama was a ho. So it was like I was the sliced bread of the family, better than the rest.

To me, Phil's jealousy was warranted. I never got why I was so special. Phil was offered the same chances I was. Grandma would've taken him in as well, but he just couldn't leave the streets alone. It was like he was possessed or somethin'.

Phil was the one who bought me my first pair of Jordans. We were only twelve at the time. He came rushing into Granny's with official red and white thirteens.

"Try these on, nigga," *Phil ordered as he handed them off to me. I nearly tripped over my feet, trying to take off them Walmart shows Granny bought. Phil was cracking up as I pranced around clutchin' ma shit like I was that nigga. I felt like a real boss.*

I remember walking home from the neighborhood store. It was me, Phil, Cyrus, and Man-man. Shit! Them niggas approached me like, "Come up outta them Jordans."

I was like, "You gon' have to take these from me body." *I was so proud of them shoes. I'd be damned if someone tried to punk me for 'em.*

"Naw, fish ain't bitin'," *I said before I threw a slew of punches. Me and my boys swarmed those eighteen- and nineteen-year-old boys like it was nothing. From then on, the hood feared me and Phil. When Phil got his gun, it was really on. Niggas wouldn't even look Phil in his eyes, for fear he would draw his weapon and bust on 'em.*

That was the beginning to the madness, though. Phil was a fucking ticking time bomb, and it was only a matter of time before somebody popped him—or me.

CHAPTER 1

Pinched

The sirens rang through the streets of Kern County, Bakersfield. A high-speed chase was in progress, and Phil was the leader.

"Hurry up, nigga, get rid of the dro. Throw it out the back, mane. We gotta move," Phil yelled at one of his goons in the backseat of his '73 Capri on 24z. Phil was biting his bottom lip cussing through clenched teeth as he cut the corner of Monroe heading toward The Bear Mountain Project. Phil cringed as he heard his newly polished rims scrape the curb.

"Fuck, bro, fuck those pigs, man. As soon as we hit the freeway we smooth sailing. Where the fuck is Shun at?" Phil felt around the lap of his jeans for his phone. He needed Shun for backup if he wasn't too good to come to the hood side of town. He'd been fucking with white bread for the last two months and still had yet to put a nigga fully on. Phil understood, but it was about loyalty and family and, as of late, he was starting to feel like the foster child that was court awarded for the money. Only, he was hungry while Shun ate.

"Nigga, where the fuck you at, bro?" Phil tried to speak loud and clear. He had Shun on speaker, but the boys were close behind.

"I'm at the tilt, where the fuck you at? You in a high-speed chase or somethin', or you watching a flick on the big screen?" Shun asked, laughing and choking on his weed.

"Naw, nigga, I'm in trouble. It's hot as fuck out here. Had to get rid of the dro. I got the Yola on me too, bro, and I ain't tryin'a ditch that shit. That's ma bread, cuz."

"Yeah, but the boys in blue on you. So you know what you got to do. You fucking around riding hella deep, like the boys ain't lookin' to pinch yo' ass. This the shit I'm talking about. You be straight jumping in shit and can't get out. Yo, you gon' have to pull over and let them pigs do what they do. We need to keep a low profile."

"You know I know the rules, nigga. You trippin'. I brought yo' ass in the game."

"Man, just pull over and let them drugs go. It's plenty more where that came from, but it's coming out of your royalties. I'm in the house, not floating the streets getting pinched by them thirsty-ass pigs. The cops ain't gon' report nothin'. They gon' flip that shit on the streets. How much bread you rollin' wit'?"

"Aww, not much. I got a couple of Gs. Had to rock with enough to make my dollas roll, you feel me?"

"No, I don't, actually. Cuz to be honest, like I said, I'm at the tilt, and you rolling hot. Get on my hype; then we can make these moves. Pull over and take the rap. You'll be out by morn. But you staying the night. I got a bad one here, and I ain't about to leave that pussy alone."

"For real? You gon' let me rot for some pussy, ma nigga?"

"Naw, you gon' simmer for some pussy. And like I keep saying, pull over. See yo' ass in the morning." Shun shook his head and hung up the phone.

"Who was that, baby?" Shun's girl asked.

"My stupid-ass cousin. I got to go to county jail in the morning to bail his ass out."

"Well, you don't have time for that shit, baby. You got work to do over here. I'm talking now *and* in the morning.

So whatever this cousin of yours is talking about is going to have to wait," Shun's girl said, licking her thick lips and swaying her legs open and closed to expose her freshly shaved pussy and hardened clit.

"You ready, baby? The pussy is calling." Her wet fingers massaged over her clit and dove into her center. Porsha's juices squirted down her fingers. She was so excited by Shun's attentiveness. Porsha continued to watch Shun as he watched her intensely as she licked her fingers and urged Shun to come and play.

Shun felt his dick rise and jump at attention to Porsha's erotic display. "I'm coming, baby. You ready to back that ass up?"

Porsha flipped over in a hurry and twerked her ass so that Shun could get a good visual of what she was working with. "I'm always ready, Daddy."

"Oh yeah," Shun said, climbing into bed and situating himself behind her. He slapped her ass before diving right in.

"Man, Phil, what you wanna do? The boys got the helicopter out. I can see the lights. Man, we gon' fuck around and get shot out here. Like you really with the shit tonight, Phil. Let's just get rid of this shit. The car, the dope, all this shit. I got kids."

"Man, shut yo' bitch ass up! I ain't about to turn over no cards. I went and got this dope and shit, and Shun just expect me to throw my money in the wind, while he eatin' steaks and potatoes. Naw, fish ain't bitin'. I got rid of four pounds of weed, I ain't gettin' rid of shit else. I'm just lightening the load for the run, ma nigga."

"Run?"

"Yeah, run. *Now!*" Phil screamed as he drove the car straight into the gate of an abandoned steel mill. Phil jumped from the car and ran like the wind with two duffle bags on his back. He didn't bother to look back to see where the hell Dré was. He just hoped he wasn't dumb enough to get caught. He would be sure to keep his mouth shut. Phil hit every backyard he knew of where there were no dogs and ducked to one of his girls' homes before hitting the main streets.

The police lights were flashing all over the neighborhood at this point, and there was no sign of Dré. "Fuck, they got his ass, I just know it," Phil said to himself as he stashed the drugs and money in an abandoned doghouse in his girl's backyard. She would know to check it and put his shit up for safekeeping. She didn't live square in the hood slums of Kern County. She lived on the outskirts in middle-class suburbia. If he was even caught in the area, the cops would just assume he was there to rob someone. After all, a nigga driving with big rims and loud music was an automatic threat to society.

Phil felt free. He had managed to stash the drugs and avoid jail. He took a huge sigh of relief as he hit the main street and walked down toward the liquor store at the corner. He buttoned his leather bomber and rubbed his hands together as he took a quick look at his surroundings. "Whew!" he said to himself as he entered the liquor store, smiling from ear to ear.

Phil greeted the store manager with a chipper, "Hello, how ya doin'?" and headed straight to the freezer. He was thirsty as shit after running damn near circles around the entire city of Bakersfield. Phil opened a can of Sprite and guzzled it before grabbing another one and heading toward the counter. He was well on his way to freedom when all of sudden, he heard the liquor store's bells chime to indicate a new customer had come in. Shortly after, loud screaming followed. Phil immediately ducked around the corner and slid behind a few unpacked boxes to conceal himself.

"Take what you want! Just get out of my store," the owner yelled at the intruders, obviously unmoved by the gun waving around his head.

"Empty the cash register," one of the robbers demanded. "Man, what you doin'?" the gunman spoke just as he was demanding the cashier's earnings. He noticed his partner shopping instead of watching the door.

"I'm getting some candy, man. Might as well. We robbin' the place, right?"

"Nigga, watch the fuckin' doe before you get us caught up in here, bro."

The gunman had lost his focus and wasn't watching the cashier's moves. He was too busy waving his gun around the room talking shit to his partner to notice that the cashier had a rifle raised to his left temple. As the gunman turned to continue on with his demands, he was met by the barrel of a gun.

"Get the hell out of my store!" the owner demanded as he cocked his rifle back. The gunman's partner dropped his chips and soda and skirted out of the store without a second glance at his partner in crime. He just bolted out the door and ran.

"Fuck this shit," the robber responded and ran out of the liquor store just as quick and fast as his no-good ditching partner.

Phil rustled to get up from his seated position in the back of the store knocking over a few of the unpacked boxes as he tried to stand to his feet.

"Who's there?" the owner yelled, his rifle still in his hands. "Show yourself!"

"Aye, it's me, sir, remember? I came in, just walked back to the freezer to grab a few sodas, but I hid when the men came in the store." Phil tried to look sympathetic about the whole mess, but he could care less. He just needed to get the hell out of Dodge. Phil held up his two soda cans and started to move toward the front of the store, all the while assuring the gun-carrying owner that he had every intention of paying for the sodas.

Phil had made his way to the counter and attempted to put a few dollars on the counter when he saw the police lights flashing in the window of the liquor store. The owner had hit his panic and emergency assistance button over ten minutes ago. The police, late as ever, finally showed up.

"Look, I'm just gon' pay you for the two sodas and get outta your store. You won't have to worry about me coming in here ever again." Phil was nervous and shaky, and the money in his hands was beginning to dampen from the sweat of his palms. "Look, man, take the money, take the fucking money." Phil was becoming increasingly nervous and agitated by the store owner's mannerisms. "Fuck it!" Phil said, and threw the money at the owner and walked toward the doors of the liquor store. It, unfortunately, was too late. Two officers ran up to the window of the liquor store, waving their guns, instructing Phil to get down on his knees and surrender any weapons he may have had on his person.

Phil shook his head and dropped to his knees yelling, "Okay, okay," and saying that he didn't do shit. He turned to the owner of the store and demanded he tell the cops that it wasn't him who had attempted to rob him blind.

The owner of the store put his weapon down and, with a look of pure evilness, said, "Officer, arrest this man. He and two other thugs tried to rob my store. What took you so long? Two of them got away."

"Fuck. Pinched! Ain't this 'bout a bitch!" Phil said to himself. He shook his head and put his hands behind his head. "Damn, Shun, this all your fault."

CHAPTER 2

Fumble

Shun's phone interrupted his sleep just in time. Porsha had managed to stay the night, and that was definitely against his rules.

"Hello."

"You have a collect call from a Phil Daniels. Do you accept the charges?"

"Yeah, put 'im through."

"Man, I didn't rob no liquor store," Phil started in before Shun said a word. He was so upset about the whole situation he could barely contain himself. "Aye, nigga, you there? I need you to swing by my girl's house and pick up that loot and the bread. I don't want her moms to find that shit in her tilt, you feel me? Plus, that nigga Dré rolling around with either a bag full of weed or a bag of my money. I didn't have the time to divide the bags. I know he didn't get caught, cuz, well, his ass would be in here with me." Phil took a moment of silence as he kicked himself for not listening to Shun in the first place. "Cutty, you there, nigga? Feel like I'm talking to God or my conscience or some shit."

Shun just sat on the phone listening to Phil dribble about the happenings of the previous night. "Yeah, I'm here, but I don't feel shit. I told you what to do. You still got caught up. Only now, you have to wait on this man to drop the charges. *If he decides to do so.*"

"Shun, I would've been in here period if I had listened to you, and you know it. Part of me thinks you want my ass locked up. I want to eat and make money too. You forgot I—"

"You put me on, right?" Shun interrupted. "Man, go somewhere with that bullshit. You gave me a pound of weed. I got it off. I graduated and came up with my own game plan, which I then offered to teach you, but you with that shit. Man, I got to go. I have some people I have to meet about some real money. You sit tight. Don't worry about the dro. If he yo' real nigga, the shit is already put up."

Shun hung up the phone without waiting for a response from Phil. Phil was partly right about his assumption. With him locked up, Shun didn't have to worry about Phil fucking up his money or being killed. If Phil got hurt in the game, it would weigh heavily on his heart because he didn't wish him any harm. He loved Phil and, if needed, he would take care of 'im. He just wished he'd listen sometimes and start using his brain. Phil was always talking that hood shit, and he couldn't stomach it anymore. Sure, he left the hood and still ended up in trouble, but it wasn't because he did something illegal. It was because he was down for his team, and he wasn't no snitch.

Shun pulled out some weed from his drawer and collected the items for his meeting. He laid out his suit and tie, his gun holster, and two weapons of choice. He was heavy in thought when he was interrupted by a woman's voice that should've been long gone.

"You aren't thinking of bailing Phil out, are you? You know he belongs there. If he'd just listened to you about the drugs and money, he wouldn't be in this mess. You have much bigger and better deals going on, baby.

There's no way you can afford to get caught up in his shit." Porsha was talking, but Shun was busy rolling a blunt and drowning her out. He was loving the sex, but he could do without all the talking. She could even refrain from cooking. He could take care of himself, make a mean steak and eggs, so her time was actually up. Shun didn't plan on sharing the blunt.

"So what time you getting up, girl? You know I got to make this money. I have a meeting with Frankie this morning, and I don't want to be late." Shun never looked up from his blunt. He was caressing and licking it closed so seductively, Porsha started to shift in her seat a bit. She was turned on by Shun in more ways than she would like to admit. She had to have him.

Porsha wasn't a girl who was easily persuaded by men. They talk a lot about nothing, and she was all about action. She enjoyed Shun's company because he wasn't real big on talking about what he had or what he could get. He was all about action. That turned her on. She was money hungry, yes, but she wasn't a lazy bitch. She would do the wifey thing, protect and serve when needed, just as long as she was taken care of as well.

Shun took two puffs of his blunt and started to get his shirt and tie together. "What you think of this blue, Ma?" Shun finally spoke as his high was rejuvenating his sense of sociability.

"It looks good, babe, as always. Are we going to talk about Phil?"

"No. You are going to get dressed and get ready to go. I lock my doors when I leave the home. No one is left behind." Shun lowered his eyes at Porsha to indicate he meant business.

Porsha couldn't deny she felt some type of way. *How in the hell can he just toss me out like I was just some skank from the club?* she thought.

"For real, Shun?" Porsha began to get her clothes together with many thoughts traveling around her brow. Shun was the kind of guy that was serious about whatever he put his mind to. He was different from junior high and high school, but he was someone she could see herself settling down with. Dancing in the club wasn't who she was. She was a dancer, yes, but her first pick wasn't sliding down some stripper pole. Most didn't get out the hood. Shun did, and that was motivation enough. Porsha didn't know exactly what he was doing, but hanging around with Phil was not in his best interest. Phil was still running around town like he the king or some shit.

"It's simple really. I'm about ma bread. You, you about all this love shit, and right now, that's not what I need. I have to keep my mind clear. My moves are all monetary. I don't have time to cater to a woman. I fuck somethin', and then I go home or they bounce."

Porsha's nose flared at Shun's ignorance. "So, money *is* your game plan. What is Phil's role? How is he going to aid you in this whole money-over-bitches outlook?"

"Now, see, this is part of the problem as well. You talking."

"Talking?"

"Yes, talking. You're adding your two cents in matters that don't concern you. It's about me, making my bread. If you must know, my cousin ain't exactly on my team just yet. I ain't sayin' that like niggas don't trust 'im. I'm sayin' I just know he ain't ready. Phil gettin' caught up in *bullshit*. So I will say this and only once more. Fuck love, fuck all this lovey-dovey shit: babe, this and that, let me cook for you, cater to you, etc. I take care of my own needs. I'm a man. I don't want you to get the wrong idea about what this is. I like you. You a bad one, and I must say wife material, but I can't go there with you right now."

"So, this is it? You have *got* to be kidding me, Shun. Just look at you. Fancy. So handsome. But such an arrogant asshole. What, you think you better than me, soldier boy? You were nothing but a scrawny nerd that could shoot a basketball."

"Mannnnn, Get outta here with all that bullshit. Spare me the basketball Hall of Fame and patriotism act. This country ain't did shit for me. I know you can dance." Shun smirked. "I ain't talkin' all that pole shit. So don't get butt hurt. I remember your dance classes and gigs." Shun licked his lips as he smiled, but he quickly recovered from his path down memory lane and got back to the point.

"Honestly, Porsha, if you want this to be a one-time thing, then it is what it is. Or you can accept the situation, slide through when I call, or when I say it's good and we do us. Other than that, if you gon' be with this drama about relationships and butting in where your nose clearly shouldn't be, then I will cut you off."

Porsha swallowed the lump in her throat. She was so appalled by Shun's illustration of her worth she wanted to slug 'im. She knew better than that shit, though. She wasn't afraid of an ass whoopin', but Shun carried a different sort of pain that bled into a fury or rage that would easily turn murderous. He was quiet when he was about to pounce. The muscles in his jaw presented, but his face seemed calm, not strained or frowned. There is where fear came into Porsha. He was emotionless in his kills, so to kill was almost soothing to him, a worry Porsha couldn't take a chance on.

"I guess I will be going," Porsha finally spoke as Shun finished up his second blunt. Shun pulled on his holster and strategically placed his weapons on each side. He was very neat, which Porsha equated to his time in the service. She had to admit that too turned her on. Even his blatant disregard for her feelings was respected to an extent because he was real about the situation and didn't want to sell her a dream, though she would have fallen for it. She wanted him to say those sweet nothings she longed to hear. She was tired of being used and abused, and the hurt and pain of it all she wore on her sleeve.

"So will I see you later?" Shun asked, grabbing for his keys and handing Porsha her purse.

"Not sure," she replied, playing her card.

"Okay," Shun said and grabbed her by the arm to assist her in her exit from his home. Porsha snatched her arm back, a bit frustrated at how quickly he dismissed her play. The truth was, Shun could care less on the surface. He knew the game, and before she even responded, he knew she was going to say some dumb shit like her exact response. It only proved his point. Drama was something he had to stay clear of. He had a meeting with a buyer that could prove to be long lasting and very lucrative.

If he got the deal with Frankie, he would have to leave the country to do the trade. He welcomed it, in need of a vacation. The only thing about this new venture was that he needed backup, and prior to that very moment, he worked solo. With Phil on and off, he wasn't sure the man could handle himself in the presence of some real shooters. This was not going to be some drug-dealing drive-by in the hood where it's hit and miss. This was the mob, and they bullets had names on 'em, and the kill was carried out personally.

There was no time for shucking and jiving. Shun hopped into his BMW and buckled up. He took one glance in his mirror to check out his grooming. Only, in his reflection was Porsha, staring him down from his front porch. Shun had to admit that look on her face scared the shit out of him. Either she was a true down-ass bitch, or she was a real bitch. Part of him wanted to find out the truths to her soul. But he knew he had to make a choice. He'd either die by the sword chasing his dreams of money and power, or he'd die in love, surely to be caught slippin' while basking in the ambience of her sex. Shun shook off the idea of reconciliation and put his pedal to metal before he jumped from his car and took her into his arms once again.

Porsha shook her head as she watched Shun clearly think about his immorality. Watching him speed away, she angrily jogged to her Mustang at full speed. She threw her clothes in the trunk of her car and jumped into the driver's seat. She watched as Shun sped off around the corner in the opposite direction of the county jail, which she figured would be his first move, but the money was calling. So she decided to make her next move as well. The game had just begun. Shun fumbled the ball. Maybe Phil could pick it up and run game. Turning her engine on, she hit the gas and headed straight to the county jail.

CHAPTER 3

Smacked

"Thanks, man, for joining me on this one, Cy," Shun said, passing him a beer.

"Man, you know I got you, bro. Where that nigga, Phil, at?"

Shun looked over at Cyrus with a displeasing look as if he had a bad taste in his mouth. He didn't want it to seem like he and Phil weren't cool. It was just that he was making moves that he needed to alone, first, before he included Phil. Shun had corporate clients that weren't always handling disgruntled business dealings and partnerships in court. "Naw, he ain't comin'. I gotta do this one alone before I pull his loud ass in. I need this to be done eloquently. We are dealing with my boy Frankie and his uncle Tommy."

Cyrus perked up when he heard the two names Shun referenced. "I gotchu," he said.

"So, what's the job?" Cyrus asked and leaned in as if overly interested.

"Just a drop-off and pickup!"

"And you trust this dude Frankie?"

"No, I don't trust anyone. He's a client, a longstanding client who offered me a more lucrative job that will set me up to lie low for a while."

"OK, cool, I gotcha, but we talking drugs and money, bro. I ain't wit' explosives and shit." Cyrus laughed but flexed his jawline quick and fast to indicate he was serious. Cyrus hadn't changed much. He was still ready to fight or shoot with little explanation but funny as hell. That was the two definitions of crazy. A nigga standing around laughin' and jokin', then all of a sudden, mad as hell. Phil used to fuck wit' 'im about his two personalities. He was definitely two-faced. Phil used to say he was mad at some bitch cuz she didn't give 'im no pussy when he started trippin' out of the blue like that. All in all, Cyrus was cool people. He was a quiet hothead, which made for a good partner in crime. His kills were done with style. Fucking with Phil, he would wake up the neighborhood. He liked to talk while he pistol-whipped niggas, like how Granny used to when they were gettin' a whoopin'.

"So we good, bro?" Shun said looking up from his beer after a moment of silence.

"We good!" Cyrus confirmed as the two men toasted to money and freedom.

Shun pulled up to Junior's home, blowing his horn impatiently. Junior bounced out of the house in a fucking sweatshirt, jeans, and Tims with his armory exposed.

"You ready, nigga?" Shun yelled out to Junior.

"Nice piece," Cyrus said through clenched teeth as he noticed Junior was freelancing with his weapon in plain sight.

Shun looked at it and frowned his lips, then shook his head. "Yeah, it's cute, but do that muthafucka shoot?"

Junior's no-job-havin' ass had the nerve to have a gold-and-black-plated nine milly with his name engraved on it. Right then and there, Shun should've seen the red flags. The man was carrying a weapon that should've been in a damn display case, not on the streets collecting bodies.

Shun hit his hands on the steering wheel as Cyrus lay in the backseat in his button down and Stacy Adams. He was hot as hell trying to put together his weapon of choice. Cyrus grunted with a loud cuss after nearly getting the black gun polish on the lap of his pants.

"What the fuck you doin'?" Shun interrupted, nervous that Cyrus had gotten his white interior dirty.

"Preparing. Just pissed that we doing this shit without Phil. How long have you known this nigga Junior?"

"Jail," Shun replied slightly under his breath. He was embarrassed that he had chosen Junior to participate. Only he didn't have anyone else, and Junior had his back in prison more than once. So he couldn't just leave Junior out of the loop. He just hoped he hadn't made a mistake.

"Jail. Why was he in there, Shun? Man, you slippin'! You sure that pussy didn't poison yo' ass? We can't get caught slippin', nigga! This shit is real. Real money and real muthafuckin' men. These men, Shun, they play with guns for fun. I'm a shooter all day, but this Junior guy? We don't know what the deal is with him. You truly don't know this fool at all. Cuz, see, in jail, we solicit those we feel may aid us in making it out alive. It's the survival of the fittest. You were selected. Consider yourself lucky. However, let me tell you, this man right here probably listened to everything you said over the course of your stay in Wasco County Prison. He dreamed of your success, your power, and his intentions of getting close to you to delve into your business worked. Now we just some sitting ducks. Cuz, this nigga right here, walkin' up to yo' shit," Cyrus said shaking his head, "is either gon' try to kill you, or he gon' wait till you love 'im like a brother, and then he gon' set yo' ass up."

Shun looked around the car pondering Cyrus's synopsis of the entire situation. Part of him was thinking the same thing. Junior could have been fronting, helping him to later help himself. He couldn't think about all that right now, though. There was money to be made.

"We will definitely have to talk about this," Cyrus said to Shun as he caught sight of Junior jogging back to the car.

Phil twiddled his thumbs as he sat in his jail cell. He was irritated as shit having to sit in jail while waiting for Shun to get there. *That nigga move slower than molasses,* Phil thought to himself. Ain't no way he was going to be sitting in some jail waiting on a decision from a judge, who more than likely wanted to hang his ass too.

Phil wasn't going to lie. He couldn't wait to lay into Shun about his latest trials. He felt some type of way about the entire deal. *What the fuck I look like giving my drugs and money up to the police and turning myself in?* Phil replayed the conversation he had with Shun over and over in his mind. Shit wasn't adding up. He understood that he was the hothead, but blood was thicker than water. At least it was in his neck of the woods.

Junior walked up to the car fumbling about his pants.

"This man can't even keep his pants up without holding them. They don't make belts anymore, my nigga?" Cyrus said to himself but made sure both Shun and Junior heard his remarks. He wasn't gon' even play wit' the nigga. One false move, one move even, Cyrus already had *pop 'im* in his mind, with or without the go-ahead from Shun.

"What's up, nigga? You ready?" Cyrus sat up to greet Junior, whistling with his teeth and looking as if he had just got a strong whiff of some bad pussy. Cyrus placed his semiautomatic on his lap. He was getting aggravated at the time it took Junior to respond.

"You ready, nigga?" Junior responded with his forehead slightly creased. Cyrus gripped the base of his gun and bit his lip hard. Flaring his nose, he simply turned his gaze to locate Shun's attention in his rearview mirror. Cyrus was definitely looking for the go-ahead to kill Junior right in front of his mom's tilt.

"Man, y'all cut that shit out. We got shit to take care of," Shun said briskly. He could already hear the drama unfolding between the two of them. "Let's just roll. My mind is on this money, man." Shun sped down the road and took the back streets to the alley and warehouse where he was scheduled to meet with Frankie.

It took Shun a little over twenty minutes to reach Frankie's little hideout, and he couldn't wait to get Junior and Cyrus out of the backseat of his car. They were both unstable. He was breaking code by asking Cyrus and Junior in, but he needed the manpower. Shun worried they might conspire to take him out as well. He pulled into his usual parking space, then jumped out, leaving the two men behind as they took their time getting out of the car. Shun walked like a man with a plan. He wore a straight face as he entered the building, buttoning his blazer.

"Frankieeeee, what's up, bro? We retro? What time the plane leave? I got my two goons with me," Shun ranted, looking around. He realized he didn't hear any footsteps follow his nor did he hear a respectable hello. Cyrus was standing close behind, quiet and observing his surroundings. "All we need is our itinerary," Shun continued. "What's the plan?" He stood with his hands folded in front of him awaiting his instructions.

Junior was fidgeting around with his gun. One of Frankie's boys noticed right away. The observant one leaned in close to Frankie to give him the news of a possible undercover mission. Frankie nodded and directed his attention back to Shun and lowered his eyes.

"You ready or what?" Cyrus jumped in. He was eyeing all three of the men. He was gripping his Magnum so tight, his knuckles were beginning to turn white.

"Excuse me?" Frankie asked. "Are you talking to me? Boys, did this young man just speak out of turn to me? Shun?" Frankie stood, blinking at Cyrus, wondering if his courage was liquor filled. "Well, are you? Are you speaking to me?" Frankie looked puzzled as he drew his gun on Cyrus.

Cyrus stood his ground looking ready to put a bullet in Frankie's scalp. Frankie stared him down for a few seconds before succumbing to his own laughter. "I see you wit' the shit. Just know I am too." Frankie winked.

Shun put his hand up to warrant a stop to the madness. "Look, bro, we here to do business. I'm about my money, not who dick is bigga. Cyrus, fall back. Frankie, let me know what the deal is."

Junior just stood there with his hands visibly shaking.

"Shun, what's up wit' ya boy?" Frankie pointed out. "I think we need to talk." Frankie gestured that Shun follow him to a secluded area of the building.

"Stay right here," Shun instructed Cyrus and Junior.

Frankie started in almost immediately. "I don't trust your boy. He's way too fidgety. We have to get through customs. You think he's going to be able to get the drugs and money through without giving us up? Seriously, this shit is not a game. My ass is on the line just as much as yours is. You think I don't have someone to answer to? Don't we all?" Frankie looked concerned as he swayed back and forth, watching Shun's reaction to his theatrics.

Shun looked confused and tired of the hesitation. He was beginning to think that Frankie was playing with his mind and money. He was ready for the bread to roll in. Shun had plans. Once he got done with this round, he would lie low for a while. This run to the Philippines would set him straight for at least a year. He wasn't greedy. He just wanted enough loot to live comfortably. The thought of going back to school crossed his mind frequently. Continuing his degree in engineering from his time of service in the marines seemed feasible.

Shun was drifting a bit in his thoughts. He was ready to jump out of the game just as fast as he'd jumped in. The thought of Porsha crossed his mind more than he would've liked to admit as well. He wasn't one for falling for the mistress. He didn't know much about Porsha and her background. He just knew she seemed solid and had his best interest at heart. The things she said about Phil were true. He was unstable, but he couldn't just turn his back on him either.

Frankie jumped into Shun's train of thought in an attempt to get his head back into the game. "Look, I don't know what's up with your boy, but we need to get that shit under control before we move forward." Frankie waited for a response.

"Agreed," Shun said, angry that he was even put in such a situation. He couldn't believe how Junior was acting. It made him look bad. Cyrus was a keeper, provided his mouth could be tamed. However, it was evident that Junior was either up to no good or scary as shit. Either way, he had to be dealt with immediately.

"Man, what you think they talking about back there?" Junior chimed in as his forehead began to perspire.

Cyrus was looking at him puzzled as ever, while Junior looked high as a kite with lips as white as snow. Cyrus got instantly hot by Junior's presentation. "Man, what the fuck is wrong wit' you, nigga? You on that shit?" Cyrus's eyes grew wide, filled with wonder. "Man, tell me you ain't on that shit!" He cut his eyes toward Junior and leaned his head close to his shoulder. He was definitely testing him then, invading another man's personal space. Cyrus felt like beating Junior gruesomely with the butt of his gun. He lifted his chin toward Junior and looked him straight in the eyes. "Nigga, you betta be cool. You fuck this shit up for us, I'm going to kill you myself. I promise."

"Man, what the fuck you think they talking about? Fuck what I'm on. I'm alert and ready to shoot these fuck boys."

This time, one of Frankie's boys heard Junior's words. "Don't matter what the boss is talking about. You just be cool, boy."

"Boy!" Cyrus jumped in, feeling froggy. He didn't want Junior to think he was protecting him at all. It was just as if Frankie's clan had disrespected him personally. Since he was standing alongside Junior with the same color skin, the term "boy" didn't sit well with him.

"You better tell your boy to calm down," the second of the two flunkies on Frankie's team announced, raising his gun.

Cyrus immediately started in ready to pounce. He was loud and obnoxious at this point. "Fall back!"

"Naw, fuck this nigga! Let's pop his ass *right here. Right now.* I'm tellin' you, something is not right. They plottin' on us." Junior was fucking sweating so hard now there were puddles of water beneath his feet.

It made Cyrus nervous as shit. A man addicted to drugs with a damn gun was reason enough for Cyrus to shoot him, not to mention Frankie's boys were getting irritated as well.

One of Frankie goons cocked back his weapon and demanded that Cyrus and Junior drop their weapons. Cyrus looked down at his gun, then back at his adversary. "Naw, I'm good. I'm not putting shit down."

Junior grew very unstable from the demand to drop his weapon. Shun and Frankie finally came barging out of the back office nearly fumbling over each other to find out what all the fuss was about.

"Girls, girls, you're all pretty," Frankie shouted, clapping his hands to restore order. "What's the problem here? Don't you all like money?"

Cyrus stood with his gun drawn. He didn't trust the men in front of him or the one standing next to him. All he could think to do was shoot first and ask questions later.

"What y'all talk about back there? I already know all about it. You think you just gon' kill me. You want to kill me? You got anotha think comin'!" Junior was obviously having some sort of paranoid attack. He waved his gun around, demanding the money and drugs, as if his intention was to rob Frankie.

Shun stepped in front of Junior and placed his hands on Junior's biceps. "Have you fucking lost your mind? I don't know what the fuck you're doing, or, better yet, what drug of choice you're on, but for one, it bet not be ma shit, and two, it bet not be the kind I deal with," Shun said once he noticed how red and wide-eyed Junior was. "You on that shit?" Shun asked, biting the hell out of his bottom lip. He wanted to kill Junior. It wasn't a good look claiming to be transporters of drugs and money, and you are a fucking addict. Shun shook Junior's shoulders and leaned in close to whisper something in his ear. It looked like a scene from *The Godfather* or something.

Junior wasn't stable, and he knew it. Shun asked Junior to just lower his weapon and chill out until the deal was made. Only, after Shun's warning, it further irritated and heightened Junior's paranoia.

Junior pushed past Shun and pulled his weapon.

Shocked and dismayed, Shun immediately started in. "Junior, what the fuck you doin', man?" Junior spoke in action and fired three shots in Shun's direction. Shun was hit twice and knocked down. Cyrus chimed right in, shooting Junior six times at close range. Cyrus was ready to fire away, gearing up to take out Frankie and his clan. Only Cyrus had solved the main issue by omitting Junior from the equation. The fucked-up part in this was that he could have omitted Shun as well.

"Frankie! Frankie! Shun's hit. We gotta get help." Cyrus panicked.

CHAPTER 4

Pussy Whipped

Porsha walked into the doors of Kern County Jail with a slight attitude. She wore a skintight black dress with red pumps. Her hair was pulled up in a princess bun, and her breasts were exposed and accented with a red lace bra. Porsha walked with an elegant sway toward the front desk. She was ready for love and war. She started and stopped as she felt a jump in her panties that was unexpected.

Thoughts of Shun's dick playing with her G-spot made her pussy twitch. Yet, she burned with anger. She took Shun's rejection harder than she herself expected. She assumed he was ready for love. His business was taking a huge leap toward monetary stability, and all she wanted to do was love and care for him. Her love for money wouldn't be denied, but she actually cared for Shun. She wouldn't be ignored either. She could give two shits about Phil. She knew he was bad news. The thing was, he was the closest thing to Shun, and she just wanted to be with him. So second best would just have to do.

Porsha waited for assistance at the window of the clerk's desk. The clerk was busy filling out some paperwork and had yet to address her. The place was filled with homeless people and drunk men. Porsha had to cover her nose and face to shield from the fumes of vomit and pee.

"Excuse me, ma'am." Porsha straightened her stance and tugged at her black minidress that rode high above her knees. Her dress left little to the imagination, but then again, that was the point. She wasn't sure how easy Phil was. She knew he wasn't a disciplined man by his track record. He was in jail based on greed. So he was a man with a weak soul.

"Money," Porsha said to herself, shifting her weight from one leg to the other. Her heels were necessary, but they were beginning to give her hell.

"Ma'am, can I get some assistance, please?" Porsha asked with a hint of irritation. She didn't want to come off like she was some ghetto hood rat, but she felt some kind of way about being ignored. The clerk was black and thought she was better than the rest of the working class in front of her desk. She was one of those fat, hairy women with a grey goatee, smirking every time she looked up from her computer and notepad. Porsha was getting angry at this point. The clerk's attitude became a sting in her craw. Her blood was beginning to boil, and nervousness followed. She sure as hell couldn't be caught by Shun at the jail bailing Phil out. How was she going to explain that shit? Especially after the way she talked about Phil previously, as if he was a walking virus. He was bad news, but if she had to, she would take him. Porsha was good at taking on cases. Phil just needed the right woman to tell him what to do. Honestly, the pussy does that if the woman behind the cat is working it correctly. A man is easily tamed by a woman's touch. Those with weak spirits, that is.

"How can I help you, ma'am?"

"Well, I'm here to pay the bail for a friend."

"Friend, huh?"

"Yes, friend!"

"Okay, so what's the name of this friend?"

"Phil goes by the name of Phil or Philly."

"Riiiggghht, the innocent one. Then again, all of our inmates are innocent," the officer commented, amused by her sarcastic undertone. Porsha just stood there with her lips pinched, trying desperately not to speak for fear she would spew something unsavory.

"How much is the bail, ma'am?" Porsha asked, avoiding the general conversation the officer was interested in conducting.

"Two grand, 10 percent!"

Porsha sucked on her teeth as she dug into her purse and pulled out a wad of cash. The officer looked on with a glow in her eyes, but a nasty look of disapproval on her brow. Porsha counted out the money slowly, on purpose, so the officer could get a good look at it. She knew she was itching to ask her where the money came from. She probably thought Phil was her pimp or some shit. Porsha thought to indulge in the officer's unspoken assumptions, but she hadn't the time.

"Here!" Porsha slid the money onto the counter. She was sad to see it go, but it was a small price to pay for her investment.

The officer counted the money at least three times before instructing one of the officers to go and fetch Phil.

"If you would just take a seat. It shouldn't be long. Just fill out these papers."

Porsha took the clipboard from the officer and headed toward a vacant seat. The eyes were heavy on her. The stench of booze and sex was heavy. Coked out prostitutes hung out on every corner of the room as if marking their territory, while drunken bar hoppers sobered up on the bench. The jail was overcrowded, and Porsha worried about possible disease if she sat down for too long. Sadly, she would have to take a chance because her dogs were barking.

She flipped through a fifteen-page discharge packet, skimming through the questions. Most of them she had no answers for. She didn't know much about Phil. Porsha filled out as much of the paperwork as she could. She didn't have the time to outline Phil's entire life, 90 percent of which she knew nothing about. Shun ranted on just enough for Porsha to pass as a friend of the family.

"Hey, you!" the officer shouted into Phil's holding cell.

"Ma cousin here?" Phil jumped up in excitement. He smoothed the front of his jumpsuit with his hands as if to iron out the wrinkles and rubbed his hands together.

"Well, if that sweet piece of ass sitting out front is your cousin, I have a proposition for you."

"What the fuck you talkin' 'bout, nigga? You betta gon' wit' that gay shit, brah. I don't give a damn if you are the law." Phil was furious that the officer had made a gay pass at him and his cousin Shun. He quickly tried to regain his composure as he thought that perhaps the officer was just trying to get a rise out of him.

The officer just laughed at Phil. He was serious about the woman, however, so he decided to inquire about the lady in the lobby once more.

"So who is the chick, your ho, your baby mama? Who?"

Phil didn't respond this time. He just stood there. He had his head and chin turned up and his nose flared as the officer took off his handcuffs and threw him his plastic bag with his belongings in them. Phil seemed to undress in one swoop. He was beaming, skinning, and grinning like a kid in a candy store. He hadn't done any real time but felt like he had been absent from civilization for a few years at least.

Phil dug through the bag a few times with a question-able look on his face. "Y'all got me for my bread and watch, I see. It's good!" Phil could feel the heat in his chest rise. It fell quickly. His only mission was to get home, take a long shower, and set on the hunt for his drugs and money.

He tossed the jumpsuit in the corner of his cell and followed the officer out into the discharge area. He signed his name hurriedly and searched the room for Shun.

Porsha noticed Phil and began refreshing her makeup. She wasn't sure he would remember her, but she wanted to make a good impression on him. Phil frequented the club where she worked, but she never had the pleasure of dancing for him. He was too loud for her, always throwing around singles as if they were hundreds.

The girls in the club actually called Shun "Hunnid." All he rolled with was a stack of hundred-dollar bills. He would spend a bill on drinks, a bill on a girl, but he never engaged with anyone on a sociable level until Porsha came along. Both Shun and Porsha would agree that he was better sober. His mental devices were well tampered with under the influence. He was a horrible drunk.

Phil looked around the room once again. He was beginning to get upset.

"Who you say made my bail again?" Phil asked the officer.

"Hey, Phil." Porsha threw her arm up and sashayed toward Phil and the officer.

"That her. She the piece of ass of I was telling you about," the officer grunted and cleared his throat as he lowered his chin and watched Porsha's every move while she approached.

"Ah, man, naw, that's the broad from the club. I wonder what the fuck she doin' here?" Phil leaned in and commented under his breath as if the officer was one of his boys. Noticing his slip in judgment, Phil looked alarmed at the officer, hoping he hadn't paid too much attention to his last statement.

"Well, since you seem to be having some difficulties with mating this one, I'll take her off your hands."

Phil didn't respond to the officer; instead, he took to eying Porsha himself in an effort to pick apart her motives.

"You ready?" Porsha stood clutching her phone, scrolling from screen to screen and reading text messages as if she was following the directions of someone. "Yessss, damn, I told you I would," Porsha recited aloud as she hurriedly texted back with a look of frustration.

Phil's eyes were dead on hers, waiting for the deceit to give her away. "Yeah, let's go."

Porsha waved good-bye to the officer who couldn't seem to stop staring at her breasts protruding from the top of her black minidress. Porsha's nipples were well defined. She couldn't hide her excitement. She was so wet she feared her juices may soon drip down her legs. It was crazy how the thought of Shun's touch could nearly bring her to come in public. Porsha took in a deep breath as she felt her clit harden and tickle the satin in her panties.

"Well, let's go," she said, erotically exhaling with a slight moan that stroked Phil's interest to probe. Porsha turned on her heel and led the way to her car.

Phil hopped in the car with her, exercising very little judgment in the matter. First question that should have probed his mind was simple. Why the hell was this broad picking him up from jail? Second, where the fuck was Shun? Third thing, a bitch comes out of the woodwork from a club—red flag automatically. What did she need? Who was she fuckin' with? Did he send her? Lastly, where the fuck was his loot? Thing was, he had better rock and roll with ole girl, temporarily, at least. Perhaps she was the smoke screen he needed to keep his affairs on the low.

Porsha switched around to the back of her whip and popped open the trunk. Phil was chill, which was a surprise to her. His ass was loud and obnoxious. That much she knew. She was waiting for him to lay into her. Her motives were clear, and the story she had for him was clear as well. It was simple. Shun said he wasn't fuckin' with him, and she found the shit foul. So she came to his rescue and thought he should know that his cousin was running major drug sales in not only corporate America, but in the hood. Territories Phil deemed as his own. The plot was thick as shit. She could care less cause, real talk. She would have been more loyal than a muthafucka to Shun, but he was playing games like his shit was platinum or somethin'.

Porsha came around to the driver's seat and got in. She immediately started in on Phil, placing her hands on his lap and traveling close to his dick. Phil's leg tensed. He could feel his shit rise. He cursed under his breath. He knew his ass was in trouble. The pussy was a severe problem he had yet to get a grip on. He already had a gang of baby mamas running around the hood.

His main bitch, however, was this nerd chick who attended California State University, Fresno. He got to see her only on holidays and a few times during the year when he drove up there to surprise her. More for his own benefit. He was scared of his attachment to Monica. He wasn't sure if she was this Goodie Two-shoes and whether he could trust her with his life.

In all honesty, Phil wasn't trying to get caught up with none of them hoes. The baby mama drama was a bit much considering he had drugs to sell, money to make, and bitches to fuck. His current girl was definitely mainstream pussy. Pussy he could bring home to moms—if he had one.

Phil's mom had been dead for ten years on account of a drug overdose, and his dad was his uncle, so his family was full of dysfunction. Love was overrated. The sound of it scared the shit out of 'im. He couldn't deny his feelings for Monica, which was the main reason he kept a close watch on her. He seriously wanted to wife Monica when the time was right, but for now, he was cool with her doing the school thing while he stacked his chips.

Phil was deep in thought but was distracted by Porsha's fondling and attempt to fuck him right in the jail parking lot. It was a dark underground parking structure, so to each his own. He hadn't had any pussy in over seventy-two hours, and he was beginning to wonder what hers tasted like and how good her pussy would feel choking the shit out of his dick.

Porsha was busy unbuttoning Phil's pants, exposing how hard he was. The head of his dick tingled and jumped in anticipation of her hot and wet mouth engulfing all eight inches of his circumcised penis.

Porsha dove in hard and hungry. She took in all of him after French-kissing the head of his dick, slowly, as if making love to it. Porsha allowed the spit from her mouth to accumulate before expelling it all over his dick. Phil moaned in excitement as he felt the wetness slide down the shaft of his penis. He responded by grabbing hold of her head and guiding her head to bob at a growing rate of acceleration. This excited Porsha as well. She began to moan and beg for Phil to come in her mouth.

Phil wasn't ready for that just yet. He wanted to feel how tight that pussy was. He grabbed Porsha by her face and kissed her deep in her mouth. Kissing hoes was totally against the rules. He didn't know what had come over him. Perhaps because he was forced to take a pussy hiatus and he was experiencing withdrawal.

"Bring that pussy here," Phil coached Porsha. She didn't need much direction. She quickly climbed onto his lap and sat directly on his dick with ease.

Phil groaned with satisfaction as he felt her wetness warm and squeeze his dick. "Fuck, you got some good pussy."

"Top of the line, baby. You like this pussy, Philly?" Porsha moaned as she rode the shit out of his dick, grinding harder and deeper with each penetration.

Phil bit his lip, desperately trying not to come too fast. But she clearly had him under her spell. Her hips were moving in such ways that brought him close to tears. She could easily make a nigga say, "I love you!" and he had the urge.

Porsha kissed Phil on his lips gently and stared deep into his eyes as she slowly twerked on his dick to music playing in the background. He was mesmerized by her beauty. Her lips were still swollen from sucking his dick. She smiled, exposing the dimple in her right cheek.

"Come for me, Daddy. Come for me." Porsha continued to grind deeper. Phil begged for more as he nearly tore the top of Porsha's black dress to get to her breast. He teased the nipple a bit, then grabbed hold of her breast with his mouth, sucking the shit out of her tits, so much so it almost hurt. Porsha swirled her hips slowly in circular motions, then in a rise and fall. She wanted to feel how deep he could go. Slowly, Porsha tightened her pelvis so her pussy hugged his dick slightly harder as she squirted continuously.

Phil moaned as he arched his pelvis to meet her every move as he climaxed. Porsha smiled, wiping the sweat from her nose with Phil's.

"Where to now?" Porsha inquired, cheesing.

"I got a few stops to make. Then you are goin' to tell me where the fuck my cousin Shun at. What was so important that he couldn't come and get me himself?" Phil replied with a look on his face that spoke of malice and foul play.

"Will do," Porsha replied, scooting off of Phil's now-limp dick and back into the driver's seat.

"Naw, I'm driving," Phil demanded, adjusting his zipper, making his way to the driver's side of Porsha's sports car.

CHAPTER 5

Loot

"Get on your knees!" Phil and Porsha yelled simultaneously. They were blowing through trap house to trap house, stealing money and drugs no matter the consequence.

"Gimme the loot!" Porsha demanded, tossing the duffle bag at one of the men and hissing for his boy to shut up and get down.

"What the fuck!" one of the men said, yelling so loud he was drooling from the mouth like a pit bull. "Do you know who the fuck I am?"

Phil shook his head and kicked the man square in the mouth. The man's head snapped back, and he bounced to the floor before coming to a rest. Phil and Porsha moved about the room like a winter breeze, collecting the money and drugs. They left no stone unturned.

Two Weeks Later
"Man, word on the street your cuz Phil and that broad Porsha got some kind of Bonnie and Clyde thing going on. I'm talkin' 'bout some real grime shit, you feel me? They kickin' in trap house doors, stealing drug money and everything. I mean, naked bitches runnin' out that muthafucka, and some mo'."

"Fuck that nigga. I get discharged in a few days. You comin'?" Shun responded with a rasp in his voice, as if smokin' on a blunt. He completely ignored Cyrus's rant. The IV in his arm was irritating. He felt a tug in his veins. His entire body was extremely sore from the shooting. "I been in here two muthafuckin' weeks. Two weeks, ma nigga, and that man ain't come see 'bout me not once. 'Round here chasin' pussy like some mutt. I'm sick to ma stomach at the mention of that bitch name too. How you know anyway, Blood? I hope his name ain't being soiled in the streets on account of hearsay, ma nigga. I have high hopes that niggas just runnin' they mouth. Cuz if he is truly runnin' behind this ho, breakin' bread and shit, then fuck it. He deserved that shit. No investigation needed. The truth always reveals itself."

"How that happen?"

Shun shook his head. His thoughts ran wild as he thought about the incident between himself and Porsha. He saved himself by runnin' from that pussy. Her shit was more poison than a muthafucka. Phil had better learn how to swim toward the exit. Pussy will get a nigga killed, *fast*.

Main reason, he couldn't fuck with Porsha on some ole boyfriend-and-girlfriend-type shit. He couldn't deny he felt some type of way. Shun was careful in his choice of words for worry his feelings would breathe life if expelled to the air. Plus, he was surrounded by some unknown niggas he knew in his heart would kill to take his place at any given moment. Shun smiled through the pain, then grimaced as he tried to sit up a bit. He went in search of his call button.

"Hey, I need somethin'," Shun snapped. He was in so much pain he was afraid he would break down in front of the pack of wolves that stood in front of him, crying like a damn baby. He was lucky. The bullets hadn't hit any major arteries, and the one that hit his belly was through and through. The bullet wound just below his clavicle bone was lodged in a very sensitive area. Doctors couldn't be certain, but their hope was that the bullet wouldn't travel, causing more issue to come about. Shun couldn't worry about that for too long. He was just happy he could feel his legs and could walk. He was mad at himself for going against his own code. It was his own damn fault, really. He was in the predicament he was in because he didn't follow the rules of engagement. He was fuckin' with too many niggas. Should have just stuck to his solo game. He was making money, but greed begets greed, and the money was calling. He couldn't just stand there and watch the next man get it.

Cyrus canvassed the area as he usually did when he was certain there was a traitor about. He stared each man down from the corner of his eye as he held his hand under his chin, speculating. Shun needed to take a few pills and get the fuck out of Dodge. There was work to be done, and the longer he sat in bed trippin' off a few gunshot wounds, the more money he would lose. Hell, Porsha and Phil were on a major come up. He was Phil's boy all day. He couldn't stand that he was allowing some bitch to dictate his next moves. One thing Shun was right about was that pussy will damn sure get a nigga killed.

Cyrus stood in the corner of the room and watched as the nurse came in to give Shun his routine meds. He knew he would be out like a light in a matter of minutes. His job as handler and bodyguard would be to clear the room so the man could get some rest. He was happy to put the bug in Shun's ear about the happenings on the streets. Shun needed to get his head back in the game. He worried about Phil. It was evident the bitch had to go. Porsha was playing that man like a fiddle. If Phil wasn't careful, he was going to end up dead one of two ways: by the pussy or by Karma.

Phil never took to robbin' the next man for drugs and money. The licks were a high school pastime. As adults, he got his drugs from suppliers and sold it legitimately. Only ass whoopin's handed out were those to fools who didn't pay on time, or buster-ass niggas snitchin' about the establishment.

Cyrus excused the men from the room so he could have a quick word with Shun before he dozed off. He was serious in his inquiries and had plans of his own but wanted to talk to Shun to get his take on the situation as well. He grew up with both Shun and Phil, but he ran the streets with Phil. His loyalties were in between. He had both their best interests at heart. It was a must that Porsha be dealt with. The question was how and who was going to carry it out.

Cyrus stepped to the edge of Shun's bed and looked down at him with a look of doom and concern. "Man, I don't want to bother you about this shit, but we need to make a move on this Porsha and Phil shit."

"What would you suggest I do about the situation? I'm not presently in a position to make many moves, Cyrus. You know me. I'm not gonna kiss nobody ass. If he feel like Porsha is the one for him, then fine." Shun was burning with anger, trying hard to make light of it. He couldn't believe how trifling Porsha's ass was. Hell, he couldn't believe he was lying in a hospital bed—shot.

"The man obviously feels some type of way about me. He hasn't come to see about me. This shit is for the birds. I want that bitch's head, real talk." Shun could feel his eyes getting heavy. "I want out of here, though, you right about that. It's time to get out of here. Shit."

Shun was fast asleep in less than a minute. His voice trailed off, and Cyrus's mind began to wander.

"Yeah, I got you, brah. You will be out of here in no time."

***

Cyrus left Shun to get some sleep. He met up with his nurse at her station and waved to get her attention. The nurse smiled at his pearly whites as she sashayed her tight scrubs over to him. He bit his lip as he searched her complete frame before speaking. She was beautiful. She was a short thang, couldn't be more than five foot three with creamy chocolate skin. She had a head full of charcoal-black hair that was parted in the middle and set behind both her ears. She certainly got his attention.

"I need you to do somethin' for me, Ma!"

"And what is that?" The nurse stood with her hands on her hips, biting her bottom lip.

"I need you to get my boy some meds. Can you do that for me?" Cyrus smiled and licked his lips as he spoke seductively.

The nurse stood for a minute as if pondering the request. "What do I get out of this?" she asked, lowering her gaze to Cyrus's dick.

"I can handle that," he smiled, showing off the dimple in his left cheek.

The nurse turned on her heel and walked speedily down to the medicine station. Cyrus made his way back to the room to prepare Shun for his departure.

"Aaahhhh!" Porsha screamed with glee as she rolled all over the bed piled high with money. She kicked and hollered about the day's earnings. Porsha's happiness drained fast, however, when she noticed Phil in a corner looking out the window with his pistol drawn. Shit was hot, and as the stealing spree continued, drug lords put a price on their heads.

"What's the matter, baby?"

"Nothin'. Just have to stay on my toes, Ma. Riches come with a price, responsibility, and Karma, all balled into one. You don't think we're able to roam freely, do you? I haven't heard from Shun either, so I'm getting worried. I hope that nigga okay. I thought the trip was supposed to be a quick pickup and back to the States. It's been two weeks at least," Phil said tapping his temple with his gun.

Porsha flared her nose at Phil's inquiries. She wasn't tryin'a hear shit about Shun and his money trails. The way she saw it, he was on the list of people to rob as well. She just needed the right time and place because she knew Phil wouldn't go for that.

"Don't trip, Phil, okay? We got to make this money and, apparently, Shun didn't care to inform or include you on his shit. So why should you be feeling guilty about your come up? Let that shit go. You can't be under that nigga wing all yo' damn life."

"What the fuck is that supposed to mean? I think you better watch your mouth. We been through a lot, and half this shit I did alone. Never been a follower, neither has he. We just wanted different things. At the time, I was so fuckin' mad at 'im cuz I felt he abandoned me. But he wanted better shit, you feel me? Felt like we could rise above the hood. Even though he ended up doin' time for the next nigga, it wasn't on no bitch shit. He went to jail for loyalty to a fuckin' country that could give two shits about him. Do you know they stripped him of all his honors? Then they just threw his ass back in the streets as if he hadn't served his country and people. So you watch what you say about my cousin. You don't know shit about our struggle. Despite his latest actions, he is all I got and never has betrayed me." Phil's voice trailed off as he thought about the times in the hood they ran from the police after stealing from the liquor store.

"Well, all that's in the past. You're with me now. We're doing just fine without Shun."

Phil looked up from his private stakeout to look Porsha dead in the face. There was something about the tone in her voice that set him off. He couldn't put his finger on it. He wasn't stupid. Porsha felt some type of way about Shun, and he was going to get to the bottom of it. However, he wasn't going to disclose his curiosity to her. He was going to go straight to Shun about the shit. He'd already smelled a rat from day one, her swooping him from jail like she was doing him such a big favor.

The sex was cool. The money was lovely, but sooner or later, their cover would be blown and going into hiding would be inevitable. Something Phil had no plans of doing. He always knew he'd go out with a bang. Whether Porsha was down with that was neither here nor there. He just figured his time of exit would be right next to his only true blood left, and that was Shun.

Porsha stormed about the hotel room packing the money up into duffle bags and pulling her tight jeans up around her thick thighs.

"Look, you want to sit in here and throw a pity party about your cousin moving on to bigger and better things, then you go right ahead. I'm about making money. That nigga could care less about you, your feelings, your money, your well-being, and the entire motions of it all. Where is that nigga now?"

Phil twiddled his thumbs and bit his bottom lip. He wasn't really concerned about Porsha's latest statements. He was trying desperately not to go upside her head. "Yeah, we shall see."

CHAPTER 6

Game Plan

By the time Shun woke up from his most recent drug-induced nap, he found himself in the comforts of his own bed. Cyrus had the room set up just like a hospital, and the nurse from his room was standing over him changing the fluids on his IV. Shun just shook his head and grabbed for the nurse's shirttail to get her attention.

"How long have I been out? You think you can help me sit up?"

"Sure. Let me just make sure your tubing doesn't get all twisted up, and I'll let you get up and get yourself dressed." Sophia taped his IV after untangling his tubing.

"You ready?" she asked.

"Damn, this shit must gon' hurt. You wouldn't be asking me if I was ready if it was a piece of cake. I guess let's just get it over with."

"Okay, I'm going to lay the bed flat real quick so I can help you scoot up. Doing it this way won't be as bad as you trying to scoot up upright."

"Okay."

Sophia let the bed down so that Shun could lie back. He nearly panicked because he felt uncomfortable, like his airways were stifled a bit. He took a few labored breaths and winced a bit with pain.

Sophia counted to three. "One, two, three, now pull." She and Shun both grunted while pulling him into a better position. She then let the bed up to a sitting position.

"There, all set." she said.

"I appreciate it. Thank you," Shun said, unsure if he was going to be able to carry out the tasks of everyday living alone. He felt strong mentally and was determined, but his muscles were weak from the past three weeks of bed rest.

"Cyrus is in the front room, so if you need anything just holler. I've got to get back to the hospital, but I'll check in on you after my shift." The nurse smiled innocently and left Shun to his own devices.

Shun observed the perimeters of his room before he made an attempt to move. He was determined. To complete the task wasn't the issue. The amount of pain he was going to have to endure was.

Shun placed his neck pillow in his mouth so that he could muffle the sounds of anguish. His stomach was sore. Each move was a task in itself. He bit down on his pillow and inched his way to the door of his room. About thirty minutes later, he made his way to the living room with his gun in his right hand. Cyrus was busy on the phone with one of his goons about his latest pickup. Shun made his way to the kitchen and grabbed himself a soda. His legs and lower back were killing him. He instantly went for one of the cereal boxes on top of the refrigerator. Shun pulled out a half of Kush and tossed it over to his dining room table. He then popped open the fridge and took a long swig of syrup, backing it with a gulp of soda.

"Damn, nigga! You good?" Cyrus interrupted Shun's entrance to intoxication beyond measure. "You feeling better?"

"I'm feeling something," Shun said, laying his gun down on the table. "I'm poppin' these damn pills like Skittles," he said as he hobbled at record speed to a chair at the living room table. Shun pulled out his chair and began to sit, inching ever so slowly into his seat. Then he began rolling blunts like he was entering a contest in the Guinness Book of Records. Shun burned the exterior of his blunt to ensure it was sealed after licking her closed. He was caressing it sweet and tenderly as if pulling the satin to reveal the core of a bitch's pussy. Lighting the bitch and inhaling her sweetness opened his mind and relaxed his muscles. The pressure in his back seemed to dissipate, and the crease in his forehead from the frustration of pain unfolded. Shun rubbed his forehead with the butt of his gun. He was in a trance, rocking slightly while he collected his thoughts.

"Phil call?" he spoke under his breath, but Cyrus caught every word.

"Not yet. We need to find out what's going on, though. You ready to hit these streets? Get some shit cleaned up?" Cyrus's nose was flared, and he was gritting his teeth. He seemed both nervous and irritated.

"Organization and planning is how I move. I can't just go in hot all the damn time." Shun was smoking on a blunt and cleaning his weapon as he talked to Cyrus about his next move. "No matter what you hear on the streets, we can't just go by that, Cy. The marines do teach you that much: discipline, loyalty, honor. Shit, these men have no idea about that."

"You still believe in that shit after they threw you to the wolves?"

"Yeah, I believe in it. I breathe it. I followed it. Can't say much about what other men do, even in the line of duty. I can only speak for myself."

"Duly noted," Cyrus responded.

"Can't wait too much longer in response to the streets, though. They talk! Loud! And when there is no movement, the takeover is inevitable."

"I'm not a gangster, Cyrus," Shun enunciated in his white valley voice. "Neither is Phil. We drug dealers, my man, supply and demand. You on some ole *American Gangster* shit. I'm not looking for all that drama, you feel me? That's how you stay alive and out of the drama of it all. Cyrus, you've got to learn how to slow down and let shit solve itself. I want to live to see the fruits of my labor."

"I mean, real talk, you think Phil know what he doin'?" Cyrus interrupted.

"I don't know. Hell, this shit he on right now, I have to admit is new to me. But our next move has got to be a strategic one."

"Dude, this ain't war. You talking like we in the Desert Storm or something."

Shun shook his head. "That's the thing, we *are* at fucking war. You think these niggas gon' let Phil just go about his business after he ran in these people shit? If he was smart, he'd be in hiding already."

"I guarantee that bitch feeding him information."

Shun looked down at the fire of his lit blunt fascinated by its burning glow. "Yeah, perhaps. But Phil ain't stupid. He got enough sense to start reading between the lines. Phil know what pussy smell and feel like. Hell, he been busy."

Cyrus fell back on the couch with laughter. "Yeah, that nigga been through Kern County like a muthafucka. I'm surprised ain't one of these bitches got to his ass."

"Don't be surprised, nigga. Phil ain't playing with these bitches. He don't mind domestic violence. It's a matter of time before Porsha catch an eye jammy. She got a mouth on her. She will get out of line." Shun's nose flared uncontrollably.

"Yeah, I feel that shit. So, what's the plan?"

"I'm going to go get the drugs from the Philippines." Shun lit another blunt and left it hanging for dear life on the edge of his lips as he finished twisting another.

"How many blunts you gon' smoke, nigga?"

"As many as it takes to keep my mind off of this God-awful pain. I need a new supply fast. How many pills that nurse give you?"

"She gave me ninety capsules. How many are you taking? I'm getting worried about you, Shun. Don't get addicted to this shit, man."

"Addicted? Nigga, I ain't some crackhead. Just need enough to get me through the day, is all, without falling prey to sleep. I got shit to do, so I can't just be taking them pills all day. Besides, I'm about to stop taking them shits cuz they damn near ain't workin' no more. You see I'm smokin' like crazy. I just rolled five blunts, and I ain't passin'."

"Yeah, I noticed. My hand been out a few times and you failed to take notice. So are we going to talk about what went down with you and Porsha, or are we going to toss that shit to the winds?"

"Fuck that bitch. She was—" Shun stopped dead in his tracks and thought about Porsha. The sex wasn't bad, and she wasn't bad on the eyes either, but she wanted too much too fast. And to go behind his back, bail Phil out, then start fuckin' with 'im. After all the shit she spoke about was beyond dirty. Shun knew her moves. He wasn't stupid. He couldn't blame Phil, cuz how was he supposed to know that was one of his chicks? Ain't no telling what the hell that woman said to Phil to get him to thinking somethin' foul was going down.

Why else hadn't he shown up to see about him? Regardless of any beef they ever had, Phil and Shun made every effort to be there for each other, no questions asked. Perhaps Phil felt like Shun made a selfish decision in meeting with Frankie without him while he waited for bail. That was the only thing Shun could think of that Porsha could use against him.

Phil was big on loyalty. It was his life, and if things were stale between them, it had to be because he thought he left him hung out to dry for drugs and money. In an effort to make peace, Shun thought about contacting Phil, but he had to be careful about his dealings with his own cousin presently. He didn't know where his mind was, and he for sure didn't want to cross paths with Porsha just yet.

Shun was smoking so many blunts his chest began to rattle a bit. He quickly tossed his lit blunt into the ash tray in an effort to regain control over his binging.

Porsha jumped into the front seat of her Mustang and slammed her fists on the steering wheel. She was so angry with herself for allowing her emotions to override reason. She was going to be stuck with Phil after all the shit they had done. There was no way she could return to work. Porsha sat still just staring out into the night. She was trying hard to think about her next move. Should she just go to Shun and ask for help? How did she get herself into this mess? her mind wondered.

"Fuck!" Porsha said to herself. She was so confused about her latest moves. Her motives were so off-kilter. Shun must've thought she was a complete whore. She hadn't seen him around town herself and had to admit she hoped to catch a glimpse of him. Unfortunately, they had to keep a low profile due to their heists. Still, it wasn't like Shun not to contact Phil, even if it was just to cuss Phil out about something.

Phil wasn't at all her type, and what started out as just a ploy to make Shun jealous had gone a bit too far. She was in too deep. A façade she knew she couldn't handle, playing the role of some badass chick, when she knew nothing of the world except what she could decipher from her nightlife at the club and movies.

Porsha was from the hills. She was rebellious, at best. Daddy bought her car, and she just stripped in the club to get a rise out of her parents. Porsha had this stupid idea that bad boys were the most loyal and confident. They had to be. They were fearless, especially when it came to the law. Daddy was always so careful, and she was tired of being so restricted.

Porsha's thoughts were flowing. "I need to end this."

"End what?" Phil asked.

Porsha hadn't noticed him as he came around to the driver's seat of the car.

"What are you doing out here? What's the matter?"

"Nothing, just thinking about our next move is all."

"Really?" Phil didn't buy anything about her statement, but he let it go. "Well, come inside. I'm hungry."

Porsha rolled up her windows and locked her car down before jumping out and following Philly inside.

"I'm going to go and see what these men doing on the block," Cy said with a hint of irritation. "You gon' be okay here?"

"Yeah, sure. I'm going to put these weapons up and take a nap." Shun was fed up with the situation. The secrecy and the feelings of abandonment and disloyalty to Phil were taking their toll. He knew better that he shouldn't travel alone, but he needed to find out what was going on with Phil. He had no plans of taking a nap. He had to find Phil and knew just where to look.

"Okay, man! I'll be back to check on you in a few hours. I'm going to pick up my bread from these cats and make sure niggas not gettin' high off ma shit or trickin' ma chips."

"I hear that!" Shun replied as he packed up his weapons and headed for his bedroom. "Lock me in. I'm going to crash."

Shun threw his icepack on the nightstand next to his bed and winced a little from the pain.

"Fuck!" he exclaimed as he peeled back the bandages on his wounds. The hole looked deep and something out of some sort of sci-fi magazine. He shook his head as he grimaced and pulled off the old bandages to put on fresh ones.

He took his time putting on fresh True Religion jeans, a wife beater, and a fresh pair of Jordans. It seemed to take forever for him to pull his leather bomber over his arms. He was so exhausted he became winded.

"So what's the game plan?" Shun asked himself, double-checking his rough hair and untamed beard and mustache. Before he could change his plan, he grabbed his keys and headed to the car.

Shun drove the streets without ease. He had only full use of one arm. The seat belt seemed to melt into his stomach, applying pressure. It was almost unbearable. With sudden movement to his arm, his collarbone was burning well up into his throat.

"Shit!" he yelped, angry at the amount of pain he was in. He felt so weak and out of sorts. He pulled up to the front of Porsha's condo. He saw her silver Mustang parked outside, so he pulled up down the block. He didn't want her to peep out of the window and see him coming. She would be sure to lock the doors and call the police then. Shun didn't know what he was thinking going to see Porsha, but his motives were to clear the air and put an APB out on his cousin. He was sure she had some indication of his whereabouts.

Shun sat in his car for a full minute, looking down at the steering wheel before wiggling out of the front seat. He moaned in agony a bit as he looked around the block to make sure no one caught him in this weak moment.

"What the fuck am I supposed to say?" Shun coached himself as he walked as briskly as he could down the block. His swag was different. He walked with a limp that was involuntary, like a pimp from the eighties. It bothered him that he couldn't walk with the confidence he presented before. The pain stabbed deep into his leg and caused a slight pang in his back.

Shun stopped right in front of Porsha's home. He felt paralyzed. He stood there pondering his approach for a minute before he could get his feet to move. Finally, he knocked on the door and rang the doorbell with confidence.

The Bonnie and Clyde duo were startled by the knocks at the door. Porsha hurriedly instructed Phil to gather all of the money and paraphernalia.

"Stay here!" Porsha demanded of Phil.

Phil looked worried but didn't say anything. Just turned on his heel and ventured out into the seclusion of Porsha's extra bedroom.

Porsha wiped the sweat from her hands before opening the door. She was sure it was the police.

"Shun!" she gasped.

CHAPTER 7

Blood on My Hands

"Porsha!" was all Shun could muster as he stared deep into her eyes.

"What happened to you? Oh my God." Porsha fell into Shun's arms, all inhibitions and anger melting away. Shun let out a loud grunt as he felt the impact of her body.

He grabbed hold of Porsha with his good arm and pulled her close against his mind's intent.

"I was shot at the meeting. Things went from bad to worse in a matter of moments." Shun shook away thoughts of death and dying as he fell into a coma of fear and uncertainty. He was taken back into the very moment where he clung to life. Money and power didn't mean so much then. Shun's eyes watered as he began explaining the events leading up to the gunfire.

"I'm glad you're OK."

"Yeah," Shun said, quickly drying up. He slid back into reality and pushed away from Porsha, to her surprise.

"Word around town is that you and Phil been kicking tough."

Porsha looked up at him with tear-filled eyes as she realized how hurt he was. "I bailed him out that day with the intention of helping. He seduced me, and I was so vulnerable. It was inevitable. I know it was wrong, and I'm sorry."

"So why hasn't he contacted me? I mean, I understand how shit happens. It just means that you wasn't really about that life, no way."

"What do you mean?"

"I mean you talking all that shit about being my wife, my girl and shit. Then you jump in bed with my cousin seconds later. You foul."

"Shun!"

"Porsha," Shun said dryly, looking at her as if he held back tears. He was in so much pain, both mentally and physically.

"Shun, I love you."

Shun looked at Porsha and then up into the air. "Don't worry about me. You do right by my cousin."

Porsha stood still for a few seconds as she searched Shun's face. She was irritated by his comment but knew she deserved it.

Phil stood just behind the door listening to the entire conversation. He couldn't believe Porsha's lying ass. She literally skipped the parts that suggested his cousin had dipped out on him. But here Shun was, showing up to who he thought was his girl's doorstep in search for answers. Phil shook his head and retreated to the back bedroom. He had to admit he was hurt about the situation. He was embarrassed that he even believed a woman over his own intuition.

The truth of the matter was he too fell for Porsha. He felt alone and betrayed. Any hopes of fixing his relationship with Shun were shattered with thoughts of fighting for the same girl. He was led to believe that Shun didn't have his best interest at heart. During the time he thought Shun had betrayed him, he fell for Porsha, partly because she was all he had. Shun seemed to be missing in action, living it up on some island—only to find out now that he was lying damn near dead in a hospital bed.

Why hadn't Cyrus come to him to let him know that his cousin was in trouble? All kinds of thoughts began to play in Phil's mind, making him both angry and confused. He fell back on the bed and grabbed hold of his head as it began to beat and throb.

"Where's my cousin?" Shun interrupted the silence.

"I don't know."

"When is the last time you saw him? I need to see him."

"Last night. I'm sure he'll be around later. You want to come back by?"

"No. Can you just have him call me?"

"Yes!" Porsha was still hanging on to the hem of Shun's leather bomber. He had to physically remove her grasp. He held her hand a bit too long, and when he noticed, he quickly shook away from her and turned to jog down the few steps on her porch. Shun nearly forgot about his injuries. He had to stop suddenly before falling face-first on the pavement below. His mind was moving much faster than his body would allow.

Phil heard his phone chime for about the thirtieth time, but he continued to ignore Brandy's calls. He couldn't wait for Porsha to bring her ass back into the back bedroom so he could lay deep into it. Five minutes was much too long to wait. He wanted to confront the situation, but it wasn't Shun's fault that Porsha was a low-down dirty bitch.

Porsha was flushed red. She stood on her porch watching as Shun got into his car and drove away. She wouldn't be able to stay with Phil if she wanted to. Her heart was Shun's. She couldn't believe the agony and pain Shun must have been in. She was deep in her thoughts.

Phil decided he couldn't hold his angry tongue any longer. He rushed from the back room with every intention of laying hands on Porsha. She was in the kitchen frantically looking for something to drink. Her hands were shaking. Phil could tell she was shaken. He hadn't actually caught sight of Shun, and he could only make out part of the conversation. However, her dishonesty was clear.

"Why didn't you tell Shun I was here?"

Porsha's eyes immediately welled with tears. "Phil, Shun was hurt bad. He was shot and nearly killed. Whatever our issues, I think you should go and see your cousin."

"I heard all I needed to hear. Now, I asked you a question. I'll handle my cousin. Truth be told, if I had been by his side, none of this would have happened. I blame you too cuz you lied to me. Had me thinkin' my cousin didn't want shit to do with me. What was the real reason behind you bailing me out? You tryin'a set me up or somethin'? Or was turning me against my blood your only mission?"

"I fucked up, Phil. I care about you, but I love Shun." Porsha braced herself for a possible physical altercation.

Phil balled his fists tight and flexed his arms down, trying hard not to raise them and thrash Porsha. He wanted nothing more than to pummel her to near death. He had risked his life and reputation for a false sense of security with this woman, when all the while, she was just using him to get back at Shun.

"I'm going to go before I kill you, Porsha. *Dead ass!*"

Porsha stared at Phil with tears in her eyes. She was upset that she hurt him, but all she could truly think of was caring for Shun.

"I'm sorry," Porsha muttered as the slam of her front door startled her.

***

Phil jumped into Porsha's Mustang and sped down the road. Porsha ran to her front door just as she heard the skid marks. All she saw was the tail end of her vehicle being stolen by Phil. She dared not call the police. She would just wait for him to calm down. He would be back.

"What it do, Ma?" Phil answered the phone in such a way that set Brandy off immediately. She was white bread, but hood as hell. She was the baby mama who gave Phil the most drama. She just so happened to be the downiest. If Phil would ever truly consider settling down, it would definitely be between Brandy and Monica. Monica was a good look because of her head. She kept it cool and in the books. Brandy, on the other hand, was a hothead. Phil knew he could ride or die with her, no doubt.

"Where the fuck you been? Been callin' yo' ass all day."

"Don't worry 'bout all that. What's the matter? How's my son?"

"Phil's good. I was just in town, and we wanted to see if you were free to kick it."

"Naw, I got some shit I gotta handle, and I don't want my li'l man out here in the midst of it, you feel me? I want you to take him back up to Merced. I'll come up there and spend a few weeks with you. Just have to iron a few things out."

"Yeah, okay! I hope you ain't trickin' yo' chips on that bitch I just saw you wit'!"

"What the fuck! You stalkin' me now, Brandy?"

"Naw, but yo' name is deep in circulation. I'm curious to know what got your dick so hard you can't think straight. I'm too through, ma nigga got his head so far up his ass he following up behind some bitch. Thought I would check this shit out myself."

"Man, leave that bitch out of yo' jealous-ass issues. She don't matter. She just a bitch from the club I got some head from."

"Nigga, I ain't dumb! The hood talkin', Phil. I hear they calling the two of you Bonnie and Clyde. Hell, you filthy rich." Brandy gritted her teeth and turned her nose up, exposing her top grill. It became obvious to Phil that Brandy's money-hungry ass wanted something from him. He couldn't be certain she wouldn't set his ass up.

Phil pulled over to the side of the road. He was more than interested in what Brandy had to say. He honestly got to thinking about all the shit he and Porsha did and how she could easily roll over on him to the police or to rival gangs. He couldn't trust a word she said.

"So what you sayin', Brandy?"

"I'm sayin' yo' ass is slippin'. I'm way in Merced, nigga, and I'm hearin' that ma baby daddy kickin' it tough with this trick from the suburbs. Hood Robin, not Robin Hood, who steals from the hood. Where they do that at?" Brandy was more than disgusted at Phil's bitchassness.

Phil was hot under the collar. His mind was wandering. He caught only one or two words Brandy said.

"I think I better make sure her ass knows what's good for her." Phil left it at that and told Brandy he would hit her later.

"No worries, Daddy," Brandy said to herself. She had a mission of her own to accomplish.

Cyrus was pissed. After perusing the blocks, he governed he found his goons cupcaking with everything that walked down the block instead of servicing customers. He ran up, busting a few heads as he gave his troops one final warning. Cyrus had plans on searching for Phil. He needed to find out where his head was at. He didn't want to cross him or Shun, but he had one thing on his mind, and that was to get rid of Porsha before she got Phil killed. Cyrus knew just where to find his pussy-crazed ass. Right at Porsha's house. Only when he got there he caught sight of her and Shun talking, so he ducked out of sight.

Cyrus waited for Shun to get into his car before he pulled up a few cars down the block. Cyrus did a small canvas of the area before he was to make his way to Porsha's home. He waited in the dark for another ten minutes to make sure all was quiet inside the residence. After the coast was clear, he bounced out of his car to approach the house. Only he caught sight of Phil bouncing outside the house slamming the front door behind him. Cyrus quickly retreated back to his car and watched Phil hop into Porsha's car and drive off.

Cyrus smiled excitedly. The bitch was left home all alone, and Cyrus was met with the perfect opportunity to clear shit up quick and easy. He waited a few minutes to see if maybe Phil was going to just round the block a few times before returning Porsha's car. He put on his "murder one" leather gloves and checked his weapon twice. The sun was beginning to set. Cyrus was getting anxiously excited to kill, as if he had a hunger for blood.

Brandy hung up the phone with Phil and immediately put a phone call in to her mother to check on little Phil. After making sure he was fine, she hopped out of her two-door Toyota and headed straight toward Porsha's crib. It was dark. She welcomed it. She didn't want Porsha to see her coming. She wanted to have a small word with her about her dealings with her baby daddy.

Cyrus saw Brandy walking rapidly down the block with a heavy puff coat and beanie hat on. At first, he thought maybe she was one of Porsha's girls from the club, but he knew Brandy's phat ass from anywhere.

What the fuck is she doing here? Cyrus thought to himself. Brandy stopped suddenly when she heard a car alarm sound. Cyrus had to duck quickly before she caught sight of him.

When Brandy felt the coast was clear, she continued on in her mission. Cyrus just shook his head and pulled out his cell phone, excited to see the catfight that was about to go down.

Brandy didn't hesitate to knock on Porsha's front door as if she were the police. Porsha was startled by the knock but assumed it had to be Shun since Phil had a key. Excited, she hopped up and adjusted her lace boy cut undies as she trotted to the front door, opening it wide without hesitation.

Brandy's head was down, and her hands were buried deep in her pockets.

"Who the fuck are you?" Porsha asked with an attitude when she realized it wasn't dick at the door.

Brandy lifted her head to look Porsha dead in the face. "Your worst fucking nightmare!" she responded, as she quickly pulled out her .22 and shot Porsha in the chest. Porsha backed into her living room. Brandy bolted past her into the house to get Phil's bags and then left the scene like a gust of wind.

After the shot rang out, Cyrus scooted down in his old-school Camaro and put the pedal to the metal, cussing the entire way back to Shun's apartment.

"Shit shit shit!" he was pissed. First of all, it was *his* job. Second, it was done so sloppy he would have to do something to make sure Brandy wasn't implicated in the murder. Brandy was a druggy, but she was still his boy's baby mama. She was under the protection rule. Cyrus couldn't tell Shun because his intentions were to kill Porsha himself, and his presence was fishy. Cyrus stopped by the liquor store so he could grab some blunt wraps and a few beers. There his wheels began to turn.

Perhaps Brandy wasn't there to check Porsha at all about Phil. Her intentions were to rob Porsha of the loot from the gate. How much did Phil know about this? Cuz how else would Brandy know what to retrieve from Porsha's apartment?

CHAPTER 8

The Culprit

"What the *fuck!*" Cyrus said to himself, rolling himself a blunt. He thought about following Brandy to let her know that he saw the shooting. She needed to keep her mouth shut. Only, he couldn't say shit because he had no business being at Porsha's in the first place. Part of Cyrus's conscience tugged at his heart. He felt like his deceptive ways would destroy his relationship with Shun. His intentions were good. Porsha was endangering the lives of both Shun and Phil. She was driving a wedge between the two of them. Cyrus knew he should talk to Brandy before her stupid ass went to Phil talking shit about poppin' Porsha, but he didn't. Brandy knew Phil was a hothead, but damn near didn't understand the complexity of the situation.

After all, Porsha was Shun's girl to begin with, another piece of the puzzle that didn't look good on Brandy's end. Just because Shun felt some type of way presently about the woman didn't mean he wouldn't ride or die for her. Cyrus could tell that he loved her.

Brandy hopped in her car, desperate to flee the scene. She was nervous and shaky. She had to get the hell out of Dodge. Her initial plan was to rob Phil, but when he didn't have the time to lounge, her plans changed. Brandy had to admit she was relieved he wasn't at Porsha's place, because she would've been forced to take the father of her son out as well.

Brandy knew the codes of the hood. She was born and bred there. However, with her present financial situation, her code of ethics were gray, at best. She couldn't return home without the money she owed to the bounty hunters collecting for drug and gambling debts.

Brandy hurriedly took off down the road. She was driving at least twenty miles over the speed limit. Sweating like a pig, she struggled to take off her puff coat. Weaving down the road, she snorted a line of coke while coasting down the avenue.

Cyrus could see how wide Brandy's eyes were in passing traffic. He pulled out of the parking lot and proceeded to follow her as she drove straight out of Kern County.

Brandy was driving so crazy, Cyrus knew she would cancel herself out. She was heading straight for a car accident. Somehow, she made it off the freeway and pulled into a quiet neighborhood just under the bridge of the highway.

Cyrus pulled up right behind her. She was so on she hadn't noticed Cyrus at all. He sat back and waited as he watched Brandy stash the duffle bag, puff coat, and gun in the trunk of the car. She wanted to get rid of all the evidence quick, fast, and in a hurry. When she was finished concealing her dirty deed, Cyrus jumped out of his car to corner her.

"Brandy!" he said, with a deep bass and rasp in his voice. She was visibly shaken and refused to turn around to face him. "It's okay. It's me, Cyrus."

Brandy let out a sigh of relief and fell into Cyrus's arms crying hysterically. "I did it! I don't know what came over me, but I did it. I couldn't stand how smug that bitch was just standing there as if she was the innocent one in all this. She has Shun and Phil bickering like they're the worst of enemies."

"I know. Now I have to clean this shit up, though, Brandy. You just basically killed this bitch unauthorized. I was there. I saw you." Cyrus noticed that Brandy failed to mention the rather large duffle bag in the trunk of the car.

Brandy stood and watched Cyrus's eyes for a few moments trying to gauge what type of repercussions she would have to endure in order for him to keep his mouth closed about the situation.

"What do I do now?"

"Nothing. Just keep your mouth closed. But first, you're going to tell me what's in that duffle bag."

Shun got back to his apartment and felt the pang of his injuries burning his back so profusely he thought about checking himself back into the hospital. Cyrus was nowhere to be found, and Phil had yet to pick up his phone. After much thought, he decided he didn't want to be alone, so he took the trip back to Porsha's apartment. He drove past first to check things out. He didn't want things to be awkward, him showing up knowing she and Phil were involved and him actually being there.

As he drove by, he noticed that Porsha's door was wide open and a figure seemed to be lying in the doorway. Shun quickly spun his car around and jumped out as fast as his body would allow. He didn't make it past the bottom stair before he noticed it was Porsha lying breathless. He fell against the rails of the porch and began to cry. How could Phil allow this to happen to a girl he was supposed to be dating? Shun was furious. He called Phil once more and was sent straight to voice mail. He didn't bother to leave a message. He quickly hung up and called 911.

Shun thought about the fact that he broke out of the hospital unauthorized. The bullet wounds suggested he was a criminal. So he made sure to let the medics know all the details and got out of there before the police came. Shun was speeding down the road. He didn't notice Phil breezing by him as he drove down the highway. Phil caught notice of him, but since Shun didn't acknowledge him, he didn't bother to do the same.

Phil slowed a few houses down the block when he saw all the commotion. He crept up slow. He didn't know exactly whose apartment the medics were at. When he noticed it was Porsha's apartment, his stomach completely dropped. All he could see was a gurney and a body covered with a sheet. He couldn't stop. He didn't know what the circumstances were. He had no choice but to keep going before anyone took notice of him. He was also driving the woman's car.

Phil's mind raced as he drove. He watched as his phone showed two missed calls. He noticed it was Shun. His first inclination was to return his call; however, he didn't know how he was going to explain Porsha's murder, being that he stormed out on her and took her car. Phil couldn't be sure who killed Porsha.

Shun hit the corner to the bar and pulled his car in haphazardly. The day had turned into evening and the dark clouds formed into a thunderous rain. He turned his car off and just sat staring at the rain beating upon his windshield. Tears began to well in his eyes. He couldn't think straight. He loved Phil but hated him at the same time. Perhaps Porsha revealed how she truly felt about him, and it set Phil off. Still, that was no reason to kill her. Could Phil have killed Porsha just to spite him?

***

Phil knew that Shun loved Porsha, but to kill her based on the fact that she chose him was some ole bitch shit. He picked up his phone and dialed Shun's number. He shook his knee waiting anxiously for him to pick up.

Shun felt his phone vibrating, but couldn't pull himself together enough to answer it. "Fuck. I gotta get ma head togetha'." Shun shook off his worries and proceeded to open his car door—only to be met by a nigga standing dead in his face with his gun drawn.

Brandy was tweaking out of her mind. Her body was moving in all kinds of directions involuntarily as Cyrus stood waiting for an answer about the contents of the duffle bag.

"Nothing, just some clothes."

"Bitch, you gon' stand here and lie to me? How long you been on that shit again? Who you owe? How did you know where to get it? You *do* know that you just signed a death wish, right? You just stole the bread from all the licks Porsha and Phil pulled around Kern County. You just implicated yourself. The only thing here is that somebody was gon' get Porsha regardless. It was just a matter of time. Phil maybe, but he would never have involved the mother of his child, Brandy."

Brandy just stood with her eyes shut, as if in some diluted trance.

"Go get the duffle bag from the car and give it me."

"I can't. I have to get that money back home before they kill my son."

"Nothing is going to happen. You just do what I say, and I will make sure you have something for that itch."

Brandy grew anxious at the thought of drugs in her system. She calmed and walked quickly to the trunk of the car and pulled out the duffle bag. She handed it to Cyrus. "What now?"

"Go home!"

Cyrus was trying desperately not to blush at his come up. He needed the money just about as bad as Brandy. He had an issue with gambling, and he owed a substantial amount of money to a very dangerous man named Tommy.

Tommy was well-spoken, educated, and ran a few clubs in Bakersfield. That was his cover. He was a cool cat, until you fucked with his money. Cyrus's gambling addiction took form in one of Tommy's most elite clubs. A few weeks later, Tommy loaned Cyrus the money to clear up his life. The mortgage was due, his wife was pregnant, Cyrus was desperate. He was in over his head.

Shun gingerly dragged his other leg out of the car to look directly in the face of the man standing with the gun.

"What can I do for you?"

"Where's Cyrus? Where's my money?"

CHAPTER 9

Sole Proprietorship

"You don't remember me, do you? Naw! How could you? You and Phil run the streets, right? We bottom-feeders don't matter. But you gon' learn today! I may be a goon, but I ride or die in all aspects of the word. This is how niggas get caught up. Sad, this truly don't have a thing to do with you and Phil. Though I reckon one of these cats gon' get they chance at poppin' the both of you. It's all about the almighty dolla, but I guess you already know that. Ya boy owe my boys some money. I ran fa him, so ma man's got a fuckin' bulldog on me, ya feel me? It's a fuckin' dog-eat-dog world. So now, you gon' have to cough up the bread fa ya boy because you vouch fo' 'im. Otherwise, he wouldn't be on ya team."

"Yo, he rock wit' me, but his debt is on his helmet."

"I didn't ask you for an explanation or a question, at that. I'm tellin' you. You got forty-eight hours to come up with fifty stacks. Cyrus owes ma people. And if I were you, I'd watch ma back. Because he got a problem. This gambling shit will get you smoked fast."

"Gambling? This nigga trickin' his chips on bets?"

"To each his own."

Right, Shun thought as he looked down the barrel of a gun. At least, this time, he had a moment to contemplate the situation. He was given a chance to look back on his life and view some of the good with the bad. The truth was, his only desire was to be comfortable. Escape the gnawing the hood had on the hem of his coat. It was like every time he tried to pull out, the bitch pulled 'im in deeper, trapping him. Then, *boom:* pregnant baby mama, drugs get a nigga caught up, do a bid in jail. Get out! Same fuckin' routine. A circle of disease, depression, and frustration.

Shun couldn't think straight. He couldn't believe this nigga wasn't man enough to confront Cyrus about his shit eitha. Except he knew exactly why he chose the wounded to take care of things. Cyrus was a fuckin' shoota all day. He didn't ask no questions. Period—before or after. That was the main reason the man was on the team. Now, this gambling shit could be a potential problem. Because if shit heated up, he could fuck around and steal from the hand that fed 'im. Thus far, he hadn't been confronted with such an issue. Just a man with misplaced anger and fear for his own life. So Shun thought better to give him a pass and simply let the man know he would relay the message.

"I'll let him know," Shun chimed in as the man was busy on the phone talking to a bitch. Shun couldn't believe it. How you a stickup king and takin' calls while you supposed to be robbin' or checkin' a nigga? Shun twiddled his thumbs as the man pointed a finger as if to quiet Shun as he finished his conversation.

"Yo!" the winded gun holder said after a full five-minute argument with his girl. He'd called her so many "bitches" and "hoes" that the "I love you" before the "good-bye" was insulting. "We clear?"

"Crystal!" Shun shut the door to his car and limped into the bar as planned. He'd had a long day. The best part of it, at that point, was he'd dodged anotha bullet.

***

Cyrus jumped into his whip and headed back to Shun's to meet up with the nurse. She was supposed to stay the night. Shun was getting better at caring for himself but needed fresh stitches on the wound on his clavicle that burst open during his exercises. He was determined to get full use of his right arm back. He felt like a cripple.

Cyrus accelerated as he got off the freeway. He sped through Kern County like he owned the place. The bag of money was sliding across the backseat, disturbing his thoughts. "I'ma pay this man this money, and then I'm not fuckin' wit' this shit no more. Do this run wit' Shun, then I'm straight," he said to himself as he noticed the money sliding about through his rearview mirror. It was like it was hypnotizing Cyrus, the back-and-forth motions calling out to him—calls he desperately tried to ignore. He knew that he wouldn't be able to get his gambling under control.

"Hey, girl," Brandy said, as she bounced into her girlfriend's house. Cindy was moving her mouth about, anxious to see what kind of goodies Brandy brought along with her. She was one of Brandy's drug-addicted friends. Brandy was excited to get high. Cyrus had done her right. He gave her a few lines of cocaine to do solo and gave her a nice supply of meth and cocaine to feed the cravings during the week while he was gone.

Cyrus told Brandy to stay put, keep her mouth closed, and do what she did best. Get high! If Phil had known she was back on drugs, he would kill her for sure. He sold the shit but was dead set against using. His kids meant the world, and he'd kill for them without question.

Cyrus was stuck between a rock and a hard place. He fed upon Brandy's addiction because he needed the money. He more than doubled the score he needed to get out of debt, and he'd keep his promise to pay the headhunters looking for her in order to protect Phil's son. Trip was Cyrus was holding on to the money because he didn't know how to let it go.

Cindy rubbed her hands together in anticipation of Brandy's candy bag. Brandy always called her drug treats *candy*. It's what kids craved, and she had a sweet tooth. Cindy was so excited she started cleaning off her area of the table so she could focus on the act of getting high.

"I did it!" Brandy spoke out of the blue. She was in full confession mode, tweaking and hitting the cigarette as if it were a blunt. Brandy couldn't hold water when she was high. She would tell the police directly if she was stopped for any reason and implicate whomever helped her if that was the case.

"You did what?" Cindy got agitated, afraid she'd used already and there wasn't much left.

"I killed that bitch. I got the bread to save my son too." Brandy was rocking hard and fast like she was in a blizzard, but sitting in a cozy temperature.

"What the fuck? Where's the money?" Cindy inquired. She knew Brandy would cut her in on the deal. She wasn't sure she would take the money, but this bitch really went and killed a bitch.

"Cyrus took it!"

Phil's concern for Cyrus's whereabouts had since turned to blind fury. He was certain he had something to do with Porsha's murder. Cyrus cleaned things up when there was too much conflicts. Porsha had become a liability. It was either his ass or someone from the blocks they'd robbed. Phil couldn't argue with the code of the streets if Porsha just got caught up. He was sad to see her go, but her death was actually a godsend. Phil could reenter society as he once knew it, placing blame for the missing funds on her.

Now this whole Bonnie and Clyde, Hood Robin thing could just die. Phil could claim her head and set search for a nigga's head. He could claim to have been Clyde and just do him. The plan was blossoming right before him as he took the drive up to Merced to meet Brandy and her son at her mom's. He was sure she'd made it by now.

Phil had to admit he missed Shun. He couldn't imagine what he must be thinking. His only family out chasin' pussy while he waited for death in his hospital room. Only, Phil felt a little bit of abandonment on Shun's part as well. Phil had yet to come to terms with the fact that Shun kept him in jail to protect him. Porsha bailed him out as a part of her own agenda. She was the real reason he was in all this mess.

"Damn, was the pussy that good?" Phil asked himself as he realized just how dumb he'd been. He prayed that his cousin would give him a chance to explain. First things first, he had to get the hell out of town for a few days until shit calmed the fuck down. He was gallivanting in a dead woman's car. The whole daddy dearest thing would be a perfect alibi, and it would shut Brandy up about his seeing little Phil on a regular basis.

Phil's phone rang for about the fifth time before he took notice. He hurried to answer without even looking at the caller ID.

"Yeah!" he answered a bit shaky.

"Baby?" Phil's collegiate queen answered properly, excited to hear his voice.

"Monica?" Phil questioned, before exhaling and curling up to an inviting spirit. He was glad she phoned. He was in need of someone he could trust.

***

Before Shun knew it, he'd downed ten shots of Henny and a cold draft. He was watching the news on the big screen when it flashed. Police were investigating a homicide that took place in the heart of Kern County earlier that evening. Shun looked on as if the news of Porsha's death didn't faze him. He was so tired of running and having to fight, he would just about trade places.

He'd almost forgotten about the little run-in he'd had with one of Cyrus's so-called runners. Shun was beginning to wonder just how solid Cyrus and his business dealings were. He laughed at himself as he thought about requiring niggas to submit a résumé before running in the same pack with him. He was dead ass. Presently, he felt well in his right to ask niggas for credentials. This drug game was legit. It was illegal, but it was still a business.

Shun was falling asleep at the bar, so the bartender asked him to call for a ride. He looked at the bartender for some time before he obliged. He didn't take kindly to direction. Shun reached into his pockets, fiddling around for his phone. He hoped that Cyrus would pick up. His wounds had begun to bleed from his alcohol intake.

Shun rang Cyrus's phone, who was talking shit as it rang.

"Yeah, what's up? Whatcha need? Aye, hit me!" Cyrus was all over the place as he answered Shun's call, busy talking to the dealer. Cyrus was so hyper he resembled a crackhead dancing after a good hit.

"Where the fuck you at? The house or at that gambling hall?"

Cyrus looked into the phone wide-eyed and quickly hung up. "Damn! What else Shun know?"

Shun was so angry he was shaking. "Did this nigga just hang up on me?" he questioned himself.

CHAPTER 10

Corporate Intoxication

Phil smiled endlessly as he chopped it up with Monica briefly. They hung up confirming that he'd come up to Fresno for the weekend. He was already on the road, so he figured he'd stop there for a few days before settling in Merced with Brandy for a few weeks. He had nothing but time. Perhaps he could figure out a place to stash Porsha's car and get something new.

Shun lay down in his bed and stared up at the ceiling. He was really trippin' off Cyrus. Cyrus was going to do what he wanted, regardless of the consequences. That was the fucked-up part because now, he was involved. Shun knew he'd be ready for the showdown either way. Money was definitely on his mind, and contacting Frankie was first on the agenda in the morning. He'd made a conscious effort to get in touch with Phil. So it was his move. He was more than willing to rectify the situation by having a meeting, but first, he had things to do as well.

The nurse paced back and forth in Shun's living room. She contemplated knocking on Shun's door to make sure he was okay. She'd heard the news about Porsha and had some concerns about Shun's dealing with things after he dragged in drunk just a few hours earlier. She'd grown quite attached to him since his shooting. Shaking the thoughts of prying further into his business, she decided against approaching him and settled for a long hot shower.

The nurse had made herself at home since her first visit. She was Cyrus's girl but had a thing for Shun. His strength and positive attitude about his injuries up until the present was an attractive trait.

Shun moaned loudly as he turned over on a sensitive spot on his side. He quickly covered his mouth in embarrassment, unintentionally sounding like a little bitch over a sore muscle. He'd really put some wear and tear on his body without being fully healed. The slight jog he had when he bounced out of his car to see if he could save Porsha was the jump-off. Then getting in and out of his car. Lastly, the alcohol didn't do him justice at all.

Sophia, Shun's stolen nurse, heard his outcry. She was soaking her thoughts under a calming warm shower when she heard Shun just as she turned it off. Sophia hadn't stopped to get fully dressed. She barely towel dried and threw on an oversized tee before rushing out of the bathroom.

"You okay? Are you pain? I think you're due for some pain meds, if needed."

Shun turned slightly to meet her presence but could barely move. "I'm not sure. I'm just in so much pain." He tried to concentrate on Sophia's question, but his eyes were wandering about her entire body. Her breasts were beautiful under her white tee, her nipples hard and looking succulent. His mouth began to water.

"I don't want any meds. I don't want to sleep. I need to think." Shun tried to sit up a little in his bed.

His muscles were chiseled and smooth around his pecs. Sophia's knees buckled a bit. Even Shun's bandages looked good.

"About?" Sophia walked over to him and touched his arm slightly. She always did this to let him know that she was going to check or change his bandages. Only this time, when she touched him, Shun reciprocated and pulled her close to him.

His hands traveled down her legs and under her shirt. He was curious to know if she was wearing panties, and was met with a pleasant surprise. She was naked. All but the tee that hung off her right shoulder. Sophia's breath caught as she awaited Shun's hands to embrace the creamy center of her thighs.

"I don't want to hurt or take advantage of you," Shun spoke, tearing his eyes away from the rise and fall of her stomach. Her breathing accelerated as his hands traveled closer to her wetness. "Please don't be afraid of me." Shun continued as he watched her eyes close.

"I know." Sophia came closer to him and eased her way in bed, climbing carefully over him. She nestled her body close to his and gently lay her head on his chest. Shun was quiet as he took in her smell. He closed his eyes and wrapped his arms around her.

"Now talk to me," Sophia said softly, as she traced circles around his chest, careful not to disturb his bandages.

The news about Porsha's death brought about the truths of her conniving, deceptive ways. News reporters were now saying the case was somewhat high profile. Porsha's father was some sort of international business owner.

"Looks like the old man got stacks upon stacks on deck," Cyrus spoke loudly over the crowd, as the news talked of the shooting. "Whoever popped her would've been better off kidnapping her and holding her for ransom." Cyrus joked as he asked to join the next hand of cards.

"You sure about that, bro? Looks like your money bag is a little light since you first entered the bar."

Cyrus's high started to immediately come down. "Come on, man, you know I'm good for it."

"Actually, you are pretty brave coming in my gambling bar as if you have paid me my money, Cyrus." A voice came from behind Cyrus that knocked the wind out of him.

Without thinking or turning around to meet his fate, Cyrus threw his cards and knocked the table over in front of him, drawing his weapon. Only, Cyrus was sloppy drunk. It wasn't a good look at all. He ran like the wind, weaving in and out of the bar, trying desperately to get the hell out of there before shots were fired. Cyrus was definitely out of breath. It'd been some time since his football days.

"Get him!" the burly man in a three-piece silk suit demanded. Three men moved swiftly to the exit of the bar.

Cyrus was happy he made it out alive. If only he could make it to his car, he'd be free and clear. He was getting nervous as he got closer to his whip. Fear began to cover him. Without a weapon, he was doomed. The clumsy drunk had dropped his gun shortly after whipping it out in the bar. He was getting sloppy, allowing his clouded emotions to override reason. Cyrus tried to think of a quick plan, but the booze clouded his vision. He could hear the three once-gentle giants right on his tail. He was fidgety. His keys fell down on the ground as he tried to put the key into the door.

Suddenly, it all went black. One of the men hit Cyrus straight in the temple, blindsiding him. He fell over like a cut tree. Blood ran from his mouth, coloring the wet pavement a nice shiny red. Cyrus's tumble to the ground was only the beginning of the thrashing. The men continued to beat him. They spit on him and demanded that he pay Tommy his money within a week. One of the bouncers joked about allotting time for him to heal his broken bones just enough to pick up the phone and let them know when and where to pick up the money. Cyrus moved about the ground, looking for help and trying to reach down into his leather bomber for a phone. One of the men looked on as he tried to get his arm free.

"You need help, Cy?" The man threw Cyrus's body over and pulled his phone out of his jacket pocket. He hit the call log and saw Shun's number at the top. He hit "call" and waited for an answer.

Sophia lay with a blank stare as she massaged Shun's dick as he spoke. He was moaning slightly with each word. She thought that was so cute. She got a kick out of how she made him feel as he lay there, baring his soul to her. She felt special.

Shun breathed in and out slowly as Sophia's soft hands made him rock hard. His mind began to wonder how sweet she must taste. He was reluctant to take things further since he was in so much pain. He didn't know what the situation was in its entirety with her and Cyrus.

Shun was in the middle of his talk about how he and Phil grew up. It was hard in the streets for the two of them, especially for Phil. With both parents on some type of drug and no positive role model to guide him, his fate had become an imprint before he could decide what he wanted. Shun had his grandmother to train him, even though back then, he couldn't understand why she was so strict. He loved her more in the present days. Because of her, he, at least, got to feel the crisp air from beyond the hood. Phil was his bodyguard back then. Shun smiled as he thought about all the fights he and Phil got into and how many times they got caught and Phil took the rap for the entire incident.

Shun began to feel guilty for not taking Phil in on his drug dealings at first. Only, he was just trying to make sure he approached his potential clients correctly. He made a calculated mistake involving Junior. Junior had had his back in prison, so he trusted him. Shun had no idea that Junior was using drugs. As for Phil, he didn't want to change Phil. He was loyal. He was just hood bound as fuck and not in tune with changes that could prove to be very lucrative.

Shun looked down at Sophia. She was fast asleep. He was in awe of her beauty, something he hadn't taken much notice of before. He was so busy being worried about money and survival that love took a backseat. He'd already lost a potential mate. He didn't want to lose another. He didn't want to involve her in the madness of his life, either.

Shun's phone began to ring loudly, awakening Sophia from her nap. She bounced up quickly, apologizing for falling asleep on him. Shun just smiled as he caught a glimpse of her clit as she gingerly crawled out of the far end of his California King.

"Can you pass me my phone, hon?" Shun's last word indicated that she now belonged to him. Sophia blushed, trying hard to hide it from him, but he could see her cheeks rise from the side view of her face. She dropped down to the floor to grab his phone.

"It's Cyrus." Sophia looked worried, as if he had caught them making love.

"Pass me the phone." Shun's attitude completely changed. He got into character just as he answered the phone.

"Yo! Where the fuck you at? What's up wit' you, ma nigga?"

"Yo, this ain't ya boy, but I'm calling with a word of advisement. You might want to get down here to your local gambling establishment and scrape ole Cy from the pavement here. I'd recommend you call a bus too. He's bleeding pretty bad." The man hung up the phone.

CHAPTER 11

The Truth Is Blinding

Monica jogged down the steps from her anatomy class excited to get back to her dorm apartment. She was so excited to see Phil. She hadn't seen him in nearly a month. With finals and all, she had to keep a clear head. Monica blushed at the thought of wrapping her arms around Phil. She so wanted to be with him on a long-term basis but knew her family wouldn't go for it.

Phil wasn't the type of dude she could take home to her father. He wasn't a dusty looking man. He was fine as wine. His lifestyle was just entirely against the rules of her father. His upbringing was the first red flag. Monica and her father didn't agree on many things. He was always so judgmental of lower-class individuals, as if it were their fault they weren't born with a silver spoon in their mouths.

Monica brushed off the ideas of her father's discomfort about her and Phil as she opened the door to her apartment.

She dropped her bags just in front of the door when she noticed Phil's leather coat draped on the back of the sofa. She was so excited she jumped up and down and ran to her bedroom to see if he was lurking about. There he was, peeking out of her closet.

"Babe!" Monica said as she ran to Phil and jumped into his arms.

Phil closed the closet door and picked up his cheer-leader and spun her around. "I missed you."

Phil smiled, kissing her deep and passionately. He felt so safe with Monica, like he was in another world. She was prissy and educated. She was black but so different from the black girls he'd encountered in the hood. Monica had class and drive. She'd never been pregnant or promiscuous. She was wife material. Only, he didn't want to involve Monica in his lifestyle. He wanted to provide a stable environment for her, which was the main reason he told her to listen to her father. Monica would do just about anything for Phil, and he was afraid she'd even drop out of school to be with him.

Phil made every effort to make their long-distance relationship work. His main concern was her education. He made sure to visit on dates of importance and listen when she was having a time at school and needed a neutral ear. Talking to her father about troubles was unheard of. In his eyes, there was nothing money couldn't solve. Phil understood the concept, but he also knew what it felt like to be alone and expected to carry the load.

Monica was like a breath of fresh air to him.

Brandy said her good-byes to Cindy and her children before hopping into her car. She was ready to get back home before Phil got there. She didn't expect him for a few days but wanted to make sure there was nothing out of sorts. Phil was a bitch about the way her home was kept, the clothes little Phil wore, and the company she kept. She most definitely had to set the stage before his arrival and let her boy toys know that she'd be unavailable for a few weeks.

Cyrus wasn't picking up his phone, which made Brandy very nervous. She was snorting and fidgeting in an attempt to get all of the coke from her line of satisfaction before hitting the road. Cyrus promised to pay the head-hunters for her. Now he wasn't answering. She was down to twenty-four hours before the men were scheduled to come after her mother and son. Brandy was confused and worried about her next move. She didn't know if she should drive home or look for Cyrus. She couldn't call Phil because then he'd know what she'd done. According to Cyrus, her head was now on a silver platter in Kern County, so her best bet was to flee the city.

Shun got dressed as fast as he could with his injuries. Sophia reluctantly helped him. She was afraid of what he was going to do. Shun was very quiet after he hung up the phone. He quietly laid out his weapons, loaded them, and stood staring into the mirror once he finally got his bulletproof vest fastened.

Sophia came over to him and wrapped her arms gently around his torso. Shun's first instinct was to push her away and knock her arms from around him. The last thing he needed was the nagging feeling that he had to return home to her. He refrained from pushing Sophia to the side. He touched her hands softly and commenced to holstering his weapons.

Shun turned around and met Sophie's gaze. "Don't worry about me. I'll be fine. I want you to lock the doors and wait for me to come home."

"Okay, okay!" Sophia nodded her head and verbally responded with a hint of worry lingering in her eyes.

"I mean it," Shun said as he kissed her on her forehead. He then pushed past Sophia and headed out the door. Shun was so worried about what he was going to find at the bar that he put a call into Phil before he turned on his car. Again, he was met with a voice messaging system.

This time, Shun was sure to leave him a message, stating that it was urgent.

Shun hurriedly drove the fifteen minutes to the gambling club. The police were still out front. One of the patrons had called the medics. Shun's stomach dropped, afraid to find out just what had gone down. He was losing people left and right, and he wasn't even on tour. While in the service, death was to be expected. Here as a civilian, he just wanted to live comfortably and perhaps have a family.

Shun walked up to one of the emergency technicians to ask about the incident.

"What happened here? I received a phone call stating that a friend of mine was in trouble."

"You know what happened here," the man responded and pinched his lips. "One of these cats got the brakes beat off 'im for fooling around with Tommy. Dude probably owed him some money. I'll say this one was a fighter. He's hanging on by a very thin thread, but he's a strong one."

Shun looked at the ground deep in thought. "Did the cops arrest the men in connection with this?"

The technician laughed at how ignorant Shun was about the situation. "Man, these cops come here on a regular basis. You know Tommy got cops on his roster. He can't be touched that easy."

"Everyone can be touched," Shun said and turned to take a peek in the back of the emergency vehicle.

"We're taking him to Kern County General, if you want to follow. There's no doubt he'll be admitted, so he'll be processed and admitted shortly after arrival. We don't know if there's any internal bleeding, so he may be prepped for surgery."

Shun just nodded. He was blacking out slightly about the entire incident. He walked swiftly. He started off with a long and wide stride but was reminded of the pain that presented full force. He shook his head and slowed to the pace of an old man the rest the way back to his car. It was cold out, and the wind was tackling his wounds. He needed to get home. He would see about Cyrus in the morning.

Sophia busied herself around Shun's home. She cleaned the kitchen and living room area before putting his clothes in the wash. Smiling, she thought about Shun and his past. He'd been so forthcoming of his fears and his plans, illegal or not. Sophia just wanted to protect him and show him how love could save him. Her fear was that he didn't want to be saved.

The thought of Shun possibly breaking her heart nearly made her pack up her things and retreat before he made it back home. She knew that if she came face-to-face with him again, he'd have to make her leave.

Sophia was busy making Shun's bed and emptying the trash when she heard a frantic knock on the door. She hurried out of Shun's bedroom and rushed to open the door.

"Hey!" Sophia exploded out of breath. She opened the door slightly irritated at whoever was knocking like the police.

"Who are you? Where's Cyrus?" Brandy walked in, slamming and locking the door behind her, waving a nickel-plated 9 mm with a sweet pink handle.

"What the—" Sophia's breath caught, and her chest pounded. She slowed her heart rate by calming her thoughts before she addressed her unwanted guest. "Cyrus isn't here. He's been gone all day. Is there something I can help you with?"

"I doubt it. What! You one of the new hoes or some-thin'?"

"No, I'm Shun's nurse," Sophia replied, trying not to take offense to Brandy's obvious disrespect. Considering she was the one with the gun, she figured she'd better just listen to what she had to say.

"Where's Shun? Cyrus took my money. I need that money. They're going to kill my mother and son in twen-ty-four hours if I don't come up with that bread." Brandy sat down, cradling her head in her hands. She was tweak-ing, and Sophia could tell. Brandy started beating herself in the head with the gun. She was so frustrated she didn't know what to do, and her high was crashing down.

"Hey, let me get you some water. Perhaps we can figure this out. You mind putting that gun away? It's making me a little nervous." Sophia walked up to Brandy slowly in hopes of encouraging her to hand over the gun.

"Get the fuck away from me, you stupid bitch. I'm not dumb." Brandy was irate and out of control, drooling as she spoke and rocking fast. She was unstable.

Shun pulled up to his home and noticed Brandy's car out front. "Oh shit! What did Phil do now?" Shun said to himself, as he struggled to get out of his car without tearing his stitches. As he got closer to the door, he could hear Brandy screaming bloody murder.

He quickened his steps to the front door no matter the pain. He could see Brandy's shadow waving a gun through the window. He knew then that Brandy was using again. She was volatile anyhow, but on drugs, she went from zero to ten in a matter of seconds. Shun pulled out his key slowly and quietly in hopes that Brandy wouldn't hear him come in.

Brandy was so out of it, she was pacing the floor and waving the gun at Sophia, demanding she get Shun on the phone. Shun crept in behind her. Sophia trailed her eyes to the floor. She didn't want to give away that Shun was in the room. He crept closer to Brandy. When he got within inches of her, he quickly grabbed her arm and confiscated her gun. Brandy flung her arms at her assailant, determined not to go down without a fight.

"Stop!" Shun ordered. "It's me, Shun!"

Brandy flew into his arms, crying out and rambling something about stealing the money from Porsha and Phil. She tried to calm herself down by breathing deeply in and out as she shook her hands to relax. "Shun, you have to help me. I can't find Cyrus. He took the money. I shot Porsha. I can't find Phil. I only took the money because they were going to kill my mother and little Phil. Please, Shun. Please! You have to help."

Shun let out a long sigh and cuss as Brandy's frame crashed into his wounded body. He looked puzzled at Brandy in her confession and was pissed that he was apparently left out of the loop on everything that he was told had taken place. Shun gingerly pushed Brandy away from him so that he could regain his composure. In that moment, he realized that those he had a little trust in, he couldn't trust at all. Brandy's shoulders shivered as she cried. Her nose was running, and panic was settling around her brow as her high began to end.

"What are you going to do?" Brandy whimpered.

Shun rubbed his face with his hand and scratched his head. He didn't know how to respond. He had mixed emotions about her killing Porsha. What had gone down? He needed to find that out first.

CHAPTER 12

Who's to Blame?

Phil lay next to Monica feeling a sense of comfort and release. He dreaded having to even get up, but he had to find a new car. He wasn't sure how far the police were in linking the missing vehicle to possible suspects in Porsha's murder. His plan was to get out of Dodge before any of that occurred.

Monica was fast asleep in Phil's T-shirt. She looked so peaceful. She had so many dreams and the potential to reach them. Phil didn't want to ruin her life with troubles of his own. He knew in that moment that he loved her. He couldn't believe it himself. Still, he had no choice but to leave.

"I'm cursed," Phil said to himself, as he quietly grabbed for his things. "It's only a matter of time before my adversary takes his turn at winning. I'll fall just as the men have fallen before me. I won't bring you down with me," Phil spoke quietly as he stared at Monica. Leaving her brought tears to his eyes. A part of him wanted her to wake up and stop him from leaving her. It was a cowardly thought. Selfishness came easy to him. For so long, all he truly had was himself. His children were those he held close, but dealing with the baby mama drama kept him at bay.

Phil swallowed the lump in his throat and reached for his keys. He quietly closed the front door and got into

Porsha's car. His plan was to stop for gas and take the trip to Merced.

Shun nearly started a fire pacing the rug on his living room floor. Beating his head with the butt of Brandy's gun, he was so upset to find that a junkie killed Porsha for money. He was so angry with Brandy he wanted to punch her in the face. Sophia was getting increasingly worried as she watched Shun's cognizance changeover. He was beastly, and Brandy's future, from her perspective, was looking quite grim.

"Shun," Sophia said softly, trying to get his attention in an effort to calm him.

"What!" Shun yelled uncontrollably. Sophia nearly jumped out of her skin. She retreated to the back bedroom and shut the door behind her. Shun walked hurriedly behind her. He wanted to stop her, but he stopped in front of his bedroom door. He didn't have time for the dramatics. He had to figure out what the next move should be. With Cyrus out of commission and Phil MIA, he didn't have a team. His injuries were far from healed, so he was limited in his plan of action, which further frustrated him. Shun stood at his bedroom door staring before he went back to address Brandy.

He was very quiet, searching for the right words for fear the anger in his chest would burst into flames. Instead of directing his full attention to the issue at hand, he retreated into the kitchen to grab a few buds of weed out of his secret stash. He needed to get high, fast. He was losing his sense of sensibility.

Shun sat down at his weed table and began to break down the weed for his blunts. Brandy looked on hungrily. He almost dared Brandy to ask for a fix. It would give him a reason to lay into her ass. He was this close to giving her a 3-D black eye. His hand involuntarily itched and curled into a fist.

Brandy sat on the couch biting her nails. She knew Porsha originally fucked with Shun, but she didn't know how deep his feelings for the girl were. She just needed the money. Plus, she was fucking with her baby daddy unauthorized, so she handled it. Killed two birds with one stone, only Cyrus played her.

"Where the fuck is Phil, Brandy? Does he know about any of this shit?" Shun said, licking his blunt to seal its intoxicating fumes.

"He isn't answering his phone. I'm worried. He was supposed to meet me in Merced."

"Why?"

"He just said that he was going to spend a few weeks with little Phil."

"All of a sudden? What does he know about Porsha? Was he in on it too?"

"No! I just needed the money. Straight-up, Shun. He didn't know shit. Matter of fact, Cyrus was the one who told me to lie low. He would take care of the debt for me. He figured if the streets found out I took the money, they would come after me for sure. Little Phil would be in the middle of his parents' fuckups. Again."

"So you gave Cyrus the money in exchange for drugs."

"No and yeah. He just offered the drugs. He knew I needed a fix. I went to my girl Cindy's as planned, stayed the night, and was getting ready to head home when something told me that I'd better find Cyrus and make sure the bread was paid before I got home. I only have twenty-four hours left."

"This is some bullshit! You know that, right? This man don't know shit about what's goin' down, and he could possibly be walkin' straight into a trap." Shun rubbed his head as he took a few hits of his blunt. "Okay, okay!" he said, rubbing the frustration from his face. "This is what we gon' do. We definitely need to call a meeting. Call these cats. See if we can get an extension. I don't know how much you owe, but now Cyrus owes Tommy as well. He in the hospital, so I know he's in danger. I need to get this meeting with Frankie together. You gon' have to lie real low. No drugs, crime, none of that shit. We have to move fast. Get that man on the phone. We need to let him know what's goin' down, ASAP!"

Brandy looked extremely worried. Shit was getting entirely too real, and she couldn't escape. Shun finished off his second blunt and left Brandy to call Phil while he worked things out with Sophia.

"Yo, nurse!" Cyrus yelled, struggling to move. "I gotta get out of here. I got shit to do."

Cyrus was more than worried that Tommy's boys were just inches away from his room. There was no way he was goin' to stay the night there.

"Yes?" an old white nurse came barreling in.

Cyrus started pulling off his oxygen mask and various tubes, looking for an escape. The big man-looking nurse slammed her swollen vein-erupting hands down on his chest, suppressing his breathing. Cyrus panicked and starting flinging his arms and legs, paging a nurse for help.

"Calm down! No one is trying to hurt you." The old nurse laughed at how paranoid he was. "Them boys must've put a hurtin' on you. I always used to tell ma boys to be careful. You may write a check your ass can't cash." The old Southern nurse chuckled as she placed the rough hospital blanket close to his chin and ordered him to get some rest.

Cyrus grit his teeth in pain and frustration. He wanted to get up and run out of there, but he knew full well he wasn't well enough to do so. His entire being was in so much pain. He wouldn't last long on the streets this way, anyhow. He looked about the room and started to think about his mom and her last days. Now here he was, perhaps close to death, and no one to see it through with him.

"I fucked up," Cyrus said to himself. He didn't know how he was going to tell Phil that he may be the reason why his son was murdered. The fact that Brandy killed Porsha and stole the money was secondary at this point. Tears filled his eyes and soon stained his stiff white pillow.

Sophia had been crying, Shun could tell. She hadn't even raised her head to meet his eyes. Her lips and cheeks were slightly swollen, as she had blown her nose. Sophia looked into Shun's eyes and gently put her hair behind her ear. "Are you hungry? Do you need pain meds?"

Shun grew instantly angry at her inquiry. "Fuck that 'you hungry?' You okay? I was the one out of pocket. I ain't used to no one genuinely givin' a fuck about how I'm doing or feel. Before, you were doing your job. Now, you here because you want to be. Because I want you to be." Shun fixated on Sophia's milk chocolate eyes as he pulled her close. "I want you to stay with me. I'm not used to this, but I want to learn with you. I'm sorry. I really am."

Sophia stepped closer to Shun. She stood on her tippy toes and kissed him gently on his lips once. Then she smiled and bit her lip before kissing Shun hungrily and passionately.

"I'm here."

***

Phil was doing great time on his small road trip. At the rate he was driving, he'd make it into Merced before dark. He noticed Brandy calling, but he simply shook his head and ignored her call. He would be there shortly. Whatever, it was could wait.

Shun ran his fingers through Sophia's hair. "I'm glad you are here, baby. I hope you'll stay for a while. I don't plan on doing none of this shit after this meeting with Frankie."

"Who is Frankie?"

"Just ma Italian homeboy. No need for you to worry. I'm just going to go and make this money and get myself out of this mess."

Sophia smiled.

"I'm going to check on Cyrus. We need to get Phil back here as well. We have shit to do. I don't want this nigga to walk into a shootout."

CHAPTER 13

The Meeting

About two hours later, Phil was pulling up to Brandy's mom's home. He was so excited to see little Phil, he could hardly contain himself. Phil Junior was his pride and joy. Back then, Phil thought he and Brandy would be together forever, being high school sweethearts. Well, Brandy was his main chick in high school. His years in grade school were spent mostly outside the school gates. He met her in his homeroom class. From then on, they were inseparable. Brandy was studious back then, so into her studies that Phil was inclined to follow the same path.

He enjoyed school. He even excelled in his classes for some time. He just couldn't take the constant scrutiny he faced back home. He was from the hood. He didn't have the sports attached to his need for education, so most thought he was a sucka; something he couldn't deal with.

Soon, Phil found himself in fight after fight. He felt the need to prove himself to those lurking about street corners, instead of using his brain to free himself from the hood mentality. Brandy and Phil separated for some time. She wanted to continue on in school. She couldn't deny she loved Phil, but she too found herself cutting class to hang out with him. She started smoking weed at first. It didn't bother Phil. Brandy was always so high strung, afraid she'd get caught cutting, but the weed relaxed her mind and allowed her to have fun.

Phil created a false sense of security for Brandy, which he would later admit. He knew he couldn't provide for her or take care of her. Encouraging her to take his path was murder, in a sense. Brandy wasn't strong willed. She fell for most of the okeydoke, and she did what Phil asked of her, no matter the consequence.

Phil parked down the road from Brandy's so the car wouldn't be directly linked to the house if, for some reason, the police did a sweep and ran the plates. He took his time cleaning out the car. He didn't leave any evidence linking him to Porsha's missing vehicle. He noticed that Brandy's car wasn't out front and figured she was at the store or something. Her mom rarely left the home.

Phil heaved the huge black garbage bag over his shoulder and carried it down the road. He was ready to start over. He had to admit he was tired.

Shun walked into Cyrus's hospital room afraid of what he might find. He was bandaged up, but his face was exposed. Doctors said he had a few broken ribs and a few cuts and bruises. Shun was relieved they hadn't killed him. That was Shun's job. If he had to put somebody down on his team, he would rather it be him.

Cyrus had a huge look of worry wrapped around his brow when he noticed Shun was in the room. He'd been standing there for about five minutes before Cyrus woke up from his nap. Startled by Shun's presence, Cyrus started looking about his bed for something to help him flee the situation. He didn't know who he could trust at that moment.

"Look," Cyrus started in before Shun could tear into him, "I was only trying to help where Brandy and the money were concerned."

"You mean help yourself." Shun buried his chin in his chest, crossing his hands in front of the zipper of his pants. He held this look of frustration and confusion that made Cyrus careful of the words he spewed.

Cyrus continued on as if he didn't notice Shun staring deep into his eyes. Shun had this stare that didn't need words attached. You often knew what was up just by his facial expressions. Shun continued to stare at Cyrus, as he waited for the conversation to continue.

"Man, I'm sorry, bro. I don't want anything to happen to Phil's kid, man. I'd do whatever was needed to prevent that shit from going down."

"We gotta get this money," was Shun's only response. "To tell you the truth, I'm tired. I just want my family to be okay. I want out of all this, man. You got yo' ass handed to you. Never thought I would see that coming. I've been shot, threatened. I think it's time for a hiatus." Shun moved farther into the room and took a seat near Cyrus's bed and began to tell him exactly what was going to go down within the next forty-eight hours.

Frankie rolled out of bed, late as always, and checked his voice mail. Shun had called numerous times. He was anxious to see what the urgency was. Shun was yelling bloody murder about getting the drugs in trade for mob connections. He sounded desperate. Frankie hurriedly dressed. Shun said they should meet, and he was down, of course. He and Shun were ace boon coons. He just didn't trust some of his following, and he wasn't about to take the wrap for anyone but Shun.

Phil got up to Brandy's door and noticed it ajar. He dropped his bag on the porch and pulled his gun out as if he were a cop getting ready to raid a home. He quietly retreated from the porch to check around back. It was unusually quiet. When he didn't hear his son playing or his grandmother blasting the television, his stomach dropped instantly.

"This bitch didn't run off with my son, did she?" Phil ran back around to the front of the home, tucking his gun, and walked into the front door. He wasn't at all prepared for what he saw.

Brandy's mom lay slain on the kitchen floor. Blood was everywhere. The house was a mess, as if someone was looking for something specific. Phil's chest began to beat so hard, he was sure his heart would burst. He leaned up against the door after closing it. He was trying to get himself together before searching the rest of the home. He feared he would find his son dead. He was starting to lose it. He said a small prayer and began to run around the home searching each room. His son was nowhere to be found.

Phil let out a sigh of relief and collapsed to his knees. He threw his head into his hands and cried like a baby. His only mission was to find out who killed Brandy's mom and if his son was next. With Brandy's record with her drug dealers, violence had been a norm for Phil Junior, and Brandy fought endlessly with the men in her life and the low-life dealers she'd cheated. He didn't want his son around the shit. It was his reason for staying away. He wanted better for his son. He just couldn't provide it at the moment.

He needed to man up and pull himself together. His son was out there somewhere, and he was wasting time crying. Phil hoped he was at a friend's house or playing at the park or something. He pulled himself up from the kitchen floor and stood with his hands on his hips trying to think.

***

Brandy was getting more and more frazzled and frustrated by the minute. Sophia didn't know what to do. The only thing she felt good about was that she was no longer armed. So if Brandy stepped to her, she'd be in for a nice ass whoopin'. She didn't have time to play with some drug-addicted buffoon. She couldn't believe what a dumb blond Brandy was. There was absolutely no sign of brain activity as far as she could tell. The fact that Brandy would dare play with the life of her child sickened Sophia, being that she couldn't have any.

"So you dating Cyrus or Shun?" Brandy made an attempt to talk to Sophia to take her mind off of things.

"I don't see how that's any of your concern. We should be trying to get in touch with Phil, don't you think? Your mother and son are in trouble." Sophia was so angry. She spoke to Brandy calm and in a monotone as she did her patients when they weren't compliant.

"I was just trying to make conversation. You don't have to be so snotty."

"Snotty?" Sophia gave Brandy a disgusted look. "Bitch, you pulled a gun out on me. Disrespected Shun's home. You are nothing but drama, and I just met your ass. You thought we were going to be friends? Please. The only thing you should be trying to do is locate Phil before Shun returns." Sophia turned on her heel and retreated to Shun's bedroom. She was making sure she had his clothes laid out and fresh bandages. He had a meeting to get prepared for.

Phil quickly dried his tears and gathered his composure. He couldn't stay there or leave his belongings. That would be murder number two he could be implicated in. He grabbed his bag from the porch and walked expeditiously down the road to Porsha's car. He got almost four cars away when he noticed a patrol car eyeing the vehicle and its plates. Phil turned around quickly and walked as fast as he could back to Brandy's home, trying desperately not to bring attention to himself. The huge garbage bag on his back would be a giant giveaway. He made a mad dash through the alley of a neighbor's home about two doors down from Brandy's home. He paused and ducked down just under the window before hopping the gate to Brandy's. He fumbled over his pants a bit and scrapped his leg during the jump, but his adrenaline was high. He didn't feel a thing. Phil bolted inside the back door to Brandy's and locked the door behind him. He quickly slid down to the floor and scrambled through the kitchen and living room to lock the front door. There he balled into a fetal position and phoned Shun.

Shun was talking to Cyrus about meeting with Frankie later that night. They were going to take the trip to Los Angeles to meet up with a few of Frankie's boys. Ones he could trust to make the trip to the Philippines. Neither Shun nor Cyrus were in any shape to fly clear across the country. It was going to be a dangerous trip, and the physical nature of it all would be strenuous.

Shun heard his phone ringing. He cut Cyrus off as he was explaining trust issues he held about Frankie, though he knew Cyrus too was in the doghouse.

"Yeah!" Shun answered without taking notice of the caller ID.

"Shun, it's Phil. You gotta help me, man." Phil hysterically broke down in tears, unable to continue.

"Where you at?" Shun's stomach dropped with worry as he listened to his cousin tryin' to regain control. Cyrus sat up in his bed despite the pain, his eyes wide, waiting to hear what was up.

Shun was getting frustrated waiting for Phil to answer his question. "Phil, you there? What's happening? Where are you? I'm coming! Just let me know where you are." Shun stood up and bolted toward Cyrus who already knew what it was. Cyrus pulled his intravenous tubes out and swung his legs from the bed as Shun threw him some scrubs from the hospital linen closet.

"I'm at Brandy's mom's tilt. Phil Junior's missing. Ma son is gone, Shun. I don't know what to do. I found Brandy's mom dead in the kitchen, and the house ransacked. Man, I'ma kill that bitch. Man, I'ma kill Brandy." Phil was beginning to break down again as he told Shun of his findings.

"Where is she?" Phil asked.

"She's at ma tilt. She confessed to murdering Porsha and stealing the money for her drug debts. I don't know, man. Right now, we need to focus on your son. Fuck that bitch for now." Shun looked at Cyrus with a stern eye. He had just saved Cyrus for the time being. He figured Phil had enough on his plate to deal with. He would have to deal with Cyrus later. Cyrus stabbed him in the back by giving Brandy drugs and taking the ransom money to cover his own ass.

"Meet me at the store around the block. I don't want to cause too much attention here at the house. I'm standing in the middle of a fucking crime scene," Phil said.

"On my way!" Shun said and hung up the phone. Cyrus nodded at Shun, thanking him for keeping quiet about his part in all the mess surrounding Phil's son.

Shun and Cyrus walked right out the front of the hospital without trouble. The staff had become accustomed to Shun and his partners in crime. They weren't being held for any criminal activity, so they were free to leave. The nursing staff had since thrown their hands up in exasperation at getting the men to stay put until their wounds were free and clear from possible infection.

Nurse Gertrude, Shun's old fart of a nurse, waved her good-bye and threw Cyrus a ziplock bag as he passed. "Hope I don't see you on the news under a sheet." Nurse Gertrude had no filter. She knew giving him medication was against the rules, but she was near retirement anyhow. They weren't going to reprimand her too harshly.

Cyrus reviewed the contents of his goodie bag as they exited the building. He was grateful for the meds. "So is Phil's son okay?" He hesitated to ask. He was scared of the answer.

"For now!" Shun said, jumping into the car. "For now," he whispered under his breath and sped off after Cyrus motioned that he was safely buckled into his seat.

CHAPTER 14

Loyalty or Power

Shun hit the freeway and drove in complete silence most of the way to Merced. His mind ran in all directions. He was so afraid that Phil would be found and killed before he had the chance to reach him. The thought of Phil hiding out just waiting for his demise burned him. He felt as though most of this was his fault. Yes, Phil was the oldest, but Shun had had the chance to get out of criminal activity, only to be found in such a mess that he too was on the verge of tears.

Cyrus was thinking long and hard about his actions as well. Perhaps it was time to seek rehab. Even if he retained the money to pay off his debt, he'd still have the gambling issue. It would just be a matter of time before he found himself in deep shit again. He prayed Frankie and his boys would come through wit' the loot, even though he didn't trust Frankie as far as he could throw 'im. There was something about them Italians that didn't sit right with him. He just knew something was up, but he couldn't put his finger on it.

Shun exited the ramp and entered the small hick town of Merced. He was nervous just drivin' around. The only reason he would dare enter into Merced was to head up to Yosemite National Park. He could rest easy in the woods. He had a cabin there just in case he needed a break from the city. Kern County, Bakersfield, was quiet, for the most part, but the hood riots were loud enough to request leave from all the madness. Shun was thinking about moving down to Long Beach. With all the money he stood to make on this last drop, he'd have more than enough to tide him over. Perhaps he would finally get the chance to go back to school. He had shared his dreams of becoming an engineer with Porsha. Thoughts of her brought his high down. Shun wasn't entirely certain he could move forward with Sophia. He was going to try, though.

Phil took a deep breath and composed himself. He finished his search of Brandy's home before walking down the block to the store. He told Shun to meet him there, not wanting any connection to the home at all. Phil took a few pictures of his son from the frames and tucked them into his wallet. He inhaled deeply and jogged down the block to the store. He hoped Shun wouldn't be long. He didn't want to find himself in another situation and go down for someone else's crime. Phil had to admit he was afraid of shopping now.

He wasn't standing out front of the store two minutes before Shun pulled up. Phil was in the worst of spirits but chuckled when he noticed Cyrus in hospital scrubs. He had no idea of his injuries.

"What the fuck happened to you, ma nigga?" Phil asked as he saw just how serious his injuries were after hopping into the backseat.

"I had a run-in with some really bad men. Caught me off guard. It's what I get. Wrong place. Wrong time." Cyrus stared out of his window into space. He was trying with all his might not to present tears.

"You okay?" Shun asked Phil.

"Yeah, physically. Just mentally drained and an emotional wreck. I am scared as shit, cuz. I just hope Junior OK. He has to be around here somewhere." Phil paused a minute before continuing to speak. His mind was racing. Ditching Porsha's car at Brandy's mom's home was sure to put his mug on a wanted poster. He just didn't have time to think of much else. The police were investigating Porsha's murder, and the pieces would fall together quickly. He didn't commit the murder, but he fit the bill.

Phil slumped down in his seat and doubled over a bit. His stomach was hurting.

"I'ma go around the school and a few neighborhood parks close by to see if we see him," Shun announced. His heart was in his throat, and his hands were sweating. He wasn't the only one perspiring. Cyrus had broken out into a cold sweat, and he suddenly felt as if his throat was going to close. He adjusted himself in his seat a few times in an effort to keep panic at bay.

"You cool?" Shun asked as he entered the street where Phil Junior attended school. His eyes grew wide when he spotted a bunch of kids standing at the gate engaged in horseplay.

"Yeah, I'm cool. Shit just trippin'. Pull up over there." Cyrus perked up when he thought he caught sight of some boys playing dice on the side of the school. Phil jolted up in anticipation.

Shun pulled up fast on the four boys playing. He startled them. They scattered, exposing Phil Junior picking up his winnings. He wasn't going to leave that behind.

"There go his rock head ass right there. He should have been home from school. Thank God he hadn't been," Phil said exhaling. He nearly fell out the car to get over to his son.

"Dad?" Junior asked with a look of confusion on his brow. "What's up?"

"Get in the car. Everything is fine, son. We're going on a little vacation."

"What about Mom? She OK?" Phil Junior hated his mom's drug addiction, but he took care of her just the same. He didn't want to leave her hanging. Phil knew as much.

"Your mom and me, we fight a lot, but I still love her. I'll make sure she's safe. Now let's go," Phil instructed one last time. Junior grabbed his backpack and slid inside the car.

"What's up, Shun? What's up, Cy? Why y'all look like y'all about to shit on y'all selves?"

Shun busted out laughing. "Shut the fuck up," he said, pulling on to the ramp to the freeway. All was well presently, but shit was still funky. It was time to get out of town.

Cyrus smiled as Shun hopped back on the freeway. They needed to hustle back to town to meet Frankie, but Phil wanted to drop his son off at the home of Janie, his local girl, first. He would stay there until they made plans to leave the city.

"Yo! About that shit with Porsha, man," Phil started in once more.

"Just forget about it. We blood. I didn't mean for you to get caught up with that broad. I didn't send her to you to occupy your time. She was on some hater shit. I told her I wasn't ready for a relationship at the time, and she went ham. She baited you, ma nigga. I'm not saying that I didn't care for her. I know after a while you did too. She was just confused about the life she wanted to have, is all." Shun quieted and turned on the radio. He didn't want to drive the entire way back in an uncomfortable silence.

It wasn't long before he hit the city limits of Kern County. Cyrus was knocked out about thirty minutes after taking a few Dilaudid. The pain brought him close to tears. Phil simply stared out of the window and watched the country pass by. He felt helpless and alone. The one thing that gave him comfort was the fact he and Shun were together again. At least he had someone to watch his back.

Shun pulled into the Chevron to gas up and phone Frankie. He was about ten minutes late for his meeting time but wanted to make sure he knew they were still on. Cyrus would have to sit this one out in the car. He would be the joke of the bunch if he rolled up in hospital scrubs. Then again, the situation was that serious. There was no need for a dress-to-impress debut. Cyrus was always ready.

Frankie picked up the phone out of breath and out of sorts, like he was running a marathon. Shun was irritated that Frankie was playing around at a time like this. Shun already knew he was up to no good, fooling around with one of these local hussies. Bottom-feeders, money-hungry mongrels, all looking for a quick way to make a dolla.

"Yo, I'm back. Meet me at the warehouse," Shun said without another word and hung up.

Frankie caught hold of his frustration but continued to handle his business. Frankie always fucked somethin' before a meeting or drug transaction. He wanted to make sure he got one last nut in case shit when bad.

"I won't be long," Frankie joked and smiled at his Puerto Rican mami as he wiped the sweat from his brow.

"Brandy, wake up! Wake up! The boys will be back in a few." Sophia came from Shun's bedroom and noticed Brandy spread across the sofa haphazardly. Sophia headed for the kitchen to make her something to eat. Brandy didn't make a sound. She looked okay from across the room, but as she got closer, she noticed how blue she was.

Sophia ran to check her pulse and pupils. She immediately picked up her cell phone to call 911, only as she proceeded to call, she noticed the empty vials of morphine on the coffee table just in front of her.

"Shit, this bitch just overdosed." Sophia knew she couldn't call it in. She had confiscated the meds from her job for Shun's pain regimen. She would be fired and lose her license. Sophia collapsed into a chair at Shun's weed table and simply shook her head. "Dumb bitch."

Shun pulled into the warehouse and hopped out of the car as if his bones were well put together. He was soon reminded of his injuries when the cold winds ripped across the wound just under his clavicle. Frankie pulled in just a few minutes later, eyes low and a few blunts in. He was loud as shit, as if the business they were conducting was legit.

Cyrus stirred and came to, but immediately lowered his eyes and got a serious look on his face once he noticed Frankie was present.

"What's the plan?" Cyrus asked Phil, groggy and irritated. "What you know about this nigga Frankie?"

"Frankie cool, bro! He was one of Shun's boys in the service. Testified as a witness to Shun not murdering dude. But Shun had to keep the code of ethics. Seemed like everybody in his platoon rolled over on him. Frankie is loud and obnoxious, but he a solid dude. This plan is all on Shun. He seems to have all his ducks in a row. So I'm just waiting on instructions." Phil looked down at the cut on his hand. He wasn't sure where he got it from, but it hurt like a bitch.

"Yeah, okay. Excuse me if I am not all that excited about Shun's marine partners. The last one shot him. I just got the shit kicked out of me. My reflexes may not be as swift this go-round."

"No worries. I'm ready! Best believe I'm ready. I can't believe Brandy's ass would endanger the life of our son. She's lost a number of brain cells since her drug use, but never has she stooped this low." Phil shook his head and tried to control his emotions. All he wanted to do was hold his son.

"I know, man. I know," Cyrus said, trailing off into a whisper. He felt so guilty about what happened to Phil's son. He wanted to confess everything to him but knew that Phil would kill him. He had to make a decision about being truthful about the situation at some point. He would rather be the one to tell him than anyone else. Shun had extended him that much courtesy.

Cyrus made his way out of the car alongside Phil and joined the two men at the center of the warehouse. Two cars joined them shortly after. The deal was all set. Shun, Frankie, Cyrus, and Phil would join two members of the Mexican mob out of East LA to make the trade. They would then trade half the money for dope to Frankie's connection, the other half of the money split between the four of them. This was the only way the two drug cartels could coexist. They traded what they needed from time to time and maintained separate territories.

Cyrus was anxious. The medicine was wearing off, and he really just wanted to get to the nearest bed.

"Shun, you think you can drop me off at my grandma house?"

"Sure. You all right, nigga?"

"Naw, yeah. Just need to lay ma ass down. Especially if we going to hit the road in the morning."

"I feel that. I'm dog-tired as well. Only I know my night has just begun. Shit, Phil is about to go ham on Brandy. I'm too busted to help that girl too. Yo! She is definitely on her own." Shun shook his head.

"Phil, let's go!" Shun called out to Phil, who was getting to know his new Hispanic brethren.

"A'ight!" Phil jogged over to Shun's car and hopped in. He was ready to hit the hay anyway. It had been a long, exhausting night.

About ten minutes later, Shun pulled into the front of Cyrus's grandmother's home. He got out gingerly and limped his way up to the front door. His granny answered almost immediately and embraced him. It was crazy how sweet and congenial Cyrus's grandmother was, compared to his hot temper. His granny was often the only one who could calm Cyrus down. Cyrus looked back with a wave and closed the door as he handed his grandmother the medication the nurse at the hospital had given him.

The entire way back to his place, Shun made an effort to calm Phil. He didn't want him to go in all crazy without thinking things through. It was quite possible that he would go off based on the mere sight of Brandy since Shun told him that she was there. Phil was calm, though, as they pulled out front.

The house was unusually dark, which Shun thought was odd being that he left the two girls home together. He pulled his keys out of his pocket and went to unlock the door. Before opening the door, he looked at Phil to get confirmation that he was going to keep his head. It was bad enough the woman had lost her mother in this situation as well. Phil nodded to let Shun know he was cool.

Shun opened the door to his crib and switched on the lights. There was Sophia, sitting in a chair in the middle of the living room with a gun pointed at her head.

"Shun, I didn't do it, I swear."

Cyrus made his way into his bedroom, relieved to see his queen-sized sleigh bed. He lay down as carefully as he could. Not five minutes later the phone rang.

"Yeah!"

"So we all set?"

"Yeah! Everything is in play. I may need a few things."

"A few things?"

"Yeah! Meds. A few more guns, and a discrete wiretap. Yo! And don't call this line again. You gon' fuck around and blow ma cover!"

CHAPTER 15

End Game

"Sophia! Baby! Calm down. What happened here?" Shun put his hands up as he inched closer to her. He didn't want to alarm her. Surprisingly, Phil was quiet. His eyes were wide with fear and hurt as he took in the scene.

Brandy was just lying there. Her chest was sunken in, and in her mouth held a few bubbles from her foaming. Phil and Shun had seen plenty of death surrounding their home. It was different, however, to see the life of a woman you loved end. Especially one who carried your firstborn.

Unable to contain himself, Phil fell to his knees. He was so upset he didn't know what to do.

"I didn't kill her. I'm going to lose my job when they come and pick up the body. I stole those drugs. I don't have anything else to live for. I don't have a family. It's just me," Sophia rambled on, looking out into space as if she was talking to someone else. Shun was so worried that she would pull the trigger before he could reach out safely and grab the gun, his hands began to sweat.

"Sophia, Brandy had a problem, okay? I don't know what happened here, but it's not worth you taking your life too. I need you. I will take care of you now. I *am* your family."

Sophia looked up from the floor and fixed her eyes on Shun's to see if she could decipher the truth. Shun held her gaze as Phil whimpered softly in the background.

"Now give me the gun, baby."

Cyrus lay in his bed thinking about his next move. He was in too deep, he had to admit. He actually cared for Phil and Shun. They had grown up together in the toughest of streets. He was rooting for Shun to make it out of the hood and stay out. Unfortunately, he was met with bad Karma. Cyrus thanked God for his blessings. He had been on the force for three years now and sworn into the DEA about ten months ago. It was his first real undercover gig. He just wished it didn't involve his old friends from the hood. For many years, Cyrus was able to keep the heat off of Phil from afar by his connection to some of the boys in blue, but lately, they were hot on his trail. Phil's drug trafficking was linked to other governing agencies that had their hands into mob money. So Phil's headstrong attitude about not fooling around with the pigs meant that he was now the enemy.

Cyrus had more than once tried to get Phil in bed with some of the local drug cartels that were shared by the Kern County Sheriff's Department, but Phil didn't believe in sharing his hard-earned cash with anyone but those who ran with him. It was a cat-and-mouse deal with him. The police would have to catch him. Knowing Phil, he wasn't going to go down without a fight. He lived and knew he would die by the gun.

Cyrus felt guilty as shit about his personal issues that were cause for suspicion. Though he was undercover, his gambling issue was very real. He had endangered the life of a very close friend's son. One that called him uncle.

Now, his betrayal was deeper than the sins he committed against his badge. Now, they ran so deep, they included those he considered blood.

Cyrus scrambled gingerly out of bed, trying with all his might not to tear anything. He needed to get his bandages changed. At the moment, he missed his little stolen nurse Sophia. He had confiscated her for Shun's medical treatments. Now he was in desperate need of some as well. It seemed as though the three of them were just trading issues of Karma and injustice all the way around. It was becoming quite a task to stay out of trouble and on the right path. Cyrus shook his head as he peeled off the bandages wrapped around his torso. The bruising on his rib cage was horrifically painful.

"Shit!" he grimaced.

"You okay, hon?" Cyrus's grandma asked as she heard him swear in passing.

"Sorry, Grandma!" Cyrus looked wide-eyed as if he were a twelve-year-old about to get reprimanded for using foul language. His grandmother just waved her finger and continued on to her room.

He rolled his head around to crack his neck and shoulder muscles. The stress of the case was really starting to get to him. A part of him wanted to drive down to Los Angeles, walk right into the precinct, and slam his badge down on his boss's desk and quit. Only, if he left it up to his colleagues, they would shoot Shun and Phil in cold blood. He knew it. That was the only thing keeping him in good spirits about his dastardly deeds. He was essentially saving Phil's and Shun's lives.

Now, the money was a different story. He had to get that money to cover his debts with not only Tommy, but a few other violent folks that held his life in the palm of their hands. Cyrus's pregnant wife, Sasha, was being watched. She was in the comforts of their home but wasn't in good company. Tommy's boys weren't going to go away without restitution, and then some. Cyrus tried to rub the frustration from his face. He was sleepy, but with so much on his mind, he just couldn't sleep.

Phil and Shun wrapped Brandy's body in a sheet and took her out to the car after midnight. They didn't want to run the risk of a nosy neighbor spotting them. Sophia was fast asleep after a long hot bath and a sleeping pill. Shun felt safe enough to leave her alone for a few to get rid of the body. Phil had turned completely numb at this point. His body was in full motion, but his mind was out to lunch. He answered on cue, simple yes-and-no questions, but feelings of anger, sadness, or confusion were met with a blank stare. Shun was afraid that Phil had cracked. He didn't want to bring up the trip. He honestly just wanted Phil to get some sleep. He needed another sharpshooter. Shun knew he would be slow reacting, but he would be the eyes and ears, no doubt.

There was plenty dirt and desert out in Bakersfield, so finding a spot to bury a body in the dead of night wasn't an issue. Shun and Phil dug for what seemed like hours. The night air was crisp. It numbed Shun enough to get through the pain of digging. He was sure his arm would hurt so bad he would damn near want to cut it off once he slowed down and brought his body to rest. His mind was gone as well for the time being. He was so worried about Sophia. He didn't realize how much he truly cared for her. She was right. She had risked so much for him, he didn't want to hurt her by bringing her into a world she wasn't accustomed to.

Phil looked into Shun's face and saw the same fears he had less than twenty-four hours ago when he made the decision to leave Monica.

"You know you're going to have to let that girl go, right? You owe her better than what you can give her." Phil didn't bother to look at Shun when he spoke. He already knew what it was.

"Man, don't I deserve to be happy sometime?"

"You selfish, bro! You know good and well you dragging that girl into some shit she may not recover from. And before you begin, I know it's her decision. I also know that she would follow you. You have to have enough sense to know that the shit ain't right, ma nigga."

Phil was getting angry as he spoke. He couldn't believe Shun on one hand, but he could definitely relate on the other. The thing was, Shun was usually the one to reason with everyone about the foul shit they were doing. In that moment, however, Phil knew that a change was going to have to come to pass. There he stood in the dead of night, adding another body to his roster. No, he hadn't killed her, but he played a part in it. The bottom line was that he was a single father now. He didn't have a mother he could just drop his kid off with so he could do his dirt.

It was time to man up, and Phil was maturing in just the last few hours. He was hurting that Brandy was gone, but she made that choice. He couldn't even place blame on Sophia. The guilt probably ate her ass up. She knew what she did was fucked up. What he wanted to know was why Brandy was back out here anyway. She said she was going home and he would meet her there.

Shun and Phil were relieved when they finally got the chance to toss Brandy's body into a deep grave and cover up the unfortunate incident. There was no way Shun was going to let Sophia go down for possible foul play or lose her license for him. After all, she was working to ensure he was okay.

***

The night's moon soon changed to a rising sun. Shun had about two hours of restless sleep. He stayed up most of the night watching Sophia sleep. Phil was still sitting up on the couch where he left him, staring out into space with his gun on his lap. Shun ventured into the kitchen to make a big pot of coffee. He needed to wake up, and so did Phil.

"You call them niggas?" Phil said. He sat stiff as a board and was militant in his speech.

"Yeah! Frankie is tryin'a get rid of this Puerto Rican chick he keep fuckin' on, and Cyrus is already on his way."

"Aye!" Phil interrupted Shun's rundown of the crew. "Did Brandy ever say why she was still out here in Kern? For the life of me, I can't get that off my mind. Like, I told her to head home, and I'd meet her there. I stopped off at Monica's, but I wasn't late cuz I left her. It's just bothering me, is all. Was she high? I mean, I know she took the morphine, but was she using again? Where she get the shit from? Cuz, yo, Shun, niggas out here know not to give ma baby mama shit." Phil was becoming more irate as he spoke.

Shun busied himself pouring the coffee. He was searching for words to clear his mind for the time being. He needed both Cyrus and Phil on this job. If Phil found out it was his partner in crime that stole the lifeline Brandy was clinging to, he would be sure to kill Cy. "Man, Brandy was on when I last saw her. She was high when she got here, ma nigga. I don't know what was going on back home. But there is nothing we can do now. Your son has to be the focus. Put this shit behind you or not."

"Okay. Somethin' ain't right, though. I been up all night trying to put this shit together."

"We'll get to the bottom of things later." Shun handed Phil a cup of coffee and encouraged him to drink up. Phil was more of a Pepsi-and-blunt guy. Shun had graduated to some of the finer things in life after fooling around with what he liked to call "White Bread."

Sophia finally came to and joined the two men in the living room. She smiled at Shun and took a seat at the kitchen bar. Shun poured her a cup of coffee and stared into her eyes as she took a long sip.

"I'm sorry," she mouthed at Shun. Shun just smiled and continued to drink.

Phil looked on at the two of them carrying on. He wanted to get up and slap the shit out of Shun with the butt of his gun. Instead, he strolled to the kitchen sink. He poured out the remaining tidbit of coffee and introduced himself to Sophia.

"You know if you stay with this man, you will most likely be killed. Since he doesn't have the balls to tell you to leave, I will. You seem like a very nice woman, and I appreciate everything you've done for my cousin, but this is for your own good." Phil extended his arm as if to show her to the door.

Sophia was shocked. Shun quietly set his cup down and began his approach in a very calm tone. "Phil, take a seat. Roll your ass a blunt. This will be your only warning." Shun was dead-ass serious, as he could feel the heat from his chest rising.

Sophia was beginning to get uncomfortable. She didn't want Shun getting into an altercation with his wounds still fairly fresh.

Phil backed up and retreated out the front door. "Don't say I didn't warn you, honey," he commented as he made his way out to smoke a cigarette on the porch. He was anxious to see Cyrus, since he seemed to be the only one left in the group who had any sense.

Cyrus bounced to the van parked a few blocks down the way from his home. He had to meet with his partner to have his wire put into his watch and make sure it was working properly. His stomach hurt as the anxiety of bringing down two of his best friends became a reality.

"You good?" Cyrus's partner looked at him to make sure his head was in the game.

"As ready as can be expected. My ribs are killing me."

"You take any meds?"

"Yup! Just not trying to get caught slippin', you know? I don't want to get too drowsy."

"Well, take a nap on the way. You trust these cats, don't you?" The agent lowered his eyes at Cyrus as if to get a glimpse into perhaps some deeper issues Cyrus may have harbored about going through with the takedown.

"What is that supposed to mean exactly? Never mind, I ain't got time for this bullshit. Test this fuckin' watch so I can go." Cyrus's hood mentality always seeped into his presence. He couldn't control it, nor did he want to.

Cyrus made sure all of his equipment worked before leaving to go meet his boys. He made the trip with ease. Phil was sitting out on the porch with a look of irritation wrapped around his face.

"What's up wit' you, ma nigga?" Cyrus greeted Phil as he bounced out of his car with as much swag as he could muster with two broken ribs.

"Ya boy!" Phil said simply and went back to his second cigarette.

"Oh boy! Well, we got shit to do. So let's get it. We don't have time to be worried about no bullshit. At least not today." He knew the game, and he knew the consequences. He was ready for the showdown with Phil. Though he didn't want to be the one to take him down, he knew it would be a situation where it was him or Phil. Cyrus's choice to become a cop was easy. After his mother was killed by a mugger when he was away in college, he trained harder than anyone in his class at the academy. He had remained off the grid. He hadn't returned home. He couldn't stomach a funeral. His focus became clear, and Los Angeles seemed like the place where he could take down some bad guys with little guilt in just how hard he came down on them. He wanted to tell Shun and Phil about his new job description, but once he got back to Kern County, the job turned to other avenues, going undercover to try to stop Tommy's illegal gambling fucked him up. He fell prey. It was just one shit storm after another. With so much going on it, was hard to choose a time, and right now would be the worst.

Frankie pulled up loud as ever, bumpin' some Iranian rap CD he got from some young cats handing out their underground music in front of the local Walmart.

"Man, turn that raggedy shit down," Cyrus said as Frankie pulled up close to the back of his whip.

"Man, you a hater!" Frankie said as he continued to walk up the pathway. "Where that nigga Shun at?"

"He in the house with his wifey cupcakin' like we ain't got nowhere to go."

"Man, shut that shit up!" Shun said as he appeared at the door. Phil hadn't taken notice of Shun's presence. "Let's go, we got a long drive."

Shun retreated back into the home to say his good-byes to Sophia before hitting the road. He was worried about leaving her alone, but he had to do what he had to do. Sophia assured Shun that she would be fine. It gave him a small window of release from his stress. But not enough to put his mind at complete ease.

Frankie and the boys jumped into Shun's SUV, and they headed out. Phil said a small prayer as they hit the highway.

***

The Los Angeles city limits couldn't have arrived any sooner. Frankie had talked the three of them into near points of vomiting. Phil had told Frankie to shut up more than a few dozen times, and Cyrus had even threatened to resort to physical violence. Cyrus was overly emotional, and Shun was beginning to take notice. He couldn't put his finger on it, but something was bothering him. Cyrus was checking his watch every five seconds as if he was waiting for something to happen.

Phil was too busy trying to educate Frankie on the ins and outs of weighing and bagging weed to take full notice of the sweat beads erupting on Cyrus's brow.

"You good?" Shun questioned Cyrus with a look of worry in his eyes. Cyrus felt instantly guilty for all that was about to transpire once the money exchanged hands.

Shun kept watch on Cyrus as he pulled into the gas station. He asked that Cyrus join him in the convenience store. He wanted help carrying a few snacks back to the car.

"I know!" Shun started in with Cyrus.

"You know what?" Cyrus asked, afraid to hear the answer to Shun's statement.

"I know what's up with you. You feeling guilty about what went down wit' Brandy. I can understand that. I know how strongly Phil feels about you. In the meantime, I'ma need you to pull yourself together. That man needs us. We need to make sure we are on point. You got me?"

Cyrus sighed hard. He was relieved. Hell, he thought Shun had made him. "Yeah, I got you. You right. I am worried like a mug. I didn't mean for any of this to happen."

"You know, if you had been up-front with us and told us what the deal was, we could have helped."

"Yeah! Didn't think I had a real problem, though, you feel me?" Cyrus said solemnly.

Shun pulled into the gates of an extravagant mansion just off the Santa Monica Pier. Frankie was joking about getting a few drinks and laying it down on one of the beaches, while Phil, Shun, and Cyrus concentrated on the armed security. The two Hispanics they met at the warehouse greeted them at the second checkpoint just after the gate.

Shun and the boys got out of the car and followed their guides down to the front entrance of the home. Shun and Phil were anxious to make the trade and get the hell out of Dodge. They had bigger things to take care of.

"So is everything ready to go?" Shun questioned.

"Yeah, we really gotta get back," Cyrus added. He was fidgety, which was making the two Mexican traders a bit cautious about doing the trade. Shun noticed his hands moving over his watch as well. He quickly tapped Cyrus on his shoulder.

Shun didn't say a word; he just warned him with his eyes that he was looking suspect. Cyrus then turned to him and told him that they needed to go. Shun held a puzzled look on his face.

"What the hell are you talking about?"

"It's a trap!" Cyrus raised his eyebrow and pointed at the two men that were standing at the end of the hall toward the entrance. "Let's get everything and get the hell out of here." Cyrus had clearly lost his mind. Four men against at least the twenty he counted, and two of his party were injured. Shun looked Cyrus deep into his eyes and could tell that he was serious as shit about getting out of there.

Shun wanted an explanation, but there was no way he was going to be pussyfooting around asking dumb questions when he knew their lives may be in danger. Phil was engaging in conversation with the traders. It made for a good cover-up from the slight mishap Cyrus and Shun had.

"Follow me!" one of the Mexican guides told them. "I have everything prepared for you."

"Great!" Phil said, rubbing his hands together. Frankie wasn't far behind, commenting on how phat the home was.

Shun, Cyrus, and Phil made the exchange with ease. It was then that Cyrus was supposed to call the dogs in to take down the entire camp. Instead, Cyrus asked for the truck that was for transporting the drugs and followed the men out back, leaving the special agents waiting at the front gate for his signal.

Shun hurriedly put all of the drugs and money into the car and gave the Mexicans a wave. Cyrus hopped in just as the rest of the crew did. "Drive!" Cyrus commanded.

Shun drove in silence for about forty-five minutes, then decided he couldn't take it any longer. He pulled over to the side of the road and demanded that Cyrus get his ass out of the car. Phil and Frankie were dumbfounded by Shun's actions.

"You good, nigga?" Shun asked aggressively. "Yo' ass been actin' weird all day. I don't want to drive another minute if we aren't on the same page."

Cyrus lowered his eyes and leaned into Shun's space. "Why wouldn't I be?" he said through clenched teeth, pushing past Shun.

Phil fell out of the truck with ease and nearly hit his leg on the front end of the truck trying to get his hands on Shun. "What the fuck is your problem, Shun? We don't have time for pit stops."

"Phil, shut the fuck up! This ain't about you right now." Shun then directed his attention to Cyrus. "What the fuck is up, ma nigga? You need to let us know what's going on right now."

Frankie started to get antsy. "We can't talk and drive? We got drugs, yo! A load of cash, and some very dangerous men waiting on a package. You think we can wrap this little fight up? It's plenty of pussy, boys, and when we get our cuts of this doe, we're going to be swimming in it."

"I'm not going no-fucking-where until I find out why and how Cyrus knew that we were going to be set up at this exchange."

"Set up?" Phil questioned, as he eyed Cyrus. "What the fuck is he talking about, Cyrus?"

"Look, this ain't the time or place."

Phil drew his weapon almost immediately when he was met with a blank answer. "Oh, I think it's the *perfect* time and place. Shun felt the need to stop and ask questions. I say we shoot and just keep it movin'. Come to think of it, you been either acting weird or MIA for quite some time now. Explain!

"Whoa whoa whoa! Look, we don't have the time for this, my African American, overly dramatic friends. We have got to get the hell out of Dodge, no matter the situation. We are out on the road, my ninjas. With a boatload of drugs and money, need I say more? I wasn't planning on getting my ass blown off today. So far, it's been a good trip. Whatever the matter, we need to take care of this in Kern County—*after* we settle the trades."

Shun looked at Cyrus with an evil eye. "I would have to agree." Shun didn't say another word. He just hopped into the front seat and waited for the rest of his party to join him. Phil's wheels were turning now that Shun decided to make light of Cyrus's funny behavior.

"Theresa, you're on," a man on the other end of the phone instructed. Theresa's job was easy. Lay up with Frankie to find out where the drugs and loot would be exchanged and lead her men there. She didn't want to do too much of anything else. She was an undercover informant for Tommy, that was all.

"Yeah!" Theresa said and hung up the phone with a huge sigh. She then put in a phone call to Frankie. She wanted to find out what he wanted for dinner. Of course, he didn't answer her voice call, but he responded almost immediately to her text. He made sure to let her know that he was on his way back from his business trip. He was exhausted, but he could eat.

Theresa made her plan of action from there. She called Tommy to let him know that the exchange was going down in just a few hours. Tommy was planning on stealing all the money and drugs and expanding his drug cartel and gambling casino. He wasn't a drug dealer; he was a man of business, and seizing both the money and drugs was a golden opportunity.

The men pulled into the warehouse to check out their come up. Frankie was rubbing his hands together, skinning and grinning. His excitement was beginning to get on Shun's nerves.

"How long before the drop?" Shun asked.

"Just a few hours. You rollin', right?" Frankie asked. He wanted to make sure Phil and Cyrus knew they weren't invited. The Italian mob had no history with the other two tagalongs, and he didn't want any confusion.

"Yeah, I'm good to go. Cyrus! You?" Shun looked at him with a look of distrust. He didn't want Cyrus out of his sight. His plan was to cut the money up and take his cut back to his place. Leave his money in a safe place before the exchange.

"Yeah, let's get to counting," Phil said.

Frankie grabbed his three bags of cash and bounced. He wanted to get back to his place, take a shower, and meet up with Shun in about an hour or so. Shun told him to be careful and meet them back at the spot.

Theresa took a long shower as she waited for Frankie to return home. She phoned Tommy to let him know that Frankie was back in town.

It wasn't long after Theresa bounced out of the shower that she heard Frankie come in. She had taken her time smoothing her body with lotion to make sure she set the scene. Frankie looked dog-tired as he heaved in three duffle bags of money. Theresa was confused.

"Babe, where's the rest of the cash? I thought you were getting a shitload of money and drugs." Theresa smiled lightly to cover up her worry.

"We did! This is my cut. We have to drop off the rest in a few hours. I just wanted to come home and shower." Frankie noticed a sense of worry as he looked into her eyes.

Theresa scratched her forehead. She was nervous. Tommy was going to kill her. She had fucked up big time.

"Where's the money, Frankie? The rest of it?" Theresa said as she pulled her gun and badge from a small seam in her panties at the small of her back. "Look, just do as I say, and I can possibly cut you a deal with the DA's office." Theresa was playing both Tommy and Frankie. Getting close to Tommy's gullible nephew Frankie was easy. Tommy used Theresa to get close to Frankie to keep tabs on him. He could trust Frankie to handle business, but at times, he could be reckless. Tommy thought that perhaps some pussy would calm him down. When Tommy sent Frankie for the drop, he trusted Frankie to bring to him what was rightfully his. Now, with Theresa showing her true colors, Tommy was sure to blow a gasket.

Frankie looked on as if he was in a fucking movie. He couldn't believe this bitch. He couldn't call for help or warn his boys. Frankie could hear the sirens coming down the road.

"Look, we don't want you or the rest of your crew. I'm undercover. I've been working to get Tommy for about six months now. He thinks I'm his girlfriend. I was supposed to set you and the boys up so he could rob you all for the loot. We were going to swarm his ass and take him down. This little bit of cash won't hold 'im. When my partner comes, we're going to arrest you, but you won't do much time for this. I don't have you on anything else."

Theresa's mouth was moving, but Frankie couldn't hear much of the words coming out of it. He was disgusted at how he'd allowed himself to be played. He just sat down on the bed and put his hands out in front of him. "Just take me in" were his only words.

"Why are we still here in California?" Phil asked as he was counting with Cyrus and Shun.

"What!" Shun said disgusted.

"Haven't we been through enough? You want the mob to come for us too? Right now, we have the chance to pay our debts and get the hell out of Dodge."

"The mob not gon' let us just walk in and out of their lair without us paying restitution," Cyrus interjected sarcastically. "You don't find the shit strange that Frankie just dipped?"

"No, Cyrus, I don't. Seeing since he said he would meet us here," Shun responded.

"All I'm saying is that I don't trust the situation at this point. So fuck what y'all talkin'. I just want me and my son to get out of this country in its entirety."

"So what you sayin' is that we just steal the entire bid and dip? What about Frankie? We just leave him to face Tommy and the mob alone?"

"Shun, how do we know that man ain't did the same to us?" Phil responded.

"Fuck this! I'm gettin' ready to call this man right now. He'll answer and set this shit straight."

Cyrus shook his head. He wasn't certain of anything anymore. The only thing he knew for certain was that he had just lost his job, so it didn't matter how shit went down at this point anymore. He was supposed to book Shun, Phil, and Frankie at the trade and bring them in then. Only, Cyrus needed the money as well. He had no choice but to roll with Shun. He was a criminal now. An agent gone rogue, and he had everything to lose. His most important assets, his wife and child. "Let's just take this money and split," Cyrus blurted.

Shun looked into space. "First things first. I gotta get Sophia, and we have to pick up Phil's son."

"I agree!" Phil said.

"Agreed," Cyrus finalized.

Frankie's phone was ringing off the hook—only he was being transported to the county jail. Theresa held the phone as she thought about how she was going to tell Tommy what went down. She waited until the police were gone to call Tommy to come over. She forwarded Frankie's calls to voice mail and kept her cool as she waited for Tommy to pull up. She was back into character and ready to spill the beans about Frankie coming back home with only two duffle bags. Her story meshed well with his plans, which were to come home, shower, and meet with his Italian mob connection.

Tommy pulled up with one of his handlers, excited to see how much money he had acquired. "Hey, sweetie, where's the money?"

"There isn't much. Probably $125,000, at the most. Plans changed. Frankie came home with only his cut. He said something about having to meet up with his boys to make the drop together." *Police show up, both Frankie and Tommy go down,* Theresa thought as she stared at Tommy testing the waters as she challenged him on his concern for his nephew.

Tommy was calm at first but was growing increasingly upset as he listened to Theresa's story. "Theresa, baby, where's the drop location?"

Theresa looked worried that Tommy was getting impatient with her. He was always so tense when it came to money. "I . . . I don't know, baby."

Tommy cocked back his hand and smacked her dead across her mouth. Theresa panicked, fell over a bit, and cried out, shocked that Tommy had struck her. She was hysterical.

"It's okay. It's okay," Tommy coached Theresa as he held her head in his hands. "It's okay, baby," he said once more—before hitting her again, this time with a closed fist. Theresa just slumped over.

"Put her in the car," Tommy ordered.

"Get those fucking cocksuckers on the phone, *now!*" Italian mob boss Joey Bono yelled.

"Frankie ain't pickin' up his phone, and neither is his boy Shun!"

"Find 'em! I don't care if Frankie is my nephew. Where's my brother Tommy in all this? He has always been weak in the mind when it came to Frankie. Those half-breeds are confused." Joey and Tommy weren't close. Joey felt that he was superior to Tommy because he was black and Italian. "I want my drugs and my money—*now!*"

"Joey! Frankie got pinched. The cops just told." One of the younger members of the crew whisked in with the news.

Joey sat up in his chair a bit and put his fat hand on his cheek. "So my drugs and money are gone?" Joey rubbed his hands together as he stared down at the boy who had given him the news. Joey was about to give the order when his phone rang. It was a collect call from the Kern County Jail. He accepted the charges.

"Frankie, you better be calling me to let me know where you stashed my money and drugs."

Frankie was confused. "What are you talking about? I was calling to make sure Shun and Phil had made the drop. I got pinched. Some undercover bitch hooked me. Now I'm looking at doing some time. Man, I hope Tommy cool. I didn't a chance to call him and warn him about this bitch."

"Oh, you won't be doing time," Joey said. "You're certain Tommy is unaware about this, uh, what did you say this bitch's name was again?"

"Theresa," Frankie replied, his voice a bit shaky as he cracked under pressure.

"Good boy," Joey said and hung up the phone.

Frankie walked back to his holding cell for the night. All kinds of things played out in his head. He couldn't believe Shun and Phil hadn't made the drop yet. They didn't need him to do anything.

All of a sudden there was a huge commotion with a group of men in the holding cell. One of them pulled out a knife and started lunging at one of the other inmates. Frankie quickly moved as the crowd seemed to be pushing toward his area of the cell. As he got up to move out of the way, one of the men pulled him into the circle. As the others surrounded him, two inconspicuous men began to stab Frankie repeatedly. Frankie fell to the floor gurgling blood and convulsing.

CHAPTER 16

Run

Police sirens rang as the unmarked police cars sped to Phil's residence in the Kern County Projects, only there was no sign of Phil. The hood was silent. Thugs stood outside the gates of Kern County Projects like foot soldiers, stiff as a board. Police barged in the project gates and set out a search of the campus and Phil's apartment. Residents were questioned, but no one was willing to give up any information on Phil's whereabouts.

No one knew of Shun's involvement. Phil made it a point to water down Shun's ability to run a crew or carry out a drug deal. Only Shun was more than capable. He was both careful and resourceful. These traits were absent from Phil's skill set. Detective Santiago had her head in the clouds, while her stand-in partner rambled on about his thoughts on the missing suspect. Santiago was worried about her partner Cyrus. She hadn't heard from him since the drug trade. She was worried sick, afraid he had gone rogue and catted off with the money. Santiago knew of Cyrus's issues with gambling and knew what a high-rolling jerk Tommy was, so naturally, she worried that Tommy may know just where Cyrus was. Santiago worried that he was underground—or in the river. She could picture his smug grin barking orders and sitting back in his chair, in show of a job well done.

Santiago had to find Cyrus and the money before Tommy or Bakersfield police did.

***

The call for Flight 119 was heard all over the airport. Shun, Sophia, Cyrus, and Phil, and Junior were hustling through the crowded corridors, desperate to make their flight to Miami.

It was a nice place to vacation, full of beaches and clubs to tour. Vacation, however, in this particular outing, was more of a run-for-your-life deal. Sophia was cursing her wardrobe selection. She wanted to look hot to trot. They were on the run, so fashion was not even on the list. Shun had a Louis Vuitton backpack full of nothing but cash and a fake ID. Phil had the same. The only thing Phil Junior had was a handheld game and his school ID for boarding purposes. Cyrus just had his fake ID.

Shun and his crew scrambled in line with the rest of the passengers. They were so nervous their hands were sweaty and visibly shaking.

Shun stepped up to the stewardess, shaking like a leaf. He was literally having a panic attack about the possibility of being caught by the police. Sure, he was nervous about the plane ride, but he was usually OK after takeoff.

"Sir?"

Shun was blank and showed no response to the stewardess.

"Your ticket, please, sir," the stewardess tried again to get Shun's attention.

Shun handed her the ticket and waited for his receipt. The attendant took one of the tickets and handed Shun the boarding pass. Shun's hands were shaking so hard it was almost as if he was using the tickets as a fan.

"Don't worry, the takeoff is the most dreaded part of the flight. At least, for me, it is." The stewardess took Shun's hand and smiled. His heart dropped from anxiety for a moment too long. His brief encounter unnerved Sophia. She cleared her throat loud as hell.

Shun retrieved his hand and whispered a thank-you and walked briskly to the entrance of the plane. Once they were all seated and fastened in, their blood pressure began to lower to a normal state. All four adults could feel their fluttering heart beat normalize.

"We made it!" Shun smiled and took Sophia's hand. "If we get out of this alive, I'm going to make you my wife," he vowed.

Sofia smiled and lay her head on Shun's shoulder. She felt safe and secure.

Phil noticed the two of them nestled together seemingly in love. He was still skeptical about Sophia's true motive for choosing the life of a runaway criminal versus her nearly six-figure nursing job. She was head nurse at Bakersfield Hospital with very high merits. Phil didn't think she was a con artist or anything. She was held in high regard for making sure his cousin had meds for his still-aching bullet wounds, but she didn't have to throw her entire life away over a few missing medical instruments, supplies, and meds. Phil assumed she was a bad girl all along. She just kept that part locked away until she laid eyes on Shun.

Still, Phil was keeping an eye on her and Cyrus. Cyrus's demeanor changed completely. The radio reported the killing of mob Boss Joey Bono's nephew in the county jail the night before. Cyrus was unusually quiet. He had been that way since shortly after the announcement of Frankie's murder. He was worried about his wife and newborn son, of course, but he was odd in his mannerisms as well. Phil couldn't put his finger on it, but he was going to get to the bottom of it.

It didn't take long for Phil Junior to fall asleep. Phil was so happy to have his son with him, he just stared at him. He didn't know how he was going to tell his son that his mother died of a drug overdose. If it was up to him, he would take the "how" out of the equation and find the time to tell Junior that his mom was in a better place.

Sophia was half-asleep, dozing on and off as she was relishing being in her lover's arms and enjoying the beautiful view. Although they were in the most dangerous position yet, she hadn't a care in the world. Sophia felt like she and Shun could take on the world. She had only known Phil for a few weeks, and she knew Phil was a catalyst. His firecracker spirit was one she wanted Shun to leave behind, but soon after getting serious with Shun, she saw that getting rid of Phil would be out of the question. The two were at each other's neck more often than not; however, if you mess with one, you mess with both.

Sophia could respect that, she just hoped that Phil's react-first/think-last attitude didn't get them all killed. She could guess that those same thoughts of worry presented in Cyrus's brow. As she gazed up and over in his direction, she could see he was filled with worry and/or nervousness He looked as if he was constipated.

Sophia liked Cyrus, but there was just something about his latest movement that suggested something else was worrying him.

Cyrus threw his head back onto his seat in an effort to try to relax. He noticed Sophia watching him from the corner of his eye, so to make sure he didn't seem out of sorts, he pretended not to notice while wiping his sweaty palms on the lap of his jeans. Then boldly, he looked Sophia right into her unwavering stare and threw her a thumbs-up to indicate things were on the up and up. Sophia gave Cy a quick nod, then lay her head back on Shun's chest. All she could do was pray for her new family. Sophia would take the scars, both physical and mental, away from Shun if she could. If she could, she would certainly take his place, in death.

CHAPTER 17

Low Life

Phil sat as still as can be. He was almost uncomfortable as Phil Junior rested his head on his shoulder. In that moment, Phil looked at his son's face and promised to give him the world. More so than that, he would protect his son at any cost. He didn't want Shun to think he had gone soft; however, his focus had changed dramatically and it was time to hang this shit up.

The pain in Shun's side was giving him the business. He was eating extra strength Tylenols as if they were Tic Tacs and downing orange juice he spiked with vodka in hopes to numb the pain. As soon as Sophia was fast asleep, he gently moved her into a comfortable position before unfastening his seat belt to take a look at his wounds. The last thing he needed was to cause attention to his injury. Shun could feel his wound pulsating as it filled with pus and blood.

As he leaned over to touch his wound as gently as possible, the plane hit an air pocket, and the turbulence threw Shun onto his side and armrest. He yelped under his breath and cussed, but he managed to keep his painful outburst quiet. Shun was starting to feel overwhelmed with all that was taking place. He feared he couldn't protect his growing family. The truth was that Shun wasn't the same man as before his tour with the marines. After he was betrayed by the flag, his honor died but never his loyalty. Loyalty, however, was what life in the hood was about. Every move he made all resulted in his return to the Kern County Projects. He was beginning to think that in some aspects, Phil was right. He lived according to the laws of the hood, and he demanded those that fucked with him to do the same. What Phil lacked in managing his small empire he filled with a spirit of relentlessness when it came to people not following orders. He was the leader and the muscle. No man would be able to simply walk into his domain without permission. He had rules of engagement, and when those laws were broken, the crime was punishable by death. Shun could dig it. He was just ready to fly sky high.

Shun grimaced a bit as he got up to go to the bathroom. He made sure to check his side for traces of blood leaking from his wound. Confident that his wound wouldn't strike the interest of others, he proceeded to the bathroom. Once inside, he lifted his T-shirt ever so gently and took a look at the damage. The gauze and tape were so matted with blood and pus, the gauze was stuck to his open flesh. His first thought was just to pull it right off in one full swing, but he knew that it would entice his skin to cry out.

Shun took a small piece of the tape off of his bandages to take a better look at the sore. It was much worse than he thought. The bullet wound was beginning to smell, and the redness spread. Taking the tape off his injury felt as if he were peeling his skin. He bit his lip and closed his eyes. He couldn't bear to look at it and admitted to himself that he was scared. The bullet wound was indeed infected, and he needed to pay a doctor a visit fast. Peeling the soiled bandages off gently and slowly, his eyes grew wide. Shun could see the pus draining from the wound and his muscle rise and fall.

Panicking, he hurriedly put some ointment on his wounds and applied a fresh stack of gauze. He stood and stared into the distorted mirror, trying to pull himself together before leaving the small airplane bathroom. He wet his face in an effort to calm his spirits and retreated to take his seat next to his sleeping Sophia.

Shun's tall frame passed through the aisle of the plane with ease. First class was a peaceful venture. He scanned the plane for the rest of his traveling buddies and caught sight of Cyrus. He was looking like he was constipated. He was sweating like a pig under a well ventilated soft breeze. Shun's forehead wrinkled. Cyrus didn't look good at all, which sent him to make a pit stop by his seat to check in on him.

Cyrus didn't notice he had a small audience watching how uncomfortable he looked. When Shun tapped him on the shoulder, he nearly jumped from his seat.

"Bro! What the fuck is up with you? You look like you gotta take a shit. You sweating under the collar. Check yo' self before you get the attention of a badge, nigga, for real, for real. These people will start to think you gotta bomb strapped to your chest or some shit."

Cyrus's stomach dropped when Shun said the word *badge*. He was leading a double life, and though Shun knew that he was a stand-up guy, he knew his confession in regards to his profession would drive a deep wedge between the two of them. "Man, it's these wings. I'm scared as shit." Cyrus knew it was far more than a plane ride bothering him, but he was glad that his anxiety fit well with the situation.

Shun looked Cyrus dead in his eyes as he spoke. He knew it had to be something more than his anxiety of flying, but he couldn't put his finger on it. Shun could understand his uneasiness. He fled from Tommy, leaving his newborn son and wife to face the music if Tommy saw fit to flush him out.

Shun felt bad that he was leaving his fam behind. He had Sophia, and Phil had his son. He wouldn't be surprised if Cyrus wasn't feeling jealous. He was alone and unable to protect his wife and son. It was Cy's call, though. There were a few holes in his story, but he would address them later. Right now, he was just interested in making sure his family was safe.

Cyrus nodded at Shun to let him know that he was feeling better and ready to get his head back in the game. Shun bought it. He returned to his seat without questioning Cyrus's ill mannerisms.

Cyrus was busy thinking about his job. He didn't know if he could trust anyone but Dana. He trusted her as his partner, but they were both high-strung believers in the badge and its oath. Cy's mind ran so much he could have sworn he could feel pressure in his head. He suddenly felt nauseated and emotional. In an effort to clear his mind, he went in search for a game to play to pass the time by.

Google had a cover story he couldn't ignore. The death of Tommy's nephew was going viral, and a few scrolls down were the fugitives about this weeklong killing spree. Cyrus felt his brow perspire. His stomach was weak. Scrolling down slowly to see the suspects wanted for the crimes, he said a small prayer.

"Fuck!" Cyrus exclaimed to himself. Fleeing with stolen property, now murder was added to the list of their crimes. He owed Tommy the money for his gambling debts. Money he acquired from Tommy's own brother, mob boss Joey Bono, and now their nephew was dead.

"They gon' kill us," Cyrus realized.

Cyrus closed his eyes and expelled a sigh of relief as he saw the drawings and names of Phil and Shun. He didn't wish any harm to his two childhood friends, but he had a wife and son to get home to. His job was his world as well.

Cyrus quickly closed his search box and took a long swig of his Hennessey and apple juice. He wasn't pleased that Shun and Phil were wanted men, but it did mean that he was in the clear of criminal activity. At least for now. Cyrus relaxed a bit and let his drink work to loosen his tight muscles. He felt so alone.

CHAPTER 18

Bye-Bye, Frankie

Phil's mind was filled with what-ifs and worry. He was scared for his son. He didn't care too much about his own well-being. He understood the life he chose to live. He would die by the hands of his brethren or end up spending the rest of his life in jail. Phil knew his fate, however, had different plans on how things would play out.

As Phil hunted for games and slot machines on his phone, his search was interrupted by an emergency broadcasting system. "Amber Alert!" Phil paused as he waited on the information for the lost child and the possible suspect. Sure enough, Phil Junior's police sketch filled the entire California database and its residents. Nervous, he powered his phone off and headed straight for Cyrus. He didn't trust a word that came from his mouth. Now, more than ever, he needed Cy to man up and spill the milk.

Phil felt played. He was surprised to know that Frankie was in jail. He thought he had fled with the dough. He knew that something was amiss, but he couldn't put his finger on it. It wasn't too astonishing that Frankie was found dead in jail. He was going to die or become somebody's bitch, that was a given. He still needed to confront Cyrus. He would start with Frankie—who, how, and why.

"So, is it true?" Phil jolted in a ploy to startle Cyrus. He figured if he scared him, he would just start telling all.

Cyrus shook for a slight second but quickly retrieved his composure. "Is what true?"

"Frankie!" Phil yelled.

"Yeah, unfortunately. They did him dirty. You know Tommy had him killed, right?" Cyrus said as he raised one of his eyebrows. He had this glaring look that suggested that he was the one pulling the strings. He didn't know for sure, but he did know how Tommy and his crew operated from previous run-ins with the gang. It didn't matter your connection or bloodline. Money and loyalty were the core of the Italian family.

"Damn, his own uncle, bro," Phil said solemnly. "That nigga's a beast." Phil was staring at Cyrus's forehead, wondering when he was going to chime in on the matter. "Yo, Cy. What the fuck, man! You look sick."

"I'm cool. Just got a ton on my mind. I miss my woman and son." Cyrus was so worried he could barely eat his lunch. He had his own set of problems with Tommy. He had to figure out how he would slip Tommy the money without Shun and Phil finding out. To tell Shun and Phil the truth could be deadly.

"Well, we better lie low. Tommy frequents quite a few states to re-up. He won't let this just go away. Shit, Tommy has killed for just under ten grand. He has probably called the entire cavalry in to ensure our capture. With a couple of hundred thousand missing, there is bound to be a price on our heads," Cy said humping his shoulders. It was too late to get sensitive about the situation. They were walking dead. "The game of it all would be in the time they managed to stay free and alive until the day came to face the music."

"Music." Phil cracked up. "Nigga, you mean death. You mighty nonchalant about this shit, Cy. I got my son to worry about. Is there something we should know? Better yet, does Shun know that Tommy had his own nephew slaughtered at the county jail, and for what? A cup of noodles for the entire D Block?"

"Let me worry about Shun, OK? I don't want that man trippin' off things we had nothing to do with."

"That's the fuckin' point, Cy. Them muthafuckas don't give a shit about Frankie, and they could care even less about us, you feel me? I have to protect my son."

"From what?" Shun interjected. Both Cy and Phil were caught in the wind with their bare asses out.

"Man, that Tommy dude had Frankie murdered in jail," Phil said.

"Yeah, I know. No use in us trying to make sense of things. Our focus is about money and safety. Now, get focused and get yo' asses back to yo' seat."

Phil shook his head as Shun downplayed the situation. He felt unappreciated after the hit and run. Shun still didn't see him as an equal. *Damn, do I have to lay my life on the line for my own flesh and blood to believe in me?*

Detective Santiago and a team of ten officers from SWAT stormed into Tommy's club.

"All right, cut the music! Everyone down!" Santiago announced. "Bakersfield Police."

Five goons stepped in front of Detective Santiago, guns blazing. Santiago held up her badge as if to ward off Tommy's boys.

"Excuse us, pig! Not sure if you know, but your badge means nothing here. This a place of business. We will show you the way out."

Detective Santiago stood her ground. "I have information involving Tommy's nephew, Frankie."

"Let her through, Jake." Tommy stepped from under the shadows and presented himself. "What did he do now?" Tommy smirked. He was so used to hearing of Frankie's shenanigans. He had inherited Frankie. He raised him since the age of five. Tommy's brother was killed in connection to some missing drugs and the killing of the cartel's drug lord's son.

Santiago cleared her throat. "He was taken into custody in connection with drug trafficking. The other two are at large. I am sorry to have to tell you, but Frankie was murdered last night in County. We think he was killed to keep quiet, perhaps from his other two partners in crime." Santiago watched Tommy's face as closely as she could in the dim light.

She was looking for some form of emotion or admission of guilt. It never came. Tommy simply turned on his heel and walked out of sight. He threw his hand up and waved to the disc jockey. As the music filled the club once more, everyone melted from their frozen state and began to dance.

Santiago was deep in thought as she approached her office. She swung into the parking space and headed straight for the tea and coffee. Santiago knew that Tommy knew about his nephew's death. She also knew that he wouldn't speak to any law enforcement about the situation either. Santiago approached Tommy just to get a read on him. He was fearless and cocky, two things that made others cringe. Dana knew that Tommy would set things in motion to avenge his family, even if Frankie was a sloppy wannabe gangsta.

Santiago was going to see if she could stir the pot a bit. Shun and his cousin Phil were on the run. The only thing she could figure was that Tommy would gather his goons to hunt the two fugitives down. More so puzzling was how Cyrus fit in the circle. He was deep undercover trying to take Tommy down. He had made a few bets at Tommy's casino. He was in over his head, Dana could feel it. She was missing something. Cyrus was missing, and he left her no clues or contact info so that she could protect him, if need be. Sipping her tea, Dana paced back and forth at her desk before plopping down in her seat. Everything reminded her of Cyrus. She was an emotional wreck.

"Santiago, Keats, get your asses in here," the sergeant came barreling out of his office. Dana rolled her eyes and followed Keats into their boss's office. She was in no mood to hear a bunch of negative reinforcement. Her partner was out in the wind God knows where, and she was stuck to play good-cop/bad-cop with a rookie detective who was still wet behind the ears.

"What's up, boss?" Keats asked overly cocky.

O'Reilly ignored him and looked completely through the new kid on the block and addressed Dana. "Detective Santiago, have you made contact with Cyrus?"

"No, not yet. We stopped by Tommy's place to deliver the news about his nephew Frankie, but that's about it."

"Shit! You don't reckon he went rogue, do you? I hate to call it, but I think he has either been made or is in too deep," Keats stated.

Dana could feel a lump in her throat swelling. She was afraid to respond verbally for fear she would get choked up and have a complete breakdown.

"No, he wouldn't go off the grid for no good reason. Something is the cause for Cy's absence."

"We don't have the time to debate any of this. Just find him," O'Reilly demanded, escorting the two detectives out of his office.

CHAPTER 19

Dana Santiago

Santiago couldn't deny her love for Cyrus, but she would never destroy his marriage with Casey. She was such a sweet girl. Seemed too soft for Cyrus. Santiago enjoyed their playful banter and partnership. The chase for the suspect and Cyrus's love made her moist, and the catch that more exciting. Dana knew Cyrus was in trouble, she just didn't know how or why.

Thoughts raged in her mind as the emotions for her partner rendered her less optimistic and prepared to handle things professionally. Fed up with tapping her pencil on the pile of late report submissions, she grabbed her leather bomber, her badge, and gun, and headed out to her vehicle One thing she loved about the Narcotics Division was ditching the uniform. Men especially treated women in uniform less than savory. She was a cop's daughter, niece, and grandchild, so choosing to be a doctor or lawyer was frowned upon.

Dana's dad didn't take too well to court-appointed lawyers. He felt that lawyers for the defense were lying scoundrels that simply made fun of the law. As far as he was concerned, lawyers were there for the win, not justice. He died a bitter old man after taking the life of another man who murdered her younger brother. He drove out to his favorite lake, had a few beers, even caught a few fish, and then swallowed his gun. Even though he committed a serious crime, no one could argue against his actions.

The man responsible for killing her mother was set free on the count of circumstantial evidence and corruption of evidence. The defense claimed the suspect was pressured into making a false confession.

Dana could care less about all the red and yellow tape her father cut through. She was just sorry that he had taken his own life for fear he would be killed in a prison full of those he put there.

Dana was so lost in her thoughts she hadn't realized she found herself just a block away from Cyrus's home. Her stomach tightened in knots because she didn't know what to do about her missing partner. Showing up at his home unannounced could prove to be a bit fishy. Still, Dana swallowed hard and parked her unmarked police car a few doors down from Cy's place of residence. She noticed a black-on-black SUV was parked in the driveway. Cy's two-door Camaro was nowhere to be found. Dana went on high alert. Her first instinct was to draw her weapon and check things out, but she didn't want to alarm anyone, especially if Cyrus had visitors from family.

Instead, she placed her weapon in front instead of her back holster and proceeded to knock on the door. She was especially nervous. It wasn't the fact that she was doing a wellness check-up. It was the fact that she would be coming face-to-face with Cyrus's wife and child. She hadn't had time to prepare a script. She was hoping to ensure she came across as a concerned member of Cyrus's team and not some jealous side bitch. She hadn't so much as kissed Cyrus, so she couldn't take pride in being the mistress either.

Truthfully, Dana's love for Cyrus was unspoken for fear he would ask for a new partner. Somehow, Dana believed that he knew how she felt. He just never played on it.

She swallowed hard and straightened her stance before knocking on the Dunkin residence. Santiago rang the doorbell for the third time. Her first thought was that no one was home, but the big truck in the driveway said otherwise.

After a few moments, Casey and her bundle of joy answered the door. Casey had only cracked the door wide enough to see who her uninvited guest was.

Dana was a tad confused. Casey had this unwavering stare that spelled *fear*—all of it.

"Daaa-na, hi," Casey said, clearing her throat.

"You OK?" she said, lowering her eyes. "Is the baby OK?" Dana was asking questions that left an open window for Casey to send her a clue about what was really going on. Dana was nervous that something was wrong with Casey and the baby. Somehow, she needed to get in touch with Cyrus. Suddenly, she felt sick to her stomach, and her intuition began to flare.

"Casey, is Cyrus here?"

Casey's eyes began to water a bit as she shook her head no.

"I understand," Dana said.

Casey's body jolted a bit as if she was being pushed. Dana noticed right away. "Do you know where Cy is? We were supposed meet up at the station, but he never showed."

Casey looked down. It was a show of panic. Dana picked up on it right away. "Can I come in?" she inquired. Casey was as stiff as a board. Then again, Dana caught the little forceful jolt she'd seen before.

"I rather you not come in at the moment. With the newborn, I have to take extra precautions."

Dana played along and giggled, "Right. My apologies. Well, if he shows, tell him to call me and check in at the station." Dana bounced down the steps to Casey's home and walked briskly to her car.

The "gentlemen" visiting Casey weren't family at all. Santiago would have to form a team to enter the home without causing harm to Casey and the baby. She paced back and forth around her car. Then she called Cyrus with no answer once again. Dana was starting to panic. The next call was to Keats. She would need backup immediately.

CHAPTER 20

Casey

Casey solemnly watch Dana walk back to her car. She was near tears watching perhaps her last chance to get away from Tommy's goons. Cyrus hadn't made good on his gambling debts. Now he had a hit on himself—and his family.

She began to cry hysterically as one of the men slammed the door and locked it.

"Casey, we don't want to hurt you or your son. We just need to get a little information from you." One of the interrogators walked around Casey as he spoke to her. Casey was breathing hard and fast, on the verge of a panic attack. The man stopped in front of her and stared into her eyes.

"Where is Cyrus?"

"I don't know," she answered.

"Casey, are you a good wife?"

"Yes."

"Devoted? Attentive?"

"I try to be."

"Good," the interrogator said, tilting his head to the sky and closing his eyes as if basking in the ambiance of his power.

"You know I can't believe that such a devoted and attentive wife wouldn't be aware of her husband's where-abouts or his problems with handling money. You know, your husband has quite the gambling problem, and he owes someone a great deal of money. Money he borrowed to ensure you and your little boy have this very roof over your heads." The interrogator took a long pause and looked Casey dead in her face once more. "Where's the money?"

"I don't know," Casey responded once more with a more confident, stern tone. She was unable to comply with the men because she didn't know about Cyrus and his gambling problem. Cy kept most of his outside ventures to the winds when came home. Only this time, the problems hunted him down. Casey searched her mind for clues to freeing herself and her son. She really relied on Dana getting her subtle gestures to indicate that something was very wrong.

Casey asked for permission to use the bathroom. The two armed men obliged. She gently laid her baby down in his basinet and proceeded to go to the bathroom with him.

"The baby stays with us," one of the armed men said. Casey sighed and reluctantly let go of the portable bassinet. She walked to the bathroom and quickly retrieved her phone from the plant behind the toilet. She texted Cyrus first. She had no idea about the troubles he was in. Now she was caught in the cross fire. Casey was so fueled with rage her character count was out on her message to Cy.

Next text was to Dana. She needed help from the one woman that was sleeping with her husband. At least, that's what she thought. All the late phone calls and long runs left Casey up late, crying, wondering.

She never spoke of it. She took what he dealt because she truly loved Cyrus. She didn't know how dark her world with Cyrus had become.

Gambling. Where did he get the money for these big-time gambling escapades? Casey was so lost in her mind that she didn't hear the loud knocking on the door. She quickly took her pants down and sat on the toilet just as one of the armed men busted in.

"What's taking so long?" he asked.

Casey hurriedly closed her legs so as not to be exposed. "My nerves are shot. It's taking me awhile. My stomach is all out of whack." She passed gas for added effect. Her body was in tune with her performance. For that, she was internally grateful.

The home invader cleared his throat, "Excuse me. Take your time, handle your business. Sorry to barge in. My partner was a little worried, that's all. I don't want to hurt you; however, he will pay it no mind. Please hurry."

Casey gave him a nod as he closed the door once more. After he had gone, she managed to retrieve the phone again to check her messages. She had no reply from Cyrus yet. Thoughts of foul play flowed like running water. She became weak and dizzy all of a sudden. Panic settled in. Casey was still healing from her C-section. The incision throbbed, and her legs were heavy. She lost her balance and fainted, hitting her head on the edge of the sink as she went down. She was out cold.

CHAPTER 21

Permission Slip

"Keats, there is something going down at Cyrus's home. I went by to check on him. He wasn't there, but Casey had some unwanted company. Can you round up a team? I'm moving to higher ground so I can keep surveillance on the home. What you want to bet those are Tommy's boys holding her hostage in the home? Either Cyrus owes them money, or he has something they are looking for."

"OK, I'm on it." Keats hung up the phone and told O'Reilly what Dana suspected was up with Casey. O'Reilly was visibly furious and told Keats to round up a crew and keep him posted. "Not a hair out of place for my daughter and grandson, you understand me?" O'Reilly warned.

Keats nodded his head to let him know that he understood everything he was asked to do, but he was stunned to find that his daughter was Cyrus's wife. *The plot thickens,* thought Keats. *Boy, oh boy, I wonder if Santiago is aware of this.*

O'Reilly slammed his door and got right on the phone. "We had a deal. What the *fuck* is going on? You have my daughter hostage. *My grandson.* I swear to God if they are harmed or mistreated—"

Tommy cut him off midsentence. "*Have you forgotten who is running this show?* I pay you to make sure my transactions are clean, and in exchange, I take care of the riffraff so that you remain the city's best choice for a healthy community. Now, if you are ready to speak to me like a man, we can discuss this issue properly."

"What is going on, Tommy?" O'Reilly asked with great irritation. He was burning with anger. No person was more important than his daughter and grandson. Cyrus had fucked up real bad this time. He had fronted Cy funds to try to win back some of his lost money, but in his heart, O'Reilly knew that Tommy would never just allow him to win the money back. It was a trap, and O'Reilly warned his son-in-law of all the consequences, but the dice entrapped his mind.

"It's obvious that one of my snot nose goons did this, because this mission hadn't crossed my desk for approval. Not that this current set of events is beyond my scope of behavioral adjustment. I just haven't gotten to that point of rage to consider murdering a woman and child. I will check him, don't you worry."

"Two of my detectives are on their way to the home now to rescue Casey. Make the call. Get your men out of there and leave Casey out of it."

"I assume my disobedient soldier took the initiative to capture his precious love to flush Cyrus out of hiding," Tommy said calmly.

"Well, there are rules to this shit, Tommy. Businesses run via protocol and permissions."

"Find Cyrus," Tommy said silently and hung up the phone.

CHAPTER 22

The Rescue

"*Shit!* They are on the move. Keats, where are you?" Dana said worriedly. Detective Santiago started her car to get a location on the two armed men that were holding Casey hostage. There were no signs of Casey or the baby.

"Keats! I'm tailing the two men that have left the Dunkin home."

"You shouldn't be going alone, Dana."

"I'll be fine. Just get there and let me know what the situation is."

"Will do. And, Dana, please be careful."

Small butterflies fluttered in her stomach that caught her by surprise. "I will," she replied with an awkward crack in her voice that she couldn't catch before her response reached her parted lips. Dana hung up and turned her attention to the black SUV pulling into Tommy's club. She slammed her hands on the steering wheel as her suspicions came to be true. *What has Cyrus gotten himself in? Has he been made, or was he just in far deeper than I thought?*

"Casey!" Dana said as she turned on her siren and sped down the block.

"Keats!" Dana exclaimed, relieved Keats had answered the phone. "Get to Cyrus's place now. *Wait for me to get there. Be discreet.*"

***

Detective Keats parked his unmarked police car about half a block from the Dunkin home, then he saw Dana pull up. Immediately, the officers entered the home, guns drawn, investigating the house. Keats said a small prayer as he surveyed the home in hopes that the sergeant's daughter wasn't found in a bloodbath. The home was eerily quiet, which made his stomach sink a bit.

Once the officers confirmed that the home was clear of any intruders, Dana rounded the hall and followed the smothered sounds of agony into the master bedroom. "In here!" Santiago screamed as she ran to Casey's side. Keats sped into the room and to a sudden halt when he discovered Casey passed out on the floor with a gash in her forehead. Dana's heart stopped. She was a cop's wife, so the urgency was critical to getting her medical attention.

Dana started checking for a pulse while Keats phoned for a bus. "Is the baby OK?" Dana said and shuddered in an effort to shield herself in case the news was horrific.

"He's fine. Asleep in his bassinet."

Dana sighed with relief as she checked Casey's pulse. She was relieved that she was still alive. Dana could hear the sirens coming, so she directed Keats to go out to flag them down. She said a small prayer and held Casey's hand until the EMTs reached their sides.

Dana loved Cyrus, but in no way did she wish harm to his wife and child. Now, however, it was imperative that she get in touch with Cyrus to let him know what has happened. Both the baby and Casey would be placed in protective custody, and as an officer of the law, he too could be transferred and place in a protective custody situation. Dana didn't want to lose her partner, but his safety was more important. Now that she locked eyes on Tommy and his gang of thugs, she was positive that Cyrus had gotten intertwined with Tommy and his many shenanigans.

Once Casey and the baby were taken to the hospital, Dana and Keats began processing the scene. Dana's mind traveled far beyond the fall. She began to wonder why O'Reilly hadn't pulled Cyrus after discovering his gambling debts instead of allowing him to hang himself. Dana pondered a bit as she stood in the middle of the living room of the Dunkin home. She had to get to Cyrus before Tommy did.

"I want you to follow the bus to the hospital. I'm going to see if those goons are still at Tommy's club," Dana directed.

"Will do," Keats said. He was very uneasy about leaving Dana to hunt wolves without backup.

"Don't worry, I'll be careful."

"Okay," he sighed.

CHAPTER 23

Fresh Start

The turbulent landing officially gave Cyrus the shits. He was so happy to be on the ground it wasn't funny. The air was warm and inviting. It was different from hot and dusty Bakersfield. Cyrus felt free from danger but guilt about his web of lies. He was going to have to come clean to Shun and Phil. The sooner the better. Cy was so lost in his mind, he didn't notice Shun's piercing stare. Shun too had become somewhat bewildered about Cyrus's disposition. Like he told Cy just a few hours prior, he understood him feeling like a pussy running and leaving his family behind, but Shun was clear that the ball was in his court that he chose to roll.

"I don't trust him," Sophia said, tearing Shun's attention from Cyrus.

"Yeah, I can see why you say that, on the outside of things, but he is good people. He is really feeling bad after leaving his wife with a newborn baby," Shun stated in a protective tone that suggested Sophia should be quiet about such things.

Phil and Cyrus carried their own suspicions about why Sophia dropped her life to be on the run with a bunch of wanted criminals. While Shun worried about Cyrus and Phil, both Cy and Phil worried that Sophia would be the death of Shun.

Shun caught sight of Phil and Cyrus staring at Sophia. They both shared a look of uncertainty. Shun took note. He didn't have the time to overthink or assume anything.

He had to admit to himself that he was becoming paranoid about the company he kept. So he needed to show he had control.

"Cy, can you come with me to get the car?" Shun asked.

"Yeah, sure." Cy complied, tearing his gaze from Sophia.

The two men went down to the airport entrance to pick up the rentals, while Sophia and Phil waited on the luggage. Phil was looking at Sophia with a side-eye, contemplating whether he was going to confront her about his suspicions or just leave well enough alone. Her entire profile didn't fit with Shun. The whole *opposites attract* shit was a myth to him. Phil felt like the connection had to be on a mutual goal.

To keep quiet was short lived. Once they got the luggage together, Phil couldn't resist fucking with Sophia's head.

"So, what's up? You really feelin' my cousin, or are you in the game for a different reason?"

"Why does malice and foul play enter your mind in every situation? No wonder Shun won't share in his dealings with corporate America. You are as crazy as I thought. I'm in love with Shun, rich or poor. Bottom line." Sophia was infuriated at Phil's line of questioning.

"There she goes. You do have a bit of nasty and aggression built up. I bet you're a beast in bed," Phil smirked. "I'm just sayin' why a beautiful woman would like yourself with a great career would pick a lowlife to run across country with. You *do* know that this will not end well. We goin' to prison or six feet under."

"I don't care. When you love someone, you accept the good with the bad."

Phil nearly fell to his knees laughing at Sophia and her fairy-tale life with Shun. "*Bitch!* This ain't no damn Cinderella story. You crazy too." He shook his head, laughing as he flagged down Shun and Cyrus. He had to blow off some steam. Phil thought ole Sophia may be a great catch on the outside, but she lacked common sense.

CHAPTER 24

Miami Vice

"Man, it sure feels good to be free," Shun gloated as he watched Sophia prance around the beach in a seductive turquoise diamond-studded bikini.

"Yes, it does. The bitches lookin' real nice too. Santa Monica ain't got shit on these Miami Vice bitches." Cyrus laughed so hard he nearly spilled his Mai Tai on his loud, colorful shirt.

"Yeah, but you ain't gon' get no pussy. Not with that shirt on." Phil laughed as he motioned for Junior to come and sit beside him. He didn't want his son out of his sight. After getting him back, he vowed to always protect his son, no matter what. This little vacation was temporary. He was anxious to get back to his stomping grounds.

Word spread fast of Frankie's death, and all fingers pointed at Shun and Phil as Frankie's accomplices in the robberies. Cyrus could keep a low profile as if he was one of their hostages or something.

Joey, Frankie's murderer and uncle, made a public appearance as if grieving, offering one hundred thousand dollars to bring to justice the murderers of his dearly beloved nephew. As the bodies piled, Phil and Shun's names hit America's Most Wanted list.

Miami was the perfect place to set up shop. A fresh start. Plenty of money and babes to manipulate. More importantly, a place where the population was plentiful.

Far more digs to get lost in. Kern County was a small town where everyone knew your name and the dirt you did. It had a good and bad side. In Kern County, they were feared and respected, if the two can truly coexist. The bad part about being known was that if, and when, they wanted to lie low, they couldn't.

Cyrus was nervous as hell. He was a wanted man, but federally, hell, Shun and Phil were wanted for the murders of thieves, drug addicts, and low-budget mobsters. He was in some real trouble. Well, maybe. They were all wanted by the mob, as well. Cyrus looked off into the sunset. He saw the sun as his beating heart. He saw his wife and son in the clouds. He had missed the birth of his son. He could imagine how beautiful he was. He felt such pain he was near suicide. Watching Phil play with his son made him want to give up everything just to risk going back to get them. He was afraid for them as well. What if Joey killed them to get to him? Was him not going back a sign of pure cowardice? Or was his staying with Shun and Phil a show of loyalty?

"Y'all ready?" Shun said, just about to pack up his sunbathing chair. He was hungry as hell, and the lobster shack was calling his name. "Sophia! Baby, come on." Sophia was still prancing about, enjoying the sun's rays and collecting seashells. She herself was feeling a sense of freedom. No intercoms or sick people to tend to. Just the crashing waves and sand between her toes.

Phil was calling for Junior to grab his sand toys and get his towel. He had yet to tell him that his mother had passed. There was something about a son and his mother. The connection was much different from son to father. She would guide him on how to treat women and how to be sensitive. Men didn't always carry those traits. Phil sure as hell didn't. He had issues with women himself.

His mother abandoned him for drugs, and his first love fell prey to them. Monica was the first he'd come to experiencing real and unconditional love. He was forced to leave her behind. He feared that the mob would track his footprints back to her as well. Only, he couldn't focus on love. He had a son to raise.

"Let's go!" Phil called out to his son once more, who seemed to be preoccupied with the magnificent lights in the waves that were brought about by the sunset.

"Coming," Phil's ten-year-old son replied.

Phil and Shun started walking back to the car with all of their beach gear. Cyrus followed close behind, as did Phil Junior. Sophia walked at an angle to keep from being tossed about by the winds. The air picked up, and off flew her sun hat. She ran, trying to catch up to it. She nearly fell trying to grab hold to her oversized, $200 bonnet.

Sophia dove down into the sand like a volleyball player trying to retrieve the ball. Barely catching hold, she grabbed for her hat. Cutting her hand on a sharp object, she was shocked by her findings. Sophia's eyes widened as she began to dig frantically. There in the sand was a badge and pouch. Sophia stood up quickly and looked inside the pouch. *Cyrus Dunkin, DEA, badge number—the whole nine.* Printed in bold, gold foil print on his business card.

Sophia looked up wide eyed with her mouth open. They weren't safe at all. The entire time, Shun and Phil were consorting with the devil. He had plenty of opportunities to bust the boys. What did he want?

CHAPTER 25

Discretion Is Advised

Sophia had to pinch her lips together damn near the entire ride home. She was itching to tell Shun about her findings, but she knew that she needed to move strategically. Telling him about the badge could set the boys ablaze, and all hell would break out. She shook the images of Cyrus's badge from her brow. She then tried to spark a conversation with Shun after noticing that he was unusually quiet.

"Hey! You OK? You haven't said a word this entire trip."

"I'm fine. maybe a bit jet lagged. I was just taking in the scenery. I realize we are on the run, but honestly, I haven't felt this free since my freshman year in college." Sophia smiled and leaned her head back as she let her passenger side seat recline. "Hey!"

"What?" Shun replied a bit startled as Sophia popped up and yelled in excitement.

"What about cooking at home? I think that we have been out under the sun all day. We could use the down-time to just unwind and bask in being free for a little while. When we are out and about, I can tell by your face that you are filled with worry. Those cute lines in your forehead deepen, and the corners of your mouth droop slightly, making for a cute, pouting facial expression."

Shun lowered his head a bit, careful not to take his eyes off the road. "I know. You, Phil, and Cyrus are all I have, and I feel as if this entire mess is my fault. I hate to suggest that Phil was right about staying right where he was comfortable, but the hood loved us. Out here, chasing corporate buyers has proved to be deadly. I don't have a solid crew. The homie from prison showed me that. We had to put him down, and I got shot in the process."

"Yeah, but we met due to that injury."

"I could have gone without the bullets," Shun stated as he winced slightly in pain. He was in dire need of medication. Part of which was why the wrinkles in his forehead presented. He was trying so hard to fight against the pain he was feeling. His facial expression showed both anguish and worry. Sure, Sophia picked up on it. She, however, couldn't think of a way to help so far from home. A hospital visit would be too daring a move considering their faces were plastered all over the eleven o'clock news across America.

Sophia looked out the window, trying to focus on Shun's words and not the feeling of betrayal growing fast in her spirit. She knew she had to tell him about Cyrus.

CHAPTER 26

Word Is Bond

Miami was the truth. Nice beaches, beautiful women, clubs on every corner. It was easy to fall prey to the night life. Shun, however, didn't have time to focus on the finer things his money could bring because he was wanted for murder. He felt bad that he had brought Sophia along for a ride that could end fatally.

Sophia was busy in the kitchen of their rented four-bedroom condo preparing dinner. She was so lost in her thoughts she didn't hear Shun calling her name. The last thing she wanted to do was to keep him in the dark about anything. She didn't want to start anything either. She had to be careful in the way she handled the situation.

"Babe, babe, what's for dinner?"

Sophia was so zoned out it was if she were under some sort of spell. Finally coming to, she bounced back into her chipper self and answered Shun's inquiry about dinner.

"I figured you boys could throw some steaks on the grill. I have already got them all prepped and ready to go."

"Oh, so you just gon' volunteer my services, huh?"

"Nooooo, babe," Sophia said flirtatiously as she moseyed over to him and planted a nice kiss on his cheek. She was anxious to get to a quiet place so that she could think of what to do about their trusted friend. Sophia thought long and hard about telling Shun that Cyrus was DEA.

She patted Shun on his chest as she lifted her lips from his. Then she skipped to the shower to hide under the warm spray.

Cyrus ran up the stairs to his room to duck away for a while and clear his head. Being on the run was starting to get to him. He was sworn to uphold the law, not break every law known to man. Thing was, the loyalty to man was far stronger than his loyalty to the badge. Right or wrong, he knew the hearts of Shun and Phil, and there was no way he was going to let anything happen to them. Even if he had to turn them and himself in, it would be done by the book and according to his call. Cyrus began to unpack his beach bag and prepare to take a shower when he realized his badge was missing.

"Shit!" He began to panic as he patted himself down as if he had pockets on his beach shorts. It has to be on the beach. Cyrus mumbled to himself, nearly throwing up in his mouth. He couldn't believe how negligent he was to lose such a thing.

Sophia stood in the shower and let the water pour over her face and head. The water was soft and warm. In that moment, she felt safe. She was happy to be free. Sure, working as a nurse had its rewards, but to be surrounded by blood and disease had truly taken a toll. She was ready to settle down and experience love. A love she had found in Shun. Sophia worried constantly about him and his need to make things with him and his cousin square. Shun's exterior was hardened by the discipline of the Marine Corps, but internally, he was a soft teddy bear who couldn't stand confrontation.

The fact that Shun took the fall for his commanding officer was proof of that. She couldn't understand why he would sacrifice his freedom for a service that pledged to protect the American people and would taunt, torment, and kill soldiers due to sexual preference. Sophia got lost in the warm waterfall as she faded into a mock conversation she planned on having with Cyrus.

Her need to protect Shun from Cyrus was growing inside her as if she were with child. "I will just confront him myself. Tell him to leave unexpectedly and say that it was best for them to split up." She would also take his cut of the money. Sophia wanted to ensure that they had the money to stay afloat until a better and safer environment was available. She sighed under the warm water of the shower as she went over her plan of action. There was one problem. What would be her recourse if Cyrus refused to leave? He had nothing to lose.

Phil watched as his son finished up his ice cream at the ice-cream parlor. It was like he was living a dream. His mind was calm of all worries, even in the face of death and capture. Shun was right about the group of men doing Phil's bidding. He knew that much to be true. He was just angry that Shun caught on to it. He was the older one, and Shun seemed to have his head on straight, even after spending a few years in prison.

Shun spent his time researching and focusing on getting his plan together once he was released. He barely talked, and he spent most of his time in the library reading up on marketing and product development. His mind was set on making money and leaving well enough alone.

Phil's goons were most likely plotting on one another for the throne since Phil was a wanted man. Phil would never admit to it, but he enjoyed feeling free. Culture shock at first, living a life outside of Kern County Projects, but feeling as if there was an entire new world outside the gates proved to be desired. A few weeks in paradise erased years of living in Kern County, and it almost made Phil forget about the fact that they were on the run.

The best part of the trip was his son. He was in and out most of Junior's life. He and Brandy often argued about her drug habits. He vowed to make it as impossible as he could to keep her away from the drugs. Phil threatened to kill anyone who sold drugs to Brandy.

"Dad?" Junior was watching as his dad stared off into space.

"Yeah, what's up?"

"You good?"

"Yeah, let's go. I'm hella hungry now."

Phil and Phil Junior grabbed their bags and headed for the car. "You think we got enough shit to play with?" Phil Senior laughed, slamming the trunk down. Phil's son laughed but soon looked solemn and out of place as he sat down in the car. Phil noticed it right away. He didn't know how to approach the situation, so he focused on fixing the radio and getting back on the road.

Phil Junior cleared his throat. "Dad, can I ask you something? It's about Mom. I don't want to pester you about it. I just want to know if she's OK, and wondered what kind of trouble you and Uncle Shun are in. I'm young, but I can pick up things being said."

"OK, ask away." Phil knew full well that he was afraid of the question and even more puzzled at what his response should be. He gripped the steering wheel preparing for his son's question.

"When is Mom coming down to be with us?" Phil Junior gazed out the window taking in the view of the tall palm trees and warm breeze. He was so excited about his mother and father reuniting he could hardly wait for his mother to come and live with them.

Phil shook his head and took a deep breath before he made an attempt to respond to his son's inquiries. He hadn't the heart to tell his son that his mother died from her drug abuse. He hadn't the time to really soak in the happenings of the night, either. He wasn't sure of Sophia's involvement in the matter, but his wife's death had to be the last thing on his mind. Right now, the safety of his son had to be number one.

"Soon . . . soon, son," Phil said simply and stared off down the road, trying to keep his tears at bay.

"Cool," Phil Junior responded sarcastically. He was young but mature in mind. He knew his mother's habits. With Phil gone, he was the one to comfort her, feed her, and bathe her. So he was smarter than Phil thought. He just wanted his father to be honest with him. After all, he was the man of the house in his own right.

Phil and Junior came tumbling in the door, rowdy and excited about all the things they bought to entertain each other.

"Shun, where you at, nigga?"

"Out back!" Shun answered as he threw the charcoal onto his grill. "Where y'all been?" he said relieved, as if safe from altercation. He was exhausted and had no energy to explain or fight with anyone.

"Aw, bro, did you miss us? We went out and got a video game system and a few games we gon' whoop yo' ass in later on. Where are Sophie and Cy?" Phil looked at Shun with the side-eye as if he suspected something was going on between the two of them.

"Aww, naw, bro, quit playin'!" Shun warned playfully. The thought of mischief tapped on his nerve for a brief second, though. "Sophia went to take a shower, and Cyrus is up in his room."

"Uh-huh!" Phil said slightly under his breath. He didn't want to stress Shun or cause him any anguish. Phil was starting to get the feel of being responsible and now with his son in tow, he had to make sure both he and Shun had their heads on straight. He would deal with the bitch if he had to. The most important thing presently was to maintain freedom and a damn pulse.

"What's up, what's on the grill?" Cyrus bounced in, jogging down the stairs.

Phil pinched his lips and looked at Cyrus with his head tilted and asked where he had been. Cyrus took offense because he was already on edge about his missing badge. He couldn't be certain if his best friends hadn't already discovered his true identity, so he had to swallow hard and go pretend as if nothing was bothering him.

Shun excused himself from Cyrus and Phil to go check on Sophia. He knew exactly where Phil was going in his line of questioning with Cyrus and wanted no part of it. Phil nodded as Shun passed.

"The steaks cool on the grill, right?" Phil asked.

"Yup! I'll be right back."

Cyrus's eyes began to water. He was sure to burst into tears if they had found out that he was the enemy.

"Nigga, you look spooked. What's up with you?" Phil asked as he handed Cyrus the last cold beer from the fridge.

"I'm good!" Cyrus replied, keeping his answers short and to the point, as if he were being interrogated.

"OK, just checking. I do have some shit to get off ma chest, though, because we brothers. You need to make sure you stay away from Sophia. I know it's pussy, and she is easy on the eyes, but that's ma cuz, and I don't want no drama between any of us. We have shit to do, and some major hittas are out here lookin' for us."

"What the fuck? Nigga, you should know me betta than that, bro. I don't have time to be thinkin' 'bout no pussy. I got a wife and brand-new baby at home that I would love to get home to. Unfortunately, I'm out here hiding out with you. And had it not been for my gambling issue, I would have ma ass in the bed with my new family. Hell, I missed out on two months of pregnant pussy foolin' round with y'all."

"Aw, naw, nigga, don't blame the hustle on me, ma nigga. You knew how I got down from the jump. Stop actin' brand new. I understand you want to be betta. Hell, now that I got ma son, that's what the fuck I'm on, but out here, we are wanted men. So we have to be careful and gettin' involved with what is keeping Shun sane is just not wise. And for the record, I could have had ma goons hit a few licks to cop that ten grand you needed to get Tommy off yo' back. But closed mouth don't get fed."

"That's coo, Phil, believe me. I know what we're up against, but I owe Tommy 100 grand. I only left my wife and son to make things seem as though they were copasetic," Cyrus said defensively but lowered his head in shame.

"You're a brave soul, my friend. You left her to stand trial for your fuckups. She don't owe Tommy shit. You do. Taking her with you could only prove that you wanted to protect her, both physically and mentally."

"*I love my wife and son!*" Cyrus shouted. His body was shaking, and he was drooling at the mouth in an animalistic manner. He quickly recovered by wiping his sweaty palms on the front of his shirt and snatched the beer from Phil's hand. Phil ignored the fact that Cyrus jerked the beer from his hand. He chalked it up to an emotional outbreak. Things that bitches do.

Phil was looking straight through Cyrus as he was talking. He couldn't believe Cyrus was bitchin' up the way he was. Part of him wanted to pop him himself. "Well, don't worry about it. They're safe now." Phil wrinkled his forehead and pushed past Cyrus as if he was uncertain that things were exactly how he made them out to be.

However, there was nothing he could do at the moment because he had no proof. But his eyes would be peeled. He'd hate to have to lay Cyrus to rest behind a bitch or a couple of dollas. They were way past that. But he had to admit something wasn't right with Cyrus's demeanor.

Cyrus could feel the heat coming from Phil's eyes as he walked past and started up the stairs. He desperately needed to get some air. He had to clear his head, and the only person he could trust was Dana. Only, he couldn't use his phone to call her. He was sure the entire police force was looking for him by now.

CHAPTER 27

Discovered

Sophia dried off in a frenzy and threw on a tank and cutoff shorts to match the heat of night. She was nervous about telling Shun her findings, but she knew that it was something that had to be done. She couldn't risk him finding out that she knew who Cyrus was before the cat was out the bag in its entirety. Sophia needed to tell him herself. She held the badge once more in her hand to make sure she was truly looking at an authentic police badge. She had placed the badge in the bottom of the drawer just in time.

Shun walked in the room with one of his eyebrows raised as soon as he saw what Sophia was wearing. "You need to take that shit off," he said.

Sophia didn't say a word. She just undressed in front of him provocatively. She then crawled onto the bed on all fours and parted her legs. Shun watched and became weak in the knees. He took a few steps back to make sure the bedroom door was locked. Sophia began to wind her hips and moan as she grew eager to feel Shun deep inside her. Shun knew as much and enjoyed taunting her without laying a hand on her. Sophia's pussy began to drip down her legs as she became wetter by the minute. Shun licked his lips. He could no longer withstand his loins aching to feel the wet and warm touch of her. His mouth watered, and he suddenly couldn't help himself. He put his hand on her back, coaching her to lean forward a bit more. She complied. Shun dove hungrily face-first licking, sucking, and eating her pussy so furiously Sophia began squirting her juice into his mouth, down her legs, and onto the bed. She begged for more. Shun complied. He dove into her with a sigh of relief. He wanted her so bad, the veins in his dick pulsated. He plunged in and out, pumping hard and fast as he dove in deeper and devoured her warm waves and soft tissue. Sophia moaned, and with each twist and turn of Shun's love, she matched every move. He groaned as he neared his peak. The sound of his groans excited her and coached her climax to resound in a beautifully conjoined orgasm.

Shun felt a release so grave to his mental health he got a headache. His mind raced so fast that he couldn't relax. Sophia rinsed off in the shower to cleanse herself and began drying off again when she noticed Shun on his knees by the bed rocking with his head in his hands. She rushed to his side nearly losing her towel.

"Are you OK, babe?"

"Yes, I think I'm just having one of those stress head-aches again," he said with a slight crack in his voice.

"Babe, how long has this been going on?" Sophia asked, slipping into her nurse mode. She realized that she had neglected a few things in regards to Shun and his recovery. She could only imagine how much pain he was going through. She was holding on to about five double-strength Norcos for him.

"I'm fine, hon. I just need some time alone. I'll get in the shower. Maybe that'll help me out," he said, directing her to the door.

Sophia stood up. "I'm going to go and check on the food real quick, then I'll come back up to give you a hand getting into the shower. Do you want some Tylenol?"

"Yes, please," he said, standing up, then lying down for a few minutes to let his head settle a bit.

Sophia left the room, closing the door softly behind her. Her thoughts were going a mile a minute. It was then that she locked eyes on Cyrus.

"Cy! Wait up!" Sophia said, jogging down the hall.

"Yeah, what's up?" he asked. He was nervous as hell and itching to get back to the beach to scan for his badge. He tried his best to fix his composure. He was so nervous he was visibly shaking.

Sophia met him down the hall. "You look like you may be in a hurry. Can I come with you?" Sophia asked.

Cyrus was taken aback by her inquiry. "Not in a hurry per se. I was going to head out to the store before dinner. I figured we could use some more beer," he responded, swallowing hard. Only his throat was crisp, dry, and he nearly choked.

"Are you OK?"

"Just need some water. Haven't been concerned about my fluid intake. I guess the men trying to kill us has taken front seat." Cyrus tried to be sarcastically humorous, but he was too tired to pull it off. Sophia just stared at him. He was uncertain of what she was actually in need of. "Can I pick up something for you? I kind of wanted this trip to give me some time to clear my head. I've been dealing horribly with leaving my son and wife."

"I can only imagine. Sure would like to tag along, though. I have some things I need to get, but I'm not too sure about some of them. I think going would be best, Cyrus. Or should I just call you Detective?"

Cyrus's eyes grew wide. He was clearly taken off guard. Not even thinking, he quickly pulled Sophia from out of the hall and into his room. "Where is my badge, bitch? I knew Shun shouldn't have trusted you. Where is it?" Cyrus was so angry, he was sweating profusely and salivating like a deranged dog.

Sophia shook herself free from his grasp. "Wouldn't you like to know. Who the hell are you? What do you want, and if you are the law, why haven't you bothered to share this information with your friends, Shun and Phil? From all the stories I've heard, they protected you. They love you. What are you planning? I can't let you hurt those boys."

"Hurt them!" Cyrus started but quickly grew quiet as he heard some movement in the hallway.

Shun had opened his door and headed down the hall to check and see what was taking Sophia so long with his water, but was detoured by the sound of muffled voices. His jaw stiffened. He was sure he could hear Cyrus and Sophia whispering about something.

"Damn!" Shun yelped as he retreated back into his room and prepared to get in the shower.

Cyrus uncovered Sophia's mouth and took a peek out into the hall to see if Shun or Phil were lurking about. When the coast was clear, he immediately started in on Sophia. "If you know what's good for you, you'll make sure you leave this information between us. I'm not going to hurt anyone. I'm hoping to fix things with the cops and Tommy. You'll just have to trust me." Cyrus brushed off everything else. He couldn't allow Sophia to think for one second that she was in control of the situation. "Do we have a deal?" he asked Sophia with a stern glare.

"Not quite. You see, Shun is in enough physical pain as it is. To hurt him mentally could get us all killed. Don't you think you should tell him who you are before he finds out about it someplace else? Furthermore, what about the fact that they are wanted? And with you a cop, I'm sure your colleagues will shoot to kill without asking any questions. Shit!" Sophia yelled, then quickly covered her mouth when she realized how much trouble they were really in. "Oh my God, Cyrus, the entire state of California is probably looking for two fugitives with a hostage, Officer Cyrus Dunkin. Shit just got real. What are we going to do?"

"Just leave it to me. You can't lose your cool. We have to stay on our toes and keep the peace between us all in this house. We are in this together, like it or not. Now go make sure Shun is OK."

"Yeah, yeah. You still aren't calling the shots. I think you should leave the money and leave here. Period. That's the only way Shun and Phil have a fighting chance against the police. With the hostage set free, they may be willing to just take them into custody."

"I can't just leave. I need that money too, Sophia. If I don't come up with the rest of the money, Tommy is going to kill my wife and son."

Sophia sighed.

CHAPTER 28

The Truth

Shun quietly shut his door as thoughts of Sophia being untrue to him hovered over his sanity. He wasn't sure what she and Cyrus could be talking about in quiet corners. His paranoia resurfaced. If he found out that Sophia was untrue to him, he wasn't sure how he would address the situation. His better judgement told him not to get emotionally involved in the first place, but he couldn't control the desires of his heart. Now, he wondered if he could muster up enough heart to rid himself of his disloyal companion if he had to.

Shun grimaced with pain as he pulled his sweaty wife beater over his head. His wounds were still healing from the heist with Frankie and his crew. Smoking, drinking, and a few Norcos would usually take the edge off of the pain, but his supply had run out. Sophie kept his wounds clean and bandaged. They couldn't risk being caught, so a hospital wasn't an option. Shun nearly passed out from the sharp pain in his side that stifled his breathing.

Sitting slumped over on the plane made him sore as well. Between Sophia's elbow squeezing against his open wounds to the armrest on his left side, he felt like a caged animal. He was distant. His head was filled with such uncertainty. He was having anxiety attacks. He was worried about having to care for Phil Junior on the run. He knew that Phil was a hothead. He was also a great father. Shun could see Phil's heart nearly flutter when he was around his son. It was a beautiful thing. But it was a horrible time. Shun wanted desperately to find a way to clear Phil's name so that he could return home, or at least live free. As for Sophie, his newfound love, well, she had risked her life and career for him. Only, he couldn't be certain that he could love and protect her as she deserved. He couldn't understand why she had walked away from her career to help a drug-dealing murderer. Still, he felt deeply for her and wanted to do right by her. Which was why he was considering asking her to leave. Shun couldn't live with himself if something happened to her, or if she was being unfaithful in any way. The only way to save her from himself was to ask her to leave.

Asking her to leave seem plausible. If she left before the cops got wind of her presence, she could skate by without so much as a scratch on her pretty lips. No one had placed a woman as part of the dynamic duo's hostage or partner in crime. But she would never leave. He knew that. He wasn't sure he could live without her either.

Shun was getting angrier by the minute. He had yet to receive the water Sophia went to get him. The water wasn't the real issue. Cyrus was, and it took everything in him not to stomp down the hall and demand answers from the two of them.

Tired of waiting on Sophia's return, Shun began to get himself ready for a bath. He was reaching for his gun holster when Sophia reached around his waist to aid him. He was startled slightly but regained his composure once he recognized the smell of her perfume.

Shun frowned a bit, feeling awkward about Sophia cozying up to him after he overheard part of a conversation between her and Cyrus.

"What were you and Cyrus chatting about? It seemed a bit sensitive since the two of you were whispering in quiet quarters."

Sophia smiled at Shun's concern and replied simply as any nurse under the HIPPA law of confidentiality would, "No worries. He is feeling distant and uncertain of his path. His son was born without his presence. He was facing the fact that his gambling issues were the cause of all his problems. He is just depressed and needs to face the issues he's dealing with. He feels alone. So we had a small conversation about the matter. He's going to make a run for beer. I told him to pick up some pain meds as well. He hasn't left yet. Is there anything else you think you need?"

"No, I'm good. Maybe you should go with him. Help him cope with whatever he's dealing with since you're his counselor and all." Shun sighed as he relaxed. He couldn't refrain from feeling her love deep within his soul. Angry or not, he felt that he should tell Sophia the truth.

"You know, Sophia, after hearing you with Cyrus, I became so angry. I couldn't understand what you could be talking about privately. The two of you barely speak. We don't have time to rub this man's head and coddle him. Do you realize the mob *and* the police want our heads? You don't have time to baby this nigga. Do you understand?" Shun knew that he was out of line, but part of what Phil said about Cy and Sophia got to him. "You sneaking around the house with this man whispering and shit." Shun's voiced trailed off midsentence. He caught himself slippin', floating dangerously toward his emotions overriding reason.

"I understand, but you don't have to worry about me being untrue to you, Shun. I love you. You are all I see." Sophia wrapped her arms around him and met his eyes as she looked up toward the sky. "I love you," Sophia said softly. Once those words departed from her lips, she could feel Shun's tense arms loosen a bit. He was a strong and disciplined man, and his heart was frozen. Sophia knew that much. Shun had had a hard life. Always doing for others. The short end of the stick was something Shun had gotten used to.

"I care for you deeply, Sophia. Loyalty is one of those things that make or break a person. I know from experience. But I will tell you this. I won't blame you if you leave. Loyalty can lead to death and further heartaches. I don't want to put you in that position. I would never forgive myself if something happened to you." Shun looked down at Sophia with high hopes on her being honest with him about what was really going on with her and Cyrus.

"Shun," Sophia interjected, "I'm a big girl. I'm not going anywhere." Sophia removed his arms from around her waist and held on to his hands. "Don't be afraid to love me. I won't hurt you."

Shun looked out the window for a few seconds too long. He began to rub his head in frustration because he knew that Sophia was hiding something. He couldn't believe that she would look him dead in the eye and lie. And on top of that, profess her love. Finally, Shun smiled and held Sophia's shoulders gently and kissed her on the forehead.

He could visibly see her heart break, but so was his. Shun couldn't possibly utter the words *I love you* to a woman that was clearly lying to him. He needed to know that she would rock with him 100 percent. He wondered how long she would keep secrets from him. He could feel his blood beginning to boil. She made no mention of talking privately with Cyrus. Phil's constant taunting of the possibilities of lust and deception between her and Cyrus played in his mind. It was like Sophia's hands were contaminated and burning holes through his skin. "I just have a lot going on is all. I have to find a way out of this mess," he said through clenched teeth.

"And we will, babe," Sophia replied. She was mulling over her threats to Cyrus who seemed hell-bent on seeing his entire plan through. He was less than cooperative when asked what he was really after. Sophia had no choice but to threaten to tell Shun about his true identity. Only, she didn't know how she would come out and tell Shun the truth without setting off a battle that would surely end fatally.

Shun ignored her. He was tired, in pain, and just wanted to calm his nerves under a hot shower. "Can you go check on the food? I want to get in the shower." Shun heard his voice crack slightly. His emotions were dangerously close to erupting. Sophia felt the same as a lump in her throat threatened to choke her.

"I'll be right downstairs if you need me," she said trying to hold back tears.

"Cool," Shun responded flatly.

CHAPTER 29

Two Birds with One Stone

Shun fell to his knees and let out a small whimper under the cool flow of the shower. The cold water stiffened his muscles, but it did wonders for the sting burning bright from his open, untreated wounds. As the shower calmed his nerves, the tears flowed, and his talk with God began. . . .

I have all these voices. Just ongoing rants that are intertwined. Slanderous remarks spewed outlandishly. Followed by a large crowd of spectators spitting on me as I jog up the stairs of the courthouse. I feel abandoned. Hate is growing deep inside me, and all I can think about is hurting those that hurt me.

These voices, they say mean, horrendous things. They threaten to kill me if I don't comply. I'm saddened by such demonic behavior, and though I call out the name of my Lord and Savior, He doesn't seem to answer.

I'm lost, afraid to share with Sophia my thoughts because she may think that I'm going mad. In many ways I am. I'm so tired of taking care of everyone around me. Just once I would like to be taken care of. I admit Sophia has been that. Ever since the shooting, she has been more than a lover. She was my nurse and best friend. There are things that blood can't seem to understand that Sophia got before I could utter the words.

I don't know what to do, God, because tonight is the first time in years that I felt such lows. My panic attacks lessened a few months after coming home from overseas, but my mental state of mind was jumbled with images of not those I killed in battle, but by those that turned on me in the trial and testified against me.

I know that taking a life is a sin, and taking my own is classified as such as well, but I can't lie and say that I haven't thought about ending it for us all. I realize I don't have a right to make those kinds of decisions; however, I need to get a grip before the voices in my head graduate to movement of my limbs. Sophia comforts me. I worry if I place too much on her. She has a ton going on as well, with the loss of her job and perhaps her nursing license if anyone found out about her medication thefts. Part of me feels deep guilt for her life falling apart. It's as if she gave it all up for me, and here I am making cowardly statements about succumbing to the voices in my head. This same woman that just professed to love me—and lie to my face. I'm not sure that I'm worthy of truth. I may be even afraid of the truths that may flow once the bow breaks. I have my secrets as well. I know of the snake in our midst. Our friend, enemy, and liar.

My mind is full of disease. So much has happened. Now, all eyes are on me, and it's up to me to make things happen and get us out of this jam. Only, I don't have all the answers, and I'm just as scared as the rest of them. In reality, as corny as this shit sounds, all I ever wanted was to be loved and respected. Only in this neck of the woods, respect means affluence. No one paid homage to bums, ex-cons, or veterans, for that matter. I could have been the most decorated soldier and still be ignored and treated as if I hadn't risked my life for this country.

I can almost hear the snickers in a crowd telling me to man up. I guess I'm supposed to thank my lucky stars for being an American citizen. Women and children are fighting wars in other countries. Well, thank you, God. I salute you for bringing me into a world to serve mankind. To be a slave for others to walk all over and trample upon. I'm not as strong as you think. I'm weak and need guidance. I could use a little help. I was the boy with high hopes for myself. I dreamed of better lands than Kern County. I believed in myself and challenged these limbs to play harder than anyone on the team, run faster, study with the due diligence to get into college. I often wonder what my life would have been like had I taken the ticket to college instead of the marines. I felt like the uniform would put a little hair on my chest, and it did. I learned a few lessons as well.

God, can you hear me?

I thank you for changing my life. I appreciate the lessons. However, I don't know how many more I can take. Thank you for removing the knife from my back. I'm sure there will be others. I can only imagine the dangers that are lurking around the next corner.

He loved Sophia with all his heart, which is what he was truly afraid of. What if he couldn't protect her from those that were after him? His only recourse would be to put her in a safe place and go after Tommy himself. Only he couldn't trust his pack. So, the plan to execute Cyrus and Tommy himself in one swing would have to suffice. Time to kill two birds with one stone.

CHAPTER 30

Damn

Rico touched down in Miami and headed straight to his girl's place. He figured he would smash first before business. He ordered some takeout and was making a stop at the store when he could have sworn he saw one of the men that frequented the bar and gambling hall.

He wasted no time to get answers about his sightings. He almost broke his phone, hurrying to retrieve it and make a call to Tommy. He could hardly wait for Tommy to answer.

"What's good? You got the next package ready for me?" Tommy added a small chuckle, trying to bring humor into a deadly situation.

"Naw, man, you know payment is due before I package and ship, but look, fam, you not gon' believe this shit, ma nigga. I mean, this is a small-ass world or somthin'."

Tommy scratched his head in frustration. "Why? What's going on?" He was hot under the collar. It was Tommy's connect. He had better have answers for the missing loot, or the entire tribe would be on the first thing smokin'.

"I'm good, I'm good. I'm always fresh. Miami weather is always a good look. I got ma all-white on and a few gold jewels to blind these bitches. You know how I do. So we good. You got that bread fo' me?"

"Yo, you know I got that work. We puttin' it in. I just need a few more days. The heat has been hot as fuck this past week."

"That's not gon' effect our sales and future business, is it, Tommy? Keep it one hunnid wit' me. I give you a week, you good. But aye, that ain't the reason I even hit you up, fam."

"What's up? What's going on?"

"Yeah, so you know them muthafuckas, the boys lookin' for from out yo' way?"

"Yeah, what about them?" Tommy sat up in his chair intrigued by the subject matter. "What's good 'bout 'em?"

"I see that cop dude that supposed to be like a hostage or some shit. He just hopped out of a black-on-black Maserati. He don't look like no hostage to me. He look like he on vacation. Either he is undercover, or he is in on whatever the other two niggas on. This could prove to be a fucked-up situation on all accounts in your situation. Tommy, how the fuck you didn't know that dude was a cop? This undercover pig been in all yo' shit. Your business dealings—you befriended him. This cop dude is an undercover pig. You seriously don't know shit about it, or you yourself could be in with the pigs and therefore, making a ploy to get me and my business shut down."

"Whatchu talkin 'bout, Willis?" Tommy said, reciting the familiar phrase from *Diff'rent Strokes* character, Arnold. "Cop?" Tommy was pissed. *You mean those two mangy mutts had a cop snooping around my establishment?* Tommy thought to himself.

"You good, nigga?" Rico interjected. Tommy was lost in his thoughts.

"Where the hell you been? News headlines this morning, blogs, etc. Every media outlet known to men is talking about the cop that is being held hostage by fugitives Shun and Phil." Rico paused as he realized the silence on the other end of the phone.

Naw, fish ain't bitin', Tommy thought to himself. *"Follow him!"* Tommy roared before hanging up the phone. He couldn't believe his ears. Shun and Phil informants?

Cyrus grabbed a few cases of beer, some juice, and a few packs of 1882s for his weed sessions with Phil and Shun. He felt like a teen again. Having Shun and Phil around was like this border of protection. Now, he may have the chance to save them for once. The two men were like his blood brothers. They fought like cats and dogs, but no one outside their circle could cause them harm. The guilt rose like thick smoke from a fire. He was choking. Every time Cy got close to telling the truth, something else would prove that the time wasn't right to talk about any of it. Now that Sophia knew his true identity, he had to ensure that she was quiet. He had to contact Dana. She was his only hope. The thing was, could he trust Dana to keep quiet? He knew she cared for him deeply, so deeply that if the risk of continuing down the path of destruction was too great, then she may pick the road less traveled and leak his whereabouts. All out of the name of love.

Dana walked in the precinct frustrated and ready to lay into anyone that may have something to say about her latest actions. Her inability to work without personal interference proved her unstable countenance. Every hour not knowing what really happened to Cyrus felt like an eternity. Sergeant O'Reilly stared at her through the blinds, working up the bravado to confront her about being late and her off-duty activities. Cyrus was her partner and one of the boys in blue. Dana would be the first to admit that she was on a war path with Cyrus gone with the wind.

O'Reilly swung his door open with such force he nearly shattered the glass. Dana rolled her eyes with a submissive attitude and whispered, "*Someone's angry.*"

When Dana entered the office, she jumped as the door of the office slammed shut. She was confused because she had followed orders since their last encounter. She had made a few runs to see if anyone saw or suspected anything.

Dana knew of Cyrus's gambling trouble from a number of sources, but she was both surprised and ashamed to know that her boss dealt with Tommy and his dirty business. She blamed O'Reilly for the happenings altogether. Dana sat down on O'Reilly's couch and dried her sweaty palms on the lap of her jeans.

O'Reilly sat on his desk peering at her with a blank stare. Truthfully, he was in a coma of thoughts on how to explain the horseshit he not only trampled over but decided to take a dive in. The money was good. A cop's salary didn't even cover the tax on his son's treatments. O'Reilly hadn't mentioned his son's illness to the fold of officers around him. He didn't want to appear weak. When Tommy approached O'Reilly with a business proposition, there was no way he could allow the offer to pass him by. In the last six months, O'Reilly's son Jacob was responding to treatment very well. Had the doctor not performed a series of unusual tests, his son would have died. O'Reilly was certain that if he used Cyrus as his undercover officer, he could find something he could use to put Tommy behind bars.

Only, he needed to make sure his son finished his treatments and his officer was safe from harm. The entire plan was off the books. He was careful. So he thought. Nevertheless, Cyrus was missing. Cy was a good cop.

More importantly, he was like a son to O'Reilly. He was excited that Cyrus wanted to transfer to his neck of the woods. Los Angeles was too fast for Casey. She wanted to move to a town that was a bit quieter and more close knit.

O'Reilly shook his head trying to refocus his attention to Detective Santiago. He needed to be rational and take on one issue at a time, even though they were all pressing.

"What's up?" Dana asked.

"Have you locked eyes on where Cyrus must be? I know this is going to a tough pill to swallow, but I need him to check in. I have reason to believe that he may be a part of this fiasco."

"I haven't." Dana kept her responses short and straight to the point.

CHAPTER 31

One Phone Call

"Shuuuunnn! If it isn't one of the most wanted dead cats in America right now. You know they want your head. What kind of nerve do you have to call me? I'm leading the pack. Which could only mean one thing: You, my foe, are calling me to tell me where I can *pick up my fuckin' money!*" Tommy snarled and glared into the mirror with a face of gloom and determination. "You know I was just thinking about you. Your name came up in a recent conversation."

"Yes and no!" Shun said sternly. He had a plan to end this foolishness with one swoop. "I would like to meet. I'll give you the cash in exchange for a truce. I don't have any business with you, and all Phil and I want to do is rest easy. We hangin' this shit up. He has his son to raise, and well, I'd like to try my hands at just being a regular law-abiding citizen." Shun spoke with a hint of compassion. He wanted to sound helpless in hopes that Tommy would feel sympathetic.

Tommy looked directly into his phone and pinched his lips at the ignorant ploy Shun tried to pull over on him. "Yeah, I got kids too. I take it mighty personal that the funds that are used to feed them was taken from my family. One would say that a violation of that sort would be cause for a violent response. A sheer sign of disrespect, if you ask me."

"I don't doubt Frankie felt the wrath of his own flesh and blood."

"Frankie's blood is on your hands, Shun. You were his partner. See, partners have each other's backs. They ensure both are on the same page in dealings, and they surely don't leave the other to rot in jail. In my opinion, you failed on all accounts."

"It wasn't my idea to rob you, Tommy."

"Oh, so you are adding snitch to the list of treachery now?"

Shun had to bite his lip at Tommy's allegation. Shun was far from a snitch. He knew what it was like to serve time for a crime he didn't commit. Once again, he found himself facing the wrath, taking the fall for others' dirty deeds. He still couldn't bring himself to tattle on his fellow man. No matter how bad things seemed, he still proclaimed to be loyal. Even to Cyrus, who he knew had to pay for his crimes.

Shun was so hot about the fact that Cyrus didn't divulge his comradery with the boys in blue it made his blood boil. He paraded around his whole life with hoodlums, sticking out like a sore thumb. Only when they were young, it was just the fact that he lived on the outskirts of the hood. He was free from the hood life and mentality. For the life of him, he couldn't figure out why Cyrus would want to hang in one of the most dangerous projects in Bakersfield. He knew he had his reasons, and he didn't fault him for it. This is what made Shun so angry. Cyrus could have come clean so many times. Yet, he remains to be dishonest about the situation. Shun suggested that he remained loyal; however, his inner spirit argued how one could be dishonest, yet loyal.

"Look, Tommy, I don't like the situation any more than you do. I just want to squash the beef so that I can get on with my life."

"See, Shun, that sounds a bit selfish to me. It's like you don't want to take responsibility for your actions. All involved are supposed to look away and just let bygones be bygones. You may not have killed my nephew physically, it may have not been your idea to take my bread, but yet and still, you participated and led the pack. So I'm confused that you would ask me to just drop all charges and go about my merry way." Tommy was beginning to think that Shun thought he was born just a few hours earlier. He felt disrespected.

"Tommy, this meeting is about making the switch, the return of your money. This doesn't mean it justifies our actions."

"No, but it shows that even though you fucked with the wrong man, you expect the issues to be dropped. Actions you and your men took and won't even stand by them. I do dirt, and that is just the game. I also stand by it. If my crew got wind that I was unsure of myself or feeling guilty about my moves, they would then question my leadership. Some may even rise up and threaten to impeach me."

Shun didn't have time to continue listening to Tommy's lectures on organized crime dos and don'ts. He really just wanted to see if he would be willing to meet so that he could get all parties involved a date and time. He had yet to break the news to Cyrus and Phil. He knew they would start barking about the idea. Tommy was still rambling about his rules of engagement when Shun interjected.

"So do we have a deal?" he said.

"No funny business," Tommy said sternly and hung up the phone.

Shun looked at the phone for a minute. He couldn't help but smirk at Tommy's arrogance.

Cyrus

CHAPTER 32

Flash

Cyrus sat in the car pondering over his next move. He popped open his new throwaway phone and powered it up. He couldn't help but blame the entire fiasco on siding with his brothers back at the force in Los Angeles. Sure, he needed the money, but it was all for not. His firstborn was still taken by his illness. Though having another child was a blessing, he and Casey both knew that the reason for getting pregnant so soon after losing Luke was to fill an empty void.

Casey had been so depressed he feared leaving her at home alone. Ironically, it was the same fear that choked him now. He felt guilty. He felt angry, and most of his hateful spirit was wrapped in trying to protect his career—and for what? To satisfy the likes of two hoodlums. Childhood friends, yes; but things change. You grow up and learn how to deal with the aches of life lessons and economic hardships.

There was a life after high school. After Shun and Phil, he too had a bond with his kind. Still, he had fallen just as Shun did. Trying to uphold the law and protect the American people landed him in witness protection and a reassignment that was less than savory. Not even a year later, he was in trouble once more. Same crime, stealing money from a major drug cartel. Now it was time to see if he could walk through fire once more and survive.

Cyrus nodded off a bit, not realizing how tired he was from all the mental stress. He dialed Dana's line and waited for her to answer.

"Dana?"

"Cyrus?" Dana anxiously answered. Sure, she recognized Cyrus's voice muffled under the soundwaves of a cheap phone.

"I'm in trouble," was all Cyrus could muster before his phone suddenly powered off. Cheap-ass phone must have had a defective battery. Cyrus tossed the phone out the window. Life in Los Angeles was a story in and of its own.

CHAPTER 33

Los Angeles Police

Day's End

Cyrus flashed back to the beginning of his shit storm with Los Angeles Police.

"Drop your gun, Tre!" Jag and Cyrus yelled out into the emptiness of the warehouse.

"Naw, y'all drop yours." Tre was shaking and sweating profusely as he pointed the gun at each one of his blood brothers. "You think I'm stupid? As many showdowns we have been through, eight fucking million ain't enough, Cyrus? Why you have to be so greedy, huh?" Tre was furious. He was also as high as a kite, and he knew that. That was the real reason Cyrus set the bounty upon his head.

"It ain't about the money, Tre, and you know it. You have become an extreme liability to the team. You of all people know what we do to dogs that are untamed. We are putting you down. Rules are rules. To die with honor, Tre, is better than being slaughtered by the pigs awaiting our fall."

Tre's head fell back laughing uncontrollably. He began to hunch over, grabbing his belly. Tre caught a cramp and nearly lost his footing. His eyes and gun never left his so-called brothers. "Honor? Don't feed me the same bullshit we tell all of our kills before taking their lives. We are work for hire. We are assassins, murderers, thieves, that proclaim to be honorable citizens for the greater good. These badges melt in our evil hands, Cyrus. Honor. You want to kill me, then come on. Commmmme ooon!" Tre yelled out, dribbling and stomping around like a drunken sailor.

"We don't have to do this, Cyrus. We're taking this too far," Jeffrey begged, lowering his weapon to the ground.

Cyrus lowered his eyes with a look so demented, one would think he was possessed. "I am my brother's keeper. We are left with no other choice. You see how sloppy he's been? This is my son's life," Cyrus said.

"He's our brother!" Jeffrey retorted.

"No, he's not. He's some drug-addicted loose-lip cop that would sell us out in a minute to avoid being brought to justice. He will sell us out, Jeffrey! This is not Tre, don't you see that?" Cyrus screamed in frustration.

Jag stood with his gun drawn, expressionless. It was clearly about the money with Jag. He was determined to keep the vows of his pack. Cyrus was leading the charge, and the order was given to take out the trash. The group had no other choice. "Rules are rules," Jag cosigned.

"Let's just divide the money and split," Jeffrey suggested.

"See, now you trippin' too. You know good and well we can't leave town. That's our asses for real. Naw, this works out just fine. We walked in and found Tre unloading stolen money from his pickup truck. We confronted him. He drew on us, so we fired. We hang our heads solemnly having taken out one of our own. Case closed. There won't even be an investigation about this because Tre is hopped up on cocaine and weed. Shit, no one will believe him anyhow. This is his third strike."

"Third strike?" Jeffrey looked puzzled as Cyrus spewed the secrets of his brethren. Both Jag and Jeffrey threw Cyrus a questioning glance.

"Oh, come on. Don't look so dumbfounded. We needed a fall guy, boys, and Tre just fell into our laps. We told this fool time and time again not to fuck with the drugs. The drugs we take we sell back to the drug lords on the streets for double the money and pardon from police. But, no, our brother had to go and get high, shameless acts of the most foolish and the one with the brightest ideas." Cyrus waved his weapon and tapped his temple with the tip of his gun, as if trying to knock his sanity back into place.

Cyrus looked off into space as he recalled his last few days with Los Angeles Police. He was as corrupt as they came, but only due to his needs. He felt nauseated about the situation as he remembered how hard his heart had become over money and his son's death. He fought hard to gain the respect of his badge back. He had once believed in its purpose. He since had to use its power.

If there was a way to predict the future, would anyone take it? Cyrus contemplated. It was three days of pure hell that drove Cyrus to the dusty city of Bakersfield. A chance for a new start. Instead, he traveled back to the hood, a lifestyle he adopted.

CHAPTER 34

Los Angeles Police

Three Days of Pure Hell . . .

"911, what's your emergency?"

"Yes, it's Mrs. Cyrus Dunkin. My son. He isn't breathing. I followed the doctor's orders. He told me that when Luke got too hot to place him in a cold bath, to try to reduce the fever. Only he started shaking violently, and now he isn't breathing. Please, help! Please," Casey cried out to the dispatcher.

"OK, Mrs. Dunkin, we'll send an EMT right away. I need you to try to remain as calm as possible. I am going to need you to do a few things and answer a few questions before help arrives."

"OK!" Mrs. Dunkin yelled and sprinted back down the hall to the bathroom where her son lay.

"OK, what is your son's name?"

"Luke."

"OK, I want you to tell me if you can still see the rise and fall of your son's chest. Sometimes in trauma, breathing stops at the fall's impact, knocking the wind out of the person's body, or in the event of a seizure, it can be perceived as a person has stopped breathing. I want to make sure he didn't just stop breathing momentarily or that his breathing is shallow."

"Ummm . . . OK, OK, yes! Yes! Thank God. He's breathing, but it is very slow and rattling a bit."

"OK, that's a good sign. Now, is he still extremely hot? *Be careful not to move him.* I don't want you to move him in case there is some trauma around his head area. Is it at all possible Luke could have hit his head?"

"Oh! No, I never left his side except to run and get my phone," Casey explained, trying to catch her breath and snap out of her disheveled mind-set. She looked around her son's head in search for blood. She didn't see anything present or spilling out from his hair at the present time.

"Mrs. Dunkin, you there?" the emergency dispatch officer asked repetitively when she noticed the silence that fell over the phone.

Casey had dropped the phone and ran to the front door when she heard the sirens approaching her quiet suburban neighborhood.

"Hey, did you hear that?" Cyrus blurted with a mouthful of steak burrito. "Turn your radio up. Sounded like my street, man."

Jag slammed his greasy taco down on his plate and pulled his radio from his belt.

"Possible Protocol 112. We need all available cars to West Chester Blvd. 8-1-9 West Chester Blvd. Again, I repeat, *we need all available cars at 8-1-9 West Chester Blvd.*"

Both Cyrus and Jag quickly wiped their mouths and leapt from their seats just outside the Mexican Cantina. Cyrus's heart was beating so fast, he felt like he was going to pass out. Jag was nervous as well. He was a permanent fixture in the Dunkin home.

Cyrus's thoughts ran wild as tears sprang to his eyes. These types of calls came in on a daily basis, and he was able to run and execute safely without a second thought. Only this time, it involved his family—and he was scared to death.

By the time Cyrus rolled up to his home, he saw a gurney being rolled toward the EMT vehicle. Cyrus sprang from his cop car while it was still coming to a rolling stop and sprinted down the street toward his home. There he fell into the arms of his wife Casey as she ran toward him, screaming hysterically and crying for his help.

"What happened, what happened?"

"I don't know . I don't know." Casey rambled on. "Luke was running a fever, so I called the advice nurse. He told me to run a cold bath. Next thing I know, he's shaking, and he became unresponsive. Cy, he just stopped breathing," Casey repeated hysterically.

"OK, OK. So, no one hurt you guys?"

"No. Goodness, no."

"All right, let's find out what's going on. You go with the EMTs. Jag and I will follow," Cyrus said, trying to be as calm as possible.

Cyrus tried hard to be strong in front of his wife. In the back of his mind, however, he was going crazy, so fearful that he was going to lose his son. He hurriedly swallowed the lump in his throat and jumped into the car with his partner.

Cyrus didn't say a word. He just spun the car around and led the emergency medical transport vehicle to clear the path to the hospital.

CHAPTER 35

Los Angeles Police

Dirt

As Doctor Helms came out to conference with the parents, the entire police force stood to greet him.

"What is it?" Cyrus was so anxious he couldn't stand it any longer.

"Your son is very sick, Mr. Dunkin."

"What are you saying? Is he going to die or something? What is it? What does he need? He can have mine, whatever it is."

"Mr. Dunkin, slow down. It's not that simple. Your son needs a kidney. His kidney is failing, and it has triggered other organs to fail. He is also very anemic, which I find is rare in children his age. He will need a few blood transfusions before we can attempt to do the surgery, *if* we find a viable kidney. There are many risks with this surgery, and being that we are dealing with a frail three-year-old boy, we need to play this smart. I know this is a very tough call, but we need to make sure that we don't do more damage than good by stressing young Luke's body out more than it already is. We don't want him to suffer."

Casey broke down to her knees as she took in the prognosis for her son. Cyrus was furious with the doctor.

"Are you fucking telling me to just let Luke die without even trying to find him a kidney? Take mine. It's easy. Where do I sign? I don't drink. I'm healthy. Why are we just standing around like there aren't things to be done? How soon do you need this done?"

"Sir, I know this is difficult, but as I stated before, this is not something that you just sign up for. Your son may reject the kidney, which means we could put him at a higher risk for a complete system shutdown. He could die on the table. I have a few donors that we can check out just to see if they are a match. Typically, we make sure that the blood type and antigens match from donor to recipient. Then we determine the health of the patient in regards to withstanding such a surgery. Right now, I wouldn't recommend surgery until we first raise his blood count. He is stable for now, but very weak. I can only allow you two to visit with him right now, and then I am going to need you to let him get some rest. We can talk about the cost of all this in the morning if you wish, or we can talk in my office shortly after your visit with Luke. We need to make sure he is medically covered for the surgery, *if* we find a viable kidney."

"No, problem," Cyrus chimed in. "I'm sure my medical insurance from the job will cover this." Cyrus held on to Casey for dear life, afraid she would crumble to the floor once more. He leaned in close to her hair and whispered softly, "Everything is going to be fine, hon. Let's go see Luke. We don't want him to worry."

Cyrus and his wife brushed past the crowd of police officers and walked down the corridor to the secured doors. He was so broken. He had to leave the waiting room abruptly, afraid that his tears would be caught by his fellow officers.

***

Jag flicked the butt of his cigarette onto the ground and kicked around the dirt a bit. He was so worried that he needed to get some air. Some of the cops began to pour out of the waiting room. It was time for them to hit the streets. Calls were coming in, and the entire force was at the hospital. Cyrus had to admit that though the secrets among cops were filled with scandal, they all came together as one in times of tragedy.

Casey stood over their baby boy in tears just watching the IV drip. It was so quiet. Luke looked so peaceful sleeping in a drug-induced coma. His heart beat was regular, and his blood pressure was satisfactory. After a moment of silence, Cyrus squeezed Casey's shoulders to encourage her to come with him. It was time to talk with the doctor about the medical procedures to come and the medical bills associated with treatment. Cyrus was confident about the surgery. Luke was a strong and stubborn little boy. At this moment, he was thankful for those traits his son had, because he needed him to fight.

Cyrus and Casey sat down in the hospital financial office to discuss the treatment costs for Luke. They waited about ten minutes, but it felt like hours. Every call that came over the loudspeaker made Casey's stomach drop. She was so afraid her son would take a turn for the worse just sitting around discussing the tedious tasks of the procedural costs. She understood the paperwork, but she was a mother as well, and right about now, the paperwork could go to hell. She just wanted her son back.

The financial advisor walked into the office and pulled his glasses from his eyes to wipe the sweat from his brow.

"Shane," he greeted and sat down to get right to the point. "Now, let's talk about what we need to do first." Shane pulled out his huge calculator, a pencil, and a notepad and began scribbling and reciting the procedure from start to finish. "Well, with pretransplant evaluation and testing, surgery, fees for the recovery of the organ from the donor, follow-up care and testing, additional hospital stays for complications, fees for surgeons, physicians, radiologist, anesthesiologist, and recurrent lab testing, antirejection and other drugs, which can easily exceed $2,500 per month, and rehabilitation, we are looking at an easy $292,874 bill. With insurance and possible savings, we can see how much of this we can deduct."

Cyrus's head was spinning. He didn't hear a word Shane was saying. The numbers threw him for quite a loop. His medical insurance only covered up to $100,000, and his savings were wiped out after the second honeymoon he and his wife took just six months prior.

"I will get the money," Cyrus said simply and stood up from Shane's desk. Without another word, he grabbed Casey's hand and led her out of the office. It was obvious to Casey that Cyrus was more than worried, but she dare not say anything to set him off. He was a beast at times like these. Cyrus didn't deal with stress easily. He didn't drink, but he gambled, and the stress would only send them deeper in debt.

Cyrus didn't say a word the entire drive home. He was focused on a plan that would go against every moral code he had, but drastic times caused for drastic measures. Casey was worried sick about Cyrus's plan of action. It was already bad enough she sat by the phone daily filled with worry.

"Things will be fine, hon, I promise. I want you to go inside, lock up, take a bath, and get yourself something to eat. I need to talk to Jag about something. I'll meet with the captain in the morning to see what type of funds we may be able to pull as well. Don't worry, OK, baby?"

Cyrus looked deep into Casey's eyes. It was his way of ensuring trust that she was all in and understood.

"Yes, baby," Casey managed to say.

Cyrus planted a kiss on her forehead and headed back to his squad car. Pulling his cell from his pocket, he quickly dialed Jag's number and told him to meet him at the spot to talk.

Cyrus walked into the tittie bar centered in the city of Inglewood's gangland isle. Neither Jag nor Cyrus were worried. Not because of their badges, but because they were regulars themselves.

Cyrus was greeted by one of the dancers. His head rocked back and forth to the twists and winding moves of his temptress. Satisfied, he slid a crisp twenty-dollar bill down the crack of her ass "Twerk!" Cyrus said in a false Boston accent as he walked off after spotting Tre at the end of the bar taking shots.

Tre hurriedly finished his drink when he spotted Cyrus coming his way. He knew how Cyrus despised drinking. It was poison, he always said, and he would be shot dead by some smooth criminal, all because he was drunk off his ass.

Cyrus, of course, noticed Tre drinking, but there were far greater things to talk about at the present time than worry about Tre and his drinking issue. Cyrus took Tre by the collar to remind him that he was a police officer. An officer of the law and on active duty. He displayed his displeasure in his behavior. It was overkill, but Cyrus wasn't in the greatest frame of mind.

"What's up?" Tre said. He had a slight shiver in his voice. The men made their way to the booth in the back of the club.

"Where's Jeffrey?" Jag questioned.

"He's on his way. I wanted to meet with the two of you first."

"Well, what's up?"

"It's about Luke. He needs surgery right away. Cas and I can't afford to pay for it. I have to find a way to get this money. I can't just sit back and let my baby die."

"OK, so what we gon' do?" Tre replied. Tre was the hit man of the group. He was a hothead and useful in many situations that were gang related. Tre rarely asked questions. He only needed to know when, where, and how much.

Cyrus's eyes welled with tears. He knew he could count on Jag to be down, whatever the case may be, but they had never done anything remotely as dirty as what he was about to propose.

"All I need to hear is that you will rock with me. I can't go this alone. I know Jag is in. He's always in. It's Jeffrey I'm a little worried about. He asks so many questions. People smell the law all over him before he can even get out of his car. Tre, what about you?"

"I'm in," Tre confirmed.

CHAPTER 36

Los Angeles Police

Shake Down

It didn't take long for the brothers to get into the gate and take over the truck full of drugs and money. The Mexican cartel set regular deliveries to businesses they owned in Los Angeles. Gathering intel for the heist didn't take much. There were several disgruntled business owners willing to give up the blueprint stock and distribution. Jag took out the driver and passenger in close range before the driver could even get the car door open.

The rest was easy as pie. Cyrus, Jeffrey, and Tre jumped into the back of the truck and waited. Jag picked them off one by one. Then they went to work. Bags of money and drugs were stacked neatly in the truck. Cyrus wasn't concerned about the drugs at all, but Tre was interested in the type of cash he could get from selling the drugs back to drug territories. Cyrus and Jeffrey brushed off Tre's idea and kept loading their truck with the cash.

The plan was to steal only the amount they needed, but they had no way of tallying how much money was in each case, so they loaded as much money as they could in a matter of five minutes. Tre loaded a few bags of cash but took at least four duffle bags full of pure uncut cocaine. Cyrus may have needs, but so did he. He could easily flip the drugs on the streets. He wasn't about to miss the come up. Plus, his plan was to get the dope *and* the money. Fuck the team goals.

Cyrus called out to Jeffrey and Jag to hurry along. It was time to move. The night was still dark, and the lights were out in the east block of Compton, so it made for a good night to rob someone blind. Cyrus and his partners rode off heading to East Los Angeles back to the warehouse where they would be safe. There, they would split the cash and make sure everyone was on point with the plan.

Once they drove into the warehouse, the boys jumped down from the truck and celebrated their riches. Cyrus placed his head in his hands and cried. He was sick to his stomach. He was both nervous and relieved.

"That was too easy," Tre said as he grabbed hold of two of his personal bags of drugs.

"What you got there?" Jag questioned. Tre was gathering bags and placing them in a small pile. "It looks like you're separating merchandise without discussing it with the rest of the group."

"Oh, naw, this is my grip. You know, the drugs you guys didn't want. I took 'em. I can get a ton of money for these drugs on the street."

Cyrus was so angry he jumped in Tre's face. "Why can't you just follow instructions? We take just enough money to cover our debts."

"We all agreed," Jeffrey said.

"What the fuck were you thinking?" Jag said enraged. "You think you can sell pure cocaine on the streets and the drug cartel not recognize that's they shit? You fucking stupid."

Cyrus didn't say a word. Jag had done a great job of explaining their thoughts and feelings on the matter. The problem now would be to get rid of the drugs.

"Tre, the drugs stay here. Right now, we don't have time to deal with the drugs. We have to count this money and get home before light. Remember, we don't know anything about the missing drug cartel money." Cyrus and Jeffrey walked over to the back of the truck and continued to unload the bags of cash as Tre and Jag started the count. They split the money up four ways. By the time the group finished counting all of the dough, they had just over 2 million dollars apiece. Well over the amount needed for Cyrus's problems, and any other problems they could imagine.

Jag smiled, and then grew sad when he realized he didn't have a soul to enjoy his newfound riches with. He figured he would stash it somewhere and invest it little by little so that no one would get suspicious.

"I think we should be left to deal with our share of the loot. We split the money and drugs, if you wish. Each man here for himself," Tre commented, looking as if he was possessed.

"Well, Tre, you do what you want. I have to get home and get this money to the hospital for my son. Please, you guys keep a low profile. All we need is to have the cops and the cartel hunting us down," Cyrus said and lowered his eyes at Tre.

"Understood."

For the next few days, it was business as usual, drug bust after drug bust, prostitutes, and domestic violence disputes. Cyrus, however, seemed on edge a bit because of Tre and his shaky behavior. It was like he was visibly shaking out of his skin at the mere sound of his name. His odd behavior was beginning to frazzle his own mind. Luke was due for surgery in just twenty-four hours, so the family was coming down from all over to make sure he awoke to support and familiar faces.

Jag was as quiet as a mouse. He was such a pen-
ny-pincher. He hadn't purchase too much of anything,
but he was eating well. Cyrus laughed at Jag as he picked
up a piece of sushi and flung it across the table when he
found out it was raw.

"You see that nigga Tre?" Jag said with a mouthful of
rice and teriyaki chicken.

"Yeah, barely, though," Cyrus responded.

"Yeah, well, he trippin'. I think he on that shit, Cyrus.
We can't afford any heat right now. The mob has a bounty
out on the men that stole the loot, and the precinct ain't
taking it lightly, either. The mob has a bounty of a million
dollars out to whoever brings us in. You know the cops
are down to bring our asses in too. At this rate, I wouldn't
be surprised if Tre didn't turn us in himself."

Cyrus didn't say much. He never even looked up from
his soup. The fact that Jag had all these ill thoughts about
one of their own made him question his integrity as
well. He understood that Tre was the least reliable of the
bunch, but to accuse him of getting high off the cocaine
was a bit farfetched—at least he hoped. It was quiet, too
quiet, and it was only a matter of time when they would
need to pin this ruse on someone. Cyrus had every intention of making sure the weakest link would suffer the
consequences of breaking the rules of the brotherhood.

"Well, I hope he cool. I have to admit I am scared for
him," Cyrus spoke finally. "I would hate to have to kill
one of our own behind such a slipup." Cyrus took a hefty
bit of his soup and flipped open his paper to check out
the headlines. Sure enough, the greatest heist ever pulled
was front and center. The blood brothers had stolen the
spotlight. Famous they were, and they couldn't even bask
in it.

Jag continued to eat quietly as he thought about
Cyrus's words. He chalked it up to Cyrus just joking

around. He figured Cyrus wouldn't dare stoop so low as to kill one of their own, although as of late, he couldn't be sure. Cyrus was much quieter than usual, as if he, too, was cooking up some sort of scheme. Still, they lived by the gun and would die by it. That was a pact Jag never questioned.

"Unit 216, we need you out at Twelfth and El Segundo, Protocol 116 in progress," Cyrus's radio chimed as the dispatcher called for all available units.

Jag dropped his chopsticks, rubbed his hands together, and pulled his police coat. Cyrus took one gulp of his soup, grabbed his things, and headed out of the small café.

"I hope to God Tre don't get there first, cuz we'll be looking at some serious time if he slips up and whispers a word out of context," Jag said. He was nervous as hell about Tre's disposition.

"Time!" Cyrus said. "We looking at a grave, Jag, six feet under. Forget your pension and retirement watch. All that gone with the wind. We better hope that Jeffrey slits his throat before Tre even breathes a word that could incriminate us."

Cyrus and Jag were first on the scene. Tre and Jeffrey soon followed, guns locked and loaded.

"What's up? Are we waiting for backup or what?" Cyrus blurted.

"Have we been waiting on backup?" Jag said to Cyrus who was acting as if he was a rookie.

"Nope, but in light of our latest dealings, I was unsure if we needed to play it safe and wait on the boys in blue to assist. Show an act of teamwork," Cyrus stated.

"Shut up, Cyrus. You thinking entirely too much now. You know good and well that ain't our style, so let's get this done." Cyrus made a note that Tre was looking a bit dehydrated and out of sorts. His mouth was snow white,

Aija Monique

and his hair and beard were untamed, something that was highly unusual for Tre. He was the pretty boy of the bunch.

Cyrus took another look at Tre; then he nudged Jag and took a look at Jeffrey to see if he too recognized how unstable Tre appeared. He was certainly not himself. He was shifting his aim, sweating profusely, and a tad jittery.

"Man, this nigga on like Donkey Kong," Jag said irritated and ready to pop Tre right where he stood. "This man gon' get us killed. Cyrus, just say the word, mane. We can't go in home with this mess going on."

"We don't have a choice. Let's get this shit done. If he screws up, shoot him and ask questions later," Cyrus instructed as he ran up the stairs to the project housing complex.

CHAPTER 37

Los Angeles Police

Act of Justice and Self-Preservation

"Jeffrey, grab the loot," Tre said, panting and moving nervously around the room. "Hey! Don't you move a fucking muscle," Tre said, pushing the barrel of his gun on one of the cartel members.

"I got it. Just be cool. We are here for the money and drugs. Period."

"Hurry! We have to clean this shit up before our colleagues get here."

"Do you know who I am?" one of the men lying on the floor said.

"I could care less," Jag said, stepping over the other bodies of the cartel.

Just as Jag made it to the entranceway, he heard a spray of uncontrolled bullets resounding. "Damn, Tre." He was on his own murdering members of the cartel.

The police sirens resounded, and the light show began on East Twenty-fifth Street. Cyrus, Jag, and Jeffrey jogged down the steps of the project stairs high-fiving and applauding the search and siege of one of the biggest drug cartels of Los Angeles.

"Drugs and money secure, slowpokes," Cyrus laughed as he punched one of the uniform cops in the shoulder.

"Yeah! Can't beat you and your crew to any of the showdowns out here in the mean streets of LA. I want in."

"You already are. The uniform is all you need. Just try pressing a little harder on the gas." Jag laughed. "You drive like you driving Ms. Daisy or some shit."

The uniformed cop was not amused at all. He was sure Cyrus knew exactly what he was referring to. He may be wet behind the ears, but he was a true white-bred hick that played dirty. It was kill or be killed out there, and he didn't mind getting his hands dirty, including dirty money. It all spent the same. Talk on the force was that the blood brothers were a force to be reckoned with. They took down more drug lords than the state of California, New York, and Florida combined.

"Where's Tre?" Cyrus nudged Jag with a worried look on his face. He was trippin' lately and screwing up some major deals. Tre was shaky at the least, dropping evidence and doing surveillance without gloves.

"I don't know," Jag replied. "Shit, go check around back. Last thing we need is that nigga fucking shit up."

"My son's life is on the line," Cyrus chimed in, whispering into his best friend, Jag's, ear. "If we must, I will take him out, blood or no blood, brother or no brother. Find him." Cyrus grunted as he holstered his weapon. He knew that they had already covered Luke's treatment. He was getting greedy. Stealing from low-life criminals proved to be worth the risk, thus far. "I'll get this paperwork complete. You and Jag get the loot and the drugs to the evidence locker and take our cut to the safe at the warehouse. I'll meet you there in an hour. We need to talk," Cyrus directed and sped down the road.

Jeffrey, Jag, and Tre headed out to the warehouse to start cleaning up their mess while Cyrus went back to the station to finish things up there.

Tre was in the backseat of Jag's car tripping, whispering to himself and loading his weapon repetitively.

"Yo, Tre, stop doin' that shit, bro. You makin' me nervous as shit with that." Jag was getting furious with Tre for his continued stupidity.

As Jag pulled into the warehouse parking lot, Tre was acting as weird as ever. He was shaky and breaking out in a cold sweat. Jag jumped from the car quickly and began unloading the truck as Tre still remained posted in the backseat.

Jeffrey pulled in to the warehouse moments later and was shocked to see Tre sulking in the car, toying with his pistol. "Bro, why are you still sitting in the backseat? We have work to do! Are you high or something? Cuz if you are, I'm telling you now you had better get your shit together before Cyrus pulls up. I'm serious." Jeffrey looked deep into Tre's face so that he could understand the sincerity and the seriousness of his words. He was worried about Tre's fate. Cyrus had made more than one comment in regards to ridding himself of Tre.

"You gotta help me, Jeffrey. Cyrus is going to kill me, I know it. He thinks I would rat us out to the boys or even the mob. I see it in his eyes. He's never liked me, Jeffrey. You know it too. Just don't let him kill me, bro. We brothers, remember?" Tre was hanging on to Jeffrey's collar for dear life, trying to convince him to save him from Cyrus's wrath. "I can't go in there. If I stay out here, I'm out in the open. He won't shoot me out here."

"Get your ass out of this car, now!" Jeffrey said low and deep. "Calm yourself and let's count this money. After this, you and I are going to have a little chat about your drug addiction and rehab."

Tre lowered his head and slowly got out the car.

"Grab a bag and let's go," Jeffrey urged as he spotted Cyrus's car pulling up. "Look, Tre," Jeffrey said, "just be cool."

Cyrus parked his car and hopped out. He walked briskly toward the warehouse entrance.

As soon as Jeffrey whispered "be cool" into Tre's good and sane ear, his entire body tensed. He started fidgeting and dropped the bag full of cocaine onto the dusty road. Suddenly, $80,000 covered the ground like snow. Cyrus was livid. Tre dropped down to his knees, scampering around, trying to save the cocaine for future use.

"Get the fuck up, Tre, we got work to do. Jeffrey, get something to clean this shit up. We may have to turn the soil a few times to get the crystals out of the dust, but if we are found, the K-9s will sniff this dope from a mile away." Cyrus was still mumbling about Tre's latest fuckup.

Cyrus raised his head and dropped the bags onto the ground just in front of him when he was met by Tre holding his rifle to his head. Jag and Jeffrey quickly responded by drawing their weapons.

Back to the present . . .

Cyrus sat still, staring off into space. The thoughts of the stolen money and his colleagues still weighed heavily on his heart. He didn't want to relive the happenings of Los Angeles Police, but the same persona he left behind, he needed for his present situation. Recalling the events during the heist helped put his mind back into perspective. Cyrus could still see Tre drooling and foaming at the mouth. He was unrecognizable. Cyrus shook his head and started the car. He had to find a better way to communicate with Dana. He couldn't be sure of Sophia's plan of action, and he wasn't going to take the gamble on his wife and son's life. He'd lost so much already.

CHAPTER 38

Phase 1

Shun and Phil sat down to have dinner. The rest of the gang were still out. Phil was preoccupied with Phil Junior, laughing and joking. Shun looked at both of them with teary eyes. Even in their present state of emergency, Shun thought he would never see the day when Phil settled down. In that same moment, Shun grew tired and weak. Emotions had taken over his mind. He looked around and noticed that Sophia hadn't come down yet. He was upset with her and her choice of clothing, but he didn't mean to hurt or disrespect her. His mind was shaken. It was filled with such uncertainty he could barely eat.

Cyrus was still out in traffic. He took the scenic ride home. His beers were lukewarm at best. He needed to speak to Dana, no matter the cost. The last thing he needed was for Shun and Phil to find out that he wasn't who he said he was. Cyrus foolishly thought that a history of friendship could hold weight over lies and betrayal in the present.

He now realized that he couldn't save Shun and Phil from the inevitable. He was along for the money, and now that Sophia knew his true identity, leaving was the best recourse. As far as for the money, his latest ventures would be for not, and he would have to make some unsavory moves to protect his safety net for him and Casey.

Cyrus took a deep breath as he pulled into the gas station. He retrieved his phone from the glove compartment and dialed Casey's number. It was time for him to come home. He needed a plan, and he needed both his girls to be active participants.

Sophia was putting on more suitable attire when she felt a sharp pain shoot around her lower abdomen. She doubled over and put her hands on the sink. She was in so much pain her arms shook, and she began to perspire. She made a quick move to the toilet as she was about to heave. She threw up violently and became dizzy.

Sophia used all the effort she could muster to call Shun's name. She was in so much pain. She became dizzy again, and she tried desperately to get back to her bed to lie down for a bit, but she blacked out and lost consciousness, the carpeting of the floor easing her fall.

Rico pulled into the gas station behind Cyrus. He was tailing him for Tommy. The concern Tommy expressed about this undercover cop business told him that his money may be tied up in all the mess. He was especially interested in finding out what the story was about this Cyrus personality. Rico stood outside his black-on-black classic Camaro and lit a cigarette. He watched as Cyrus used the phone.

"Fuck!" Cyrus barked in frustration.

Rico decided that it was the appropriate time to introduce himself. "You good, bro? Car trouble?"

"Naw, I'm good. Just trying to get a hold of my wife and check on my son." Just as the words fell from Cyrus's lips, he knew he had said too much. He didn't know who this man was. Cyrus hurriedly took the nozzle from his car and proceeded to get in his car.

Rico noticed how nervous he got, but he didn't want to make him feel uncomfortable. "Have a good night," Rico yelled and put out his cigarette. He watched Cyrus drive out and get back on the freeway as he followed cautiously.

Shun was especially quiet. He had his mind on the meeting with Tommy. He would forgive Cyrus if he came out and told the truth. It was in his best interest. Phil wouldn't hesitate to put him down. It was the code of ethics they all followed. Every dog has its day. Coming clean was the only way to avoid death. Shun bit into his steak and potatoes and guzzled down his ice water. Phil noticed Shun's forehead wrinkled with stress and worry.

"What's good?" Phil said after excusing Junior from the dinner table. "Everything good with you and Sophia? I knew it. I knew that bitch wasn't no good. What are we going to do to get rid of her? We can't just keep lugging her around." Phil was just running off at the mouth. He hadn't noticed Shun rise from his seat.

"Watch your mouth," Shun warned. His arms were at his side, fists balled and his forearms' veins pulsating.

Phil ignored his cousin's words of advice and suggested he sit down. His head wasn't straight. "Did you really just stand from your seat, like you was gon' fight me? Not over no bitch, I know."

Shun didn't say a word as he heard his name and a thump coming from upstairs. He turned on his heel and ran up the stairs.

"Sophia?" Shun called as he started up the stairs. He grew worried as he didn't hear her respond the second time he called her name. He made his way to their bedroom. At first sight, he didn't see her. As he moved farther into the room, he could see Sophia's arm lying on the floor. She was a few feet from the front of the bed. He ran to her side.

"Phil!" Shun screamed as he tried to wake Sophia up. She was bleeding from a gash on her forehead. He checked her pulse and felt around her face and neck and was relieved to find that she was warm and still breathing. "Phil!" Shun shouted once more.

"I'm comin', nigga. What's going on?" Phil rushed up the stairs. Junior followed close behind, shaken and worried. When Phil saw Sophia lying on the floor in a pool of blood, he asked his son to wait in their room. "What the fuck happened?"

"I don't know. She's out," Shun said, trying to compose himself.

"Let's get her to the bed. You need to snap out of this shit. Snap out of it and let's get her to the damn bed," Phil said, trying to get Shun to realize that shit was real.

"We need to call for an ambulance. Her pulse is strong, but she still hasn't woke up." Shun was pacing the floor back and forth. During all his confusion, he realized that Cyrus had yet to return as well. Everything was falling apart, and he didn't take well to not being in control of his own destiny.

"Have you lost your fuckin' mind? We aren't law-abiding citizens. Go and get some ice and a few towels. Maybe the cold water will shock her awake." Phil was slipping right into nurse mode. It was that or face the music. He just wasn't ready for that. He wasn't going to lose his son to the system. All they could do was pray that with natural healing mechanisms, she would pull through.

***

Cyrus pulled in behind Shun's rental and took a deep breath. His heart was pumping so hard and fast he was afraid he was having a heart attack. Once he could gather his composure, he tried Casey's phone once more. It was late, but with the new baby, he was sure she was up at all times of night. Once again, however, he didn't get an answer. His heart sank. All he wanted was to hear her voice and make sure she and the baby were doing OK. After hanging up, he quickly dialed Dana to get some answers.

"Hello," Dana answered on the first ring. She had just gotten out of the shower and changed into her bedclothes.

"Hey, I am sorry about earlier. I tried calling from a nontraceable phone."

"Are you OK? Where are you? I've been worried sick. So much has happened," Dana said with a hint of sadness. She couldn't begin to figure out an appropriate time to tell him Casey was dead. She hadn't found out any info about his son and social services. She knew those two things would kill him.

"I need you," Cyrus blurted out. He was feeling extremely vulnerable alone.

"I'm here," Dana replied. She felt his words throughout her body. She closed her eyes as her nipples increased in size and her love began to pour down her legs.

"I need your help. First, I need you to know that I'm not involved in everything going on with Shun and Phil. I'm not a hostage either. I've been working a case against Tommy and his illegal gambling halls for over six months now."

"Shit, Cyrus, why was I out of the loop?"

"Look, I know. O'Reilly didn't want to involve you. He needed things to stay and look as normal as possible.

I was newly transferred here, so I became the perfect candidate for this position. I am going to bring Shun and Phil in myself. They're my childhood friends. There's a large amount of bullshit flying about the two of them as well. Long story short, we're on the run, and I know we're wanted; however, if we just give up and come home right now, Shun and Phil won't make it to the precinct for booking."

Cyrus swallowed hard. He was so emotional and weary he couldn't bear to hold his feelings in any longer.

"What can we do?"

"Well, there's something else pressing that we can't afford to mess up."

"What's that?"

"There's a girl with us. The nurse that treated Shun is with us. She quit her job and has been with Shun ever since."

"Go on," Dana said through clenched teeth. She was stewing about the fact that Cyrus was running around with some woman.

"Sophia quit her job after falling for Shun. She was cool, and I was very happy for him— till she found ma fuckin' badge in the sand at the beach. I don't trust her. She basically confronted me a few hours ago asking me to leave empty handed. That, I can't do."

"So, you were working with Tommy too? Why didn't you tell me? Did you think that you couldn't trust me with that level of information? Because now, we're here in deep shit, and it's looking pretty dark, Cyrus."

Cyrus looked down and sulked a bit. "I know I fucked up. I couldn't take the chance that something could happen to you based on my gambling debts. I need to get rid of Sophia before she blows my cover. I'm skating on thin ice."

Dana perked up after hearing that Sophia was Shun's piece of ass. She would do anything for Cyrus, good and evil. Still, she needed to find out if he was as corrupt as Sergeant O'Reilly. The gambling debt was an addiction, but he was still a good cop, at least she hoped so. "Kill her?" Dana questioned.

"We won't have to. We will just make her an offer she can't refuse."

"And what would that be?"

"Shun! If she really loves him, she will get the money needed to cover the debts."

"And if she doesn't take the bait?"

"We will cross that bridge when we get there."

"Where are you?"

"Miami."

"Okay, I'll let O'Reilly know and catch a flight there."

"No. O'Reilly can't be trusted."

"OK," Dana said without question. She knew she had witnessed "O" talking to Tommy outside of the club, and she hadn't had the time to research what dealings the two of them were operating under the table.

Cyrus said good-bye and simply hung up the phone. He didn't want to linger on the line too long. With Sophia's ongoing interest in his motives, he didn't want to add fuel to the fire. He grabbed his hot case of beer and stumbled in the door as if he had been mugged.

"What's the word?" Tommy said without a greeting or any formalities.

"I got eyes on Cyrus. I'm sitting right outside his place. They must feel safe and secure with their new move. The blinds are open, and there's smoke coming from a barbeque pit. I'm hungry as shit now," Rico said with a small chuckle. "Now on to the real, do we need to take care of this issue tonight?"

"No! Not yet." Tommy stared into the night. He didn't want to make any sudden moves. For all he knew, O'Reilly was playing him as well. Why else would Cyrus infiltrate his club? O'Reilly wasn't pleased with all the heat his club was mounting. It was just supposed to be about making a little money on the side. Leave well enough alone, the drugs were going to get on the streets anyhow. Cyrus stumbled itching to scratch a gambling addiction, and Tommy was happy to oblige. He also knew what he was doing by giving the loan to Cyrus. He wanted to lock him in so that membership to his club was inevitable.

"You sure? All I need is the word," Rico said.

"Naw, we good. I want to wait and see what their next move is. Plan to track movement. Gon'!" Tommy hung up the phone and went back into his suite. A couple of his girls were awaiting his presence. With fruit and wine on deck, he didn't want to waste any more time on Shun and his sloppy business practices. He would get back to uncovering his crimes after he got some pussy.

CHAPTER 39

Truth if You Dare

Dana's hands wouldn't stop shaking. She took her seat on the plane, and a wave of emotion fell over her. She began to weep and pray, asking God for answers. She didn't know how in the world she was going to greet Cyrus, and then tell him that his wife died on her watch.

Her stomach began to turn. Quickly, she unbuckled her seat belt and made a beeline to the bathroom.

"Ma'am, we aren't cleared to move about the aircraft. Please take your seat," a flight attendant yelled and ran down the aisle in an attempt to rescue Dana from harm.

"I'm fine. Go away. I just get nervous at the start of a plane ride is all. I'll be out in just a few," Dana said amidst the dry heaves and dizziness. She took a deep breath and rinsed her mouth out, then splashed some water on her face and returned to her seat.

"You OK?" an older gentlemen asked, seated next to her. "Good thing your seat is the aisle one, huh?" he laughed. After he didn't receive a smile in return, he cleared his throat and opened his book. Dana's eyes were watering, and the lump in her throat was nearly choking her. She just kept telling herself that everything was going to be OK. Once she could get to Cyrus, everything would be OK.

***

Shun sat on the edge of the bed praying. He could hardly wait until Phil left the room. The tears were on the cusp of falling in front of him. In that moment he knew that he couldn't bear to lose Sophia. The nature of them meeting was tragic, but she had become his lifesaver. The thought of losing her caused physical pain. He raised up from the bed a bit trying to stand. The twinge of pain startled him, and he doubled back onto the bed.

Sophia moaned and groaned as she came to. Shun turned around too fast for his growing pain to greet her. He was so happy that she was awake, he forgot about the sign of death piercing his side.

"Don't move," Shun said.

"Why? What's wrong?" she asked.

Shun got up and closed the door. He was wincing with pain. Sophia tried to get up, but her head was pounding. She could feel the warm blood oozing from her head. "What's happened?"

"I don't know exactly. Phil and I found you passed out on the floor. You scared the shit out of me. Do you remember anything?"

"Not too much. I just felt sick to my stomach and dizzy. I think that maybe I waited too late to eat. I don't remember hitting my head or anything after that."

"Just rest," he said, reaching for the Tylenol on the bedside table. "Here's something for the pain." Shun passed Sophia two pain pills and took four for himself. He waited for her to take hers, then kissed her gently on her forehead.

Shun bounced down the stairs as if he wasn't in serious pain. He met Cyrus's gaze. Cyrus was scarfing food down as if he hadn't eaten in days. "What's up with Sophia? She OK?" he asked, feeling awkward about inquiring in the first place.

"She good, bro," Phil yelled from across the room. He was playing the video game with Junior, but his attention was on Cyrus. He hadn't said two words to him since he returned from his three-hour trip to the store just up the street.

Shun stared at Cyrus. He was actually waiting for him to explain his whereabouts. Cyrus ignored Shun's unwavering stare and just kept eating. He didn't want to stir up any drama around the house, but he was getting tired of the quiet stares.

"Where have you been?" Shun asked Cyrus with clenched teeth. "Please don't lie to me. I'm not sure I can take it." Shun stood in front of Cyrus waiting for him to respond.

Cyrus let out a sigh and shook his head. "I'm not the enemy, Shun. I went out for a drive. Didn't know that I was a hostage or something. I can come and go, can't I?"

Shun smirked. "I don't care what you do, as long as you're honest about it. My family depends on that. If you're feeling like a prisoner, then you're welcome to leave." Shun pointed to the door.

"Chill, before this shit get outta hand. If either one of y'all start fightin' in front of ma son, I'ma whoop both y'all's ass!" Phil chuckled, but he meant every word.

"I went for a drive. I have a lot on my mind, and I just wanted to see if I could get some rest about leaving Casey. I just wanted to hear her voice, but she didn't pick up. It made things so much worse. I just drove." Cyrus started to break down. Shun could feel his pain. Just moments before, he thought he was going to lose Sophia. He felt bad for Cyrus. He couldn't have made the same decision. Still, it was the matter of his true identity that needed to be ironed out. Shun bit his lip and began making something for Sophia to eat. He didn't want to leave her alone for too long.

***

"Keats, my office please," O'Reilly said.

Keats hurriedly packed the files on his desk and headed to O'Reilly's office. "This can't be good," he murmured in passing. He knew it would only be a matter of time before he found out that Santiago was missing in action.

"Santiago?" O'Reilly said before Keats made through the door. "Before you lie, please be aware that your job is at stake. I don't want you to lose your badge as well."

"I don't know where she is. She just told me that she needed some rogue time, and that she couldn't tell me where she was going."

"Did she leave any instructions?" For a moment, O'Reilly looked panicked and worked up. Something that Keats noticed. "I just want to make sure she's OK."

"She'll be fine," Keats said with his forehead wrinkled. He then stood, turned on his heel, and left the sergeant's office. Keats didn't bother to stop at his desk. He needed to get in touch with Dana fast. In no way did O'Reilly buy his ignorance to the entire mission Santiago was on. He knew that she was going to meet Cyrus in Miami, and he knew that O'Reilly had some unsavory business dealings with Tommy, as well. No doubt Keats was worried. He needed to give Dana a call to give her a heads-up about the situation at home.

"Tommy."

"What! You don't have control of your team? You need my assistance?" Tommy didn't give O'Reilly a chance to govern the conversation. He was so red in the face about Cyrus being a cop, he couldn't see straight. He wouldn't let that cat out of the bag just yet. If he was going to go down for his street crimes, he was going to make sure he took O'Reilly with him.

"I just wanted to know if Santiago has come by your place to maybe question you about anything."

"Yeah, she did, actually. She came by to let me know that someone killed my nephew in County a few nights ago. Why? What's up with her?"

"Nothing. Just wondered if she had the pleasure of meeting you and whether you gave her a hard time."

"Naw, not this time. She was very disrespectful. She came in hot with backup, shut my place down. I let her live, though. No blood on my hands this time, but there won't be another pardon," Tommy said with a deep stern voice that sounded both monstrous and parental. "I gotta bust a few moves. Stay out of my way. Don't worry, I'll let you know when and where to be," Tommy assured O'Reilly and hung up before waiting on a response.

CHAPTER 40

Love Kills

Shun watched as Sophia slept. The dim light began to peek through the blinds, which set a soft gold glow against her skin. He traced the outline of Sophia's lips and brushed his thumb across her cheek and down her jawline. He would kill for her. She gave up her life for him, and to that very moment, he continued to ask why someone as beautiful and responsible could fall for him.

Shun didn't seem to think he deserved love or a second chance, for that matter. The one thing he did well ended in jail time and being stripped of his honor. Shun felt his days were numbered. He could accept living and dying by the gun. It was what he was trained for. Losing Sophia was what was going to break him. His true weakness was in her embrace. Love would be the death of both him and Cousin Phil. Shun kissed Sophia's forehead and rocked her gently in his arms. If there was some way he could ditch the call of death, he would run off to a tropical island and never look back. Only, Phil and his son were in this, as well as Cyrus and his family.

Shun thought that silence was a show of loyalty to his platoon, but there was no honor in that. True honor would rest in the man that betrayed his country to step forward and take responsibility for his own actions. Shun played the events of that night over and over again. He often wondered how different his life would have been if he had turned a blind eye to the happenings deep in the barracks. What-ifs seemed to flood his mind. He was happy to still be alive. In the last few months, his life was a movie: fast cars, women, drugs, and money. Of course, things would end badly. He had the perfect cocktail for malice.

Sophia motioned and winced with pain. She had some pain in her head, but most of her discomfort was from her mental state of mind. She couldn't place what made her so sick in the first place. She hadn't eaten anything out of the ordinary. She agreed she was dehydrated; however, she couldn't be sure she could chalk it up to a hot day and little fluids.

Sophia sat up and took Shun's hand. "I love you," she said softly.

"I love you too," Shun replied without hesitation.

Dana flagged down a taxi at the airport and instructed the driver to take her to the Faena Hotel in Miami Beach. She wanted to shower and rest a bit before letting Cyrus know that she was in town. She hadn't told him that she would be literally coming down to Miami, but she figured he had enough sense to know that she would come at the drop of a hat. He was her partner, and she knew he would do the same if she needed him.

Dana dried her hair and unpacked a few of her belongings. She was anxious to see Cyrus, but dreading the news she would have to share. She could feel a lump burning in her throat. She contemplated not telling him because he was going into battle, mentally and physically. Finally, she picked up her phone to call him. As the phone rang, she became so nervous she was visibly shaken.

***

Cyrus paced the floor of his bedroom, trying to keep his mind clear of thoughts of his impending demise. He was so confined to his mind he jumped when his phone rang. His heart rate accelerated. He quickly picked up the phone. "Dana?"

"Cy, can you meet me?"

"Yeah, but where? How?"

"I'm at the Faeona Hotel. Room three twelve."

"OK, on my way," he said and hung up. Cyrus bounced down the stairs in a hurry. He met Phil's gaze as he hit the bottom of the stairs.

"What's up, bro? You good?" Phil asked.

"Yeah, I'm going to go for a ride to clear my head a bit," Cyrus said, praying no one asked to join him. He was anxious to see Dana and find out what was really going on in his hometown. He didn't wait for a reply or an approval from Phil. He left swiftly.

Sophia slowly got out of bed and walked cautiously to the bathroom. She looked at her face in the mirror. Her nose was red, and her eyes were a bit puffy. She turned on the shower and carefully took off her clothes. The warm water was refreshing. She felt her muscles relax, and the tension in her limbs melt away. She thought about her next move in regards to Cyrus and decided that she needed to tend to her own health issues.

Phil and Phil Junior got dressed and went out for lunch. Phil needed to come clean about Brandy's death. He didn't want any secrets between the two of them. He drove quietly to the restaurant. He was busy going over how he was going to break the news.

Junior was surprisingly quiet as well. He was beginning to worry. With Sophia getting sick, and his mother
out and about, Junior was a ten-year-old man. He had
protected his mother at any cost.

Cyrus knocked on Dana's hotel room door excited to
see her. As soon as she saw Cyrus, she jumped in his
arms, hugging him so tightly he was losing oxygen. He
welcomed the long embrace. Realizing the true reason for
her presence, Dana let go of him and backed away with
tears welling in her eyes.

"What's wrong?" he asked.

Dana began to cry.

Cyrus was holding back a lump in his throat as well
and suddenly felt rage building. "What's going on?"

"Casey's dead."

"Noooo!" Cyrus let out a scream and noise of despair
that frightened Dana. He clenched his fist and punched a
hole in the bathroom door. There he stood with his back
turned to Dana. "Where is my son?"

Junior took a huge bite out of his burger and downed a
long swig of his drink. Phil watched him. He didn't know
what he was doing, and he feared that telling him would
ruin their new relationship. That was the last thing he
wanted. Loyalty was his rule, and he wouldn't walk away
from truth, no matter how bad it hurts.

"Junior, I need to talk to you about your mom."

"Great!" Junior perked up. He just knew that his mom
was going to pop up somewhere in the restaurant. He
started looking around the booths and tables for his
mother.

"No, son, she's not here." Phil started to get sick to his stomach. He was getting nervous. He was sweating under the collar and scared he would lose his son forever.

"Dad, what happened? She doesn't want to get clean, does she? We can make her, can't we?" he said, confused.

"No, not that, son. I am so sorry, but your mother passed away," Phil said, scared for Junior's reaction.

Junior just stared off into space. *You killed my mother*, he thought to himself.

Sophia sat on the toilet in the convenience store bathroom staring at the pregnancy test. She was so scared. How could she raise a child on the run? If she was pregnant, she would have to either give up the baby or give up Shun.

To Be Continued . . .

ORDER FORM
URBAN BOOKS, LLC
300 Farmingdale Road, NY-Route 109
Farmingdale, NY 11735

Name (please print):_____

Address:_____

City/State:_____

Zip:_____

QTY	TITLES	PRICE

Shipping and handling: add $3.50 for 1ˢᵗ book, then $1.75 for each additional book.
Please send a check payable to:
        Urban Books, LLC
Please allow 4-6 weeks for delivery